# EXPLORING THE HIDDEN POWER
# OF FEMALE SEXUALITY

# Exploring
# *the* Hidden Power *of*
# Female Sexuality

## A WORKBOOK FOR WOMEN

*Maitreyi D. Piontek*

☥ WEISER BOOKS
York Beach, Maine, USA

First published in 2001 by
WEISER BOOKS
P. O. Box 612
York Beach, ME 03910-0612
www.weiserbooks.com

**Note to the reader:** This book is intended as an informational guide. The remedies, approaches,
and techniques described herein are meant to supplement, and not to be a substitute for, professional medical
care or treatment. They should not be used to treat a serious ailment without
prior consultation with a qualified healthcare professional.

**Library of Congress Cataloging-in-Publication Data**

Piontek, Maitreyi D.
  [Tao der weiblichen Sexualität. English]
  Exploring the hidden power of female sexuality : a workbook for
  women / Maitreyi D. Piontek.
        p.  cm.
  Includes bibliographical references and index.
  ISBN 1-57863-218-8 (pbk. : alk. paper)
  1. Sex instruction for women. 2. Sex—Religious aspects—Taoism.
  I. Title
  HQ46.P48613 2001
  613.9'6'082—dc21                                        00-069323
                                                              CIP

Illustrations by Aruna Palitzsch, Aruna Communications, Berlin
Author photo by Manik Germann
Typeset in 11/14 point Centaur
Cover design by Kathryn Sky-Peck
Printed in the United States of America

EB

07 06 05 04 03 02 01
7  6  5  4  3  2  1

# CONTENTS

# LIST OF ILLUSTRATIONS

# LIST OF EXERCISES

I would like to give special thanks to the people close to me who supported me in realizing this book: to my parents Bayar and Gianni, Ajito for being my friend, Aruna for the beautiful illustrations, Tushita and Beatrice for their open ears, and Carsten for being my sinologist consultant and friend. And a special thank you to Deva Nando Breitner for helping me write this book in English.

I would like to thank all the women in my workshops for all those hours, days, and weeks of mutual meditation we shared, especially Michelle, Ines, Gaby, Marilene, Elisabeth, Margit, Isabelle, Katherina, Maya, Annemarie, Werfeli, Beatrice, Daya, Sandra, Blandiene, Sabina, Nina, and all the others. In our mutually experienced silence and laughter, new doors always opened up.

I would like to thank Mantak Chia for who you are and how you are. Even though our approaches are very different, you have always been a great inspiration and challenge for me. How boring if we all were the same!

Writing this book has filled me with gratitude, especially toward my meditation master Osho. The deeper I enter into the treasures of the Tao, the more I realize how much the thousands of hours sitting in his presence has affected my life and my inner path.

In love and thankfulness,


Maitreyi

# INTRODUCTION

Women's reality is changing rapidly. To be a woman today is both challenging and confusing. On the one hand, we are still involved in the traditional role of caretaking and being identified with others, and on the other, we are trying to live with a more complete sense of self. We are accepting this challenge of change and exploring new possibilities, becoming courageous and responsible enough to expose ourselves in business, politics, education and many stimulating careers. We women are flexible by nature, so we are able to adjust to changing circumstances.

Up to now, most women who have been successful in the world are those who adjusted to the male value system. To keep up with the ambitious pace of modern life, women have emphasized the performance of masculine qualities. To become recognized experts in particular fields, women have sharpened their minds and become calculating, aggressive, dominating, and outgoing.

The new millennium requires that we now find new ways to heal ourselves and the world: therefore it is necessary that we realize our responsibility and explore new possibilities and dimensions of femininity. If we are to understand our female essence, we must come to terms with our sexuality and recognize the opposite poles of masculinity and femininity within and without. We live in a male-dominated society that is extroverted, full of activity, excitement, and tension. Sexuality clearly reflects this social phenomenon, as it is mainly focused around male desires. Sexuality is deeply engraved with male behavior patterns and fantasies that honor maximum excitement. Yang-predominant sexual behavior is full of tension and it's climax oriented. As a consequence of this sexual orientation, little importance is given to female qualities, such as love, empathy, stillness, and depth. Rather than searching within to get in touch with our own nature, we started to imitate men and have learned to play the male game at work, in sport, and also in sex. But unfortunately, it is simply not possible for our potential to blossom out of male behavior patterns and male qualities. On the contrary, it takes us farther away from our real roots, and deep within this behavior makes us very, very unhappy.

My understanding of sexuality is based on a natural balance of yin and yang, the harmony of female and male. When male (yang) and female (yin) energies are not balanced, sexual behavior spirals more and more out of control. At its extreme, it escalates into sexual perversion, child abuse, or even violent sexual acts, rape, threatening physical harm or even death to generate sexual excitement. It would be too simplistic to make men fully responsible for this development. In our society, sex is also out of balance because we women, while being more sexually free for the last forty years, have not yet really assumed our full sexual responsibility.

Until now, fulfillment of female sexuality has not been given much importance. Women's traditional sexual duty has been to give pleasure and satisfaction to men, and to give birth to as many sons as possible. This view of our sexual role is still very common and deeply rooted in society. So far, we have had little opportunity to perceive our own needs and desires, or to develop a sexual identity. The majority of women do not experience the healing power of womanhood and a fulfilled sexuality that spans an entire life. The current state of affairs surrounding sexuality calls upon today's women to become more independent, and to find inner fulfillment, rather than continuously looking for love and appreciation in the outside world. I encourage women of all age groups to unearth the treasures of female sexuality, developing the feminine power of healing love, which is also our contribution to a more natural and joyful society, to nourish and heal our world.

## Being a Woman is a Responsibility

Too many women still avoid facing their own situation regarding sexuality, or they may be unable to truly surrender. This is due in part to personal fears, mental blocks, or personal and collective experiences. But women also know they have a sexual responsibility of some kind. To take on that responsibility, women will have to develop these healing female sexual qualities within themselves. Getting to know their own womanhood with all its personal desires, limits, and wounds is a significant part of that. This can enable women to live their sexuality according to personal conviction and in tune with their personal truth.

Sexuality is discussed openly through the media, but this doesn't mean that we women have become more natural and relaxed about our sexuality. Nor has it made it easier to understand our sexuality any better. On the contrary, we are constantly fed inaccurate, misleading information. For the most part, we are being manipulated for commercial and entertainment purposes.

This commercially produced image of women, how we are supposed to feel, what we should like, and how we should be, has been created mostly out of male fantasies. For us women, this can be an irritating and confusing predicament. Unconsciously, we are absorbing these images in each cell of our body and being. This means we try to adjust ourselves to these artificial images. We are trapped in an absurd situation where we try to be ourselves according to superficially imposed male ideas. The price women pay in their hope to be taken care of, or loved and accepted, is too high. We pay for it with our needs, feelings, and beliefs.

## How Important is Sexuality?

Women still think that enjoying sex is selfish. But sexuality is not just the satisfaction of an instinctual urge or a pleasant way for nature to ensure reproduction. Its possibilities reach far beyond this. Because many women are not in touch with their intrinsic nature, they end up playing a role that does not really suit or nourish them. They are easily manipulated or abused and find themselves playing the victim role, or are humiliated and hurt over and over again. They do not learn to access their own internal strength so their sexual potential remains hidden. With the help of the Tao, I want to invite women to explore sexuality, so we all are able to feel it as a part of our whole being.

Women who are ready to come to terms with their sexuality, and who want to find new ways to experience it are still a small minority. In fact, the overwhelming majority of women live in a social situation where it does not even come to their minds to ask themselves, "Do I have a fulfilled sexuality?" or, "Is this all there is?" Millions of women are living in very primitive circumstances in little villages, in India for example, far below the subsistence level. Most of them are not able to read or write, and their religion and society have dictated that they worship their husband as a god. For women in these circumstances, whether they have an orgasm or not, or if it is clitoral, vaginal, or even "cosmic" is simply not an issue.

In Muslim and African communities, it is still the custom to circumcise small girls, to cut out the clitoris or the lips of the vulva. Every so often a girl dies after this painful procedure, which is often done without any anesthesia. The tradition is practiced today in over twenty-two countries. The endless pain and lack of respect which so many women have borne through the ages has become part of our collective consciousness. And this shared collective experience is what still connects and unites all women.

## The Collective

In psychology, the term "collective" refers to the psychic (of the psyche, not intuitive) contents of the mind that belong to an individual, to a social group of people, to a nation or race, or to all of humanity as a whole. The modern concept of a collective consciousness was originally formed by C. G. Jung. This collective consciousness determines the behavior of a group and the content of their minds: their norms, views of life, customs, symbolism, and their sexual habits. The stronger the collective, the more meaningless the "I" becomes. The less we have developed and experienced our individuality, the more we are ruled and identified with the collective. The uniqueness of the personality is absorbed and loses its independence. We, as individuals, turn into an expression of the crowd.

People who live their lives unconsciously, without any inquiry or investigation, become like a channel; they are an open invitation for the pattern of the collective mind to act through them. That's how the predominant structures of society—the traditions, religions, and the sexual roles of women—get passed on through the womb, unfiltered, from generation to generation. Now the time has come where women, at least in some parts of the world, are free to give a completely new contribution to the collective, with new qualities and new possibilities.

We cannot afford to ignore the vast possibilities of womanhood. Most women are not aware that it is possible to unfold the potential of female sexuality, whether we are living in a perfect relationship, having great sex, or becoming a mother. Our possibilities go beyond our involvement in outer circumstances and can unfold irrespective of them. But these restrictive ideas about being a woman, based on dependency, are deeply engraved in our unconscious mind. The collective mind is flowing through our blood and soaking our bones with this ancient conditioning. The hidden power of sexuality reveals itself by learning the art of swimming against the mainstream.

## Sexual Liberation

The bad news is that there are no valid role models for the modern woman today. The good news is that we do not need them! Over years of working with women, individually and in various workshops, it is confirmed again and again, that we do not need outer images or pictures. Every woman is carrying unlimited wisdom and strength within, and the Tao can help us get in touch with these inner treasures.

As long as we have not liberated the feminine healing power that sleeps within us, we will be hurt and humiliated over and over again, until the healer is healed. When a woman has access to her well of inner strength, she will also have the desire and courage to set herself free from the archaic chains and limitations that burden her sexuality. Women's liberation is an implosion, an explosion inward, a quantum leap that gives inner space and independence.

In the process of this liberation we are lead through all the pain we carry within, and through all the injustice to which we have been exposed over centuries. To liberate female sexuality means to free ourselves from the boundaries of identification with others who limit our perception of the vast possibilities we have in being a woman. To develop an independent sexuality based on free choice is not just the foundation of a more fulfilled life; it also carries with it the possibility of influencing the collective soul with more pleasant, joyful, and loving qualities.

## Does Western Sexual Therapy Work?

I have often been asked why, as a modern Western woman and as a sexologist, do I work with an Eastern method like the Tao? The answer is very simple. Ever since I can remember, Western health and therapeutic models have never really convinced me of their effectiveness. They seem coincidental, unnatural, and unable to touch the real depth of our being, unable to find the genuine root of a specific problem. Even when they come wrapped in convincing and impressive theories, they seem but superficial. I am not generally against Western science and therapy. But when it comes to female sexuality and its understanding, development, and treatment, I prefer a model that presents an overall view and expands our vision to allow us to understand our lives through a holistic approach. The Taoist methodology has the tools to make this possible.

Many Western sexual therapists, doctors, and psychologists are still stuck deep in infancy. The state of neurosis and frustration they carry within limits their capacity to understand and help people. I am often deeply shocked when I hear about some of the bizarre methods therapists are using to try to heal their clients' sexual problems. Some patients, especially women, wind up even more disturbed and confused by the "therapies." We hear that abuse or voyeurism has unfortunately become rather common in therapy today. I feel that to unfold the feminine essence we need to use methods that go beyond therapy, methods that are ruled by spirituality and love, and that suit the female nature.

On my first trip to India in 1978, I attended a series of lectures held by the Indian mystic Osho, and he talked about the Tao. That was my first contact with Taoism. At that time I was learning my first Chi Kung form, the Eight Brocades, had my first acupuncture session, and prepared my first Chinese herbal teas. At the time I did not realize that these healing arts and health exercises were all rooted in the Tao. All I knew about the Tao was that there were two wise men involved in the tradition, Lao Tzu and Chuan Tzu. I was just interested in the tantric way, the way of love, surrender, and dissolving the ego.

In 1986, I met the Taoist Master Mantak Chia and was initiated into the internal work of the Tao, including the sexual practices. I was quite overwhelmed by these techniques. They were very powerful and had a strong effect on my body and my energy. At that time the intensity of the energy work was very exciting, but not very nourishing and healing. Only later on, when I became more sensitive to female energy patterns, did I understood the negative side effects that the exercises can have on the female body. To be able to balance out the meditation and energy work, I decided to study traditional Chinese medicine, nutrition, and the basics about the healing herbs. Through these studies, the pieces of the puzzle began to fall in place for me.

I started on this journey with the Tao exclusively to benefit my own inner growth and meditation. Eventually, I realized that it could also be a useful tool for my work with other women. It was beautiful to observe that what worked for me also helped others. I opened my work to the Tao, and together with all the women who were attending my workshops, we surrendered more and more to the silent power of the feminine, and the secrets hidden within started to unfold.

## For Women Only

With this book I am addressing women only. It is not my goal to reach men so they are able to understand women. My only intention in writing this book is that women find a deeper understanding of their own female sexuality. While lecturing on issues of female sexuality, I keep observing an interesting thing. The men who are present at these lectures are either bored or offended. This is not my intention. While writing this book, I did not want to consider male feelings and social conditioning. I do not expect that men will understand or like this book.

I am a woman writing for women. It is a book originating out of my experience as a woman. I do not just want to reach your sense of logic or intellect. I would like to reach your whole being. While writing the book, I have surrendered to female intuition and the female principle so that they can guide me. I did not want to impress or discourage you with amazing phrases and great ideas. And I do not want to make you feel insecure about yourself by presenting perfect, idealistic images and conditions. I will give my best so that you will be able to deepen your understanding and your experiences to recognize the pattern of your sexuality, so you will be able to allow your feminine potential to unfold from the strength within.

## What This Book Has to Offer You

This book is a comprehensive introduction to the holistic female sexology of the Tao. It is based and rooted in the traditional Taoist view of life, and traditional Chinese medicine. It includes playful exercises to try, as well as practical hints for healing. And it is written to inspire and encourage you to look at different aspects of sexuality from the female point of view, so you are able to explore and experience your inner world at your own individual pace.

This book is written to help you increase your perception of your sexuality, especially if you are interested in liberating your sexuality from the personal and collective patterns and ideas. It is written so you can learn to develop and explore new healing qualities. It will also help you discover your shadow sides and taboos. Fear, insecurity, jealousy, mental blocks, ignorance, power games, and borrowed concepts or fantasies are the obstacles that are preventing femininity from flowering.

In this book you will find sections dealing with emotions, sexual techniques, sexual development, problems and misunderstandings, dealing with male sex, healing love, and sex in everyday life. Along with theoretical explanations, I have provided many healing exercises to try. They are divided into categories that are clearly identified in the margin. The different categories are:

> "Try This!"
> "Go Deeper!"
> "Hints for Healing!"
> "My Diary!"
> "Watch Out!"
> "Healing Points!"

You will not find universally applicable instant recipes in this book to change your life. Instead, you will find an inspiration to discover your own truth. I am not attempting to write a complete or perfect book; this would not correspond to the Tao. Rather I would like to encourage you to get to know yourself better, until you become an expert at self-healing. While reading this book you may be moved to go beyond your limits and your wounded personality to discover your own truth and wisdom within.

To deepen your experiences it is recommended that you get yourself a beautiful diary. You will find some questionnaires in the text, and to derive the most benefit from them, I recommend that you give yourself enough time to reflect on the questions and let them touch you. Write down your experiences and insights in your diary to deepen the inner process that is initiated. It is up to you how deeply you want to get involved with your personality and your sexuality. I would like to invite you to open yourself to the Tao. It will provide you with all the help that you need.

# How to Use This Book

*Part One*

# THE
# BASICS

# Chapter 1

# TAO

The Chinese character Tao stands for origin, intelligence, truth, a higher spiritual principle, the path, the journey, the traveler, the goal, to be.

**Origin and Essence of the Tao**

*The Tao that can be told*
*is not the eternal Tao.*
*The name that can be named*
*is not the eternal name.*
*The nameless is the beginning of heaven and earth.*
*The named is the mother of ten thousand things.*[1]

That is the beginning of the *Tao Te Ching*, the words and teachings of the mystic Lao Tzu, who lived a few thousand years ago. He is considered the founder of the Tao. The main aim of the Tao is to bring our lives, including our sexuality, in harmony with the Universe, with nature, and with our personal environment. For me, the Tao also symbolizes that which is unknown, something exotic that cannot be defined. I would like to encourage you, especially when it comes to sexuality, not to avoid and ignore the unknown and exotic or strange, but to integrate and accept it as an aspect of life. Let the unknown inspire you on your path.

Chinese symbol representing the Tao.

---

[1] *Tao Te Ching*, Gia-Fu Feng and Jane English, trans. (New York: Vintage, 1972), p. 11.

The path of self-discovery is as diverse as the different people to walk the path. Every human being is unique and is living in a unique surrounding, so there can never be a general rule applicable for everyone. It is the responsibility of each individual to find the way and the true purpose of his or her own life. You are the only one who can decide what is good for you and what you need. Nobody except you has a real interest in your being, or the sensitivity to understand it. No one else has the ability to perceive your personal needs, or your boundaries and limits. The Tao asks you to develop your inner strength and liberate your sexuality in order to live your individuality.

*Roots of the Tao*

The roots of Taoism in China reach back to the time of the Yellow Emperor and the mystic Lao Tzu (2600 B.C.) These two men are traditionally known as the founding fathers of the Tao. Taoism is not a religion in the sense that most Westerners understand, but a way to become spiritually, emotionally, and sexually independent. In their search for immortality, the Taoists have been very determined to explore all the many aspects of life. On their intense search, they gathered great wisdom and a deep understanding of human nature.

Taoism, simply put, is the science of life, a science that endeavors to include all the many aspects of human life within it. It is formed from the collective wisdom of millions of people, and has been passed from generation to generation over many centuries. This treasure of wisdom has been condensed in a collection of books called *Tao Tsang.*[2] That collection has 5,484 volumes in it by now and covers many fields of knowledge, ranging from astrology to medicine, agriculture, herbology, architecture, Feng shui, war strategies, and of course, sexology.

The wide spectrum of the Tao Tsang gives us a glimpse of how vast the skills of Taoism are. Many of the old scriptures, especially the instruction on inner alchemy (the work on the inner self), are encrypted in a language of symbols. So only those who were able to understand this language had access to

---

[2] The *Tao Tsang* is available in Chinese. Some of it has been translated into English.

these ancient secrets. The techniques and the texts where traditionally only passed on to chosen adepts or within the lineage of families that carefully guarded these secrets. These precious pearls of wisdom are still preserved intact today. They have survived all the barbarian wars and battles that have plagued China over the ages.

In China, many different schools arose out of the goal to enter the Tao, all with different approaches and different methods to explore, train, and refine the inner-self. The deep longing to enter into a space of "open emptiness," to merge with the unlimited energies of the universe, motivated seekers in these schools to find ways to create the ideal internal environment for this to happen. They started to experiment with different methods of self-cultivation to prepare themselves for the ultimate experience to merge with the Tao. Becoming totally open and empty is a main prerequisite to become one with the Tao. Only in a state of surrender and silence is it possible to receive the divine heavenly energies. For most of the disciples of the Tao, though, it was not possible to surrender directly to the pathless path without any form or structure and to disappear into the ocean of vast emptiness.

*The inner training*

To make it easier for them to enter "the state of nothingness," they started to experiment and develop many different powerful techniques to "conquer" their nature. Disciples from "the school of the south" had to undertake arduous physical training to raise their level of energy, while disciples from other schools where just sitting silently, and others focused more on their meridians and energy points, also known as acupressure points.

But at the same time, there have been people who misinterpret the Tao and go astray from its higher perspective, turning away from the path of self-knowledge and meditation. These people have used Taoist practices to strengthen the ego, rather than to dissolve it, or to gain power over others. The Taoist energy work and sexual practices can be misused by immature people, or by those who are ignorant of the higher principles the Tao embodies. These people then wind up caught in a self-deception in their opinion of themselves and their accomplishment, and they lose the way of the true Tao.

**Wu Wei**

The essence of the Tao is rooted in depth and in open nothingness, and its door opens through emptiness and stillness. The path leading to the essence of the Tao is known as "wu wei." It means non-doing, and this concept embodies the main Taoist approach to life; to allow life to flow naturally and not to interfere or fight the flow of the Tao. I am convinced that most of the Taoist energy work, physical training, and sexual techniques have been developed by men for men. The essence of the Tao corresponds with the female principle; therefore it cannot flow through a male body naturally without an intense preparation.

**The Main Pillars of the Tao**

The Pakua.

The Pakua is a Taoist symbol, and its eight sides symbolize different aspects and qualities of life. The octagon represents the holistic approach of the Tao, demonstrating that each area is just one aspect of the whole and only when merged together do they become a strong unity. People often believe that when they are having a sexual problem, they need to be focused mainly on sex, and must solve the problem through sex. The approach of the Tao is different. If one area has become weak or is in disharmony, Taoist practice begins by using all the other pillars to strengthen and nourish the weak one, until it has the strength to heal itself easily and naturally.

### 1. The Tao of Philosophy
The first pillar is called Philosophy. Just being interested in sex won't be enough of a motivation to transform your sexuality. To explore virgin territory, you need a solid motive, the right attitude, and knowledge about the cosmic laws and patterns surrounding sexual energy.

The first pillar is asking you to reflect deeply about the purpose of life, to question and examine your own sexuality. The Taoists have become great experts in the science of life and have developed a profound teaching about energy. Their understanding is based on the concept of chi.[3] Chi initiates change, movement, life, and death. The Taoists consider life as an expression of chi that manifests itself in different energy patterns.

*The energy patterns of the Taoist cosmology are:*

- *Wu chi*—original state of absolute openness and unity;
- *Yin* and *yang*—the laws of duality;
- The three treasures—*ching, chi-chi,* and *shen;*
- The change of the *five elements;*
- The *meridians.*

Later on these points will be discussed in detail.

### 2. Tao of Preventive Health Care and Self-Healing

In old China, a doctor was paid a salary only as long as his client remained healthy. If the client became sick, he was not paid anymore. So it was in the doctor's interest to develop methods to maintain patients' health and vitality, and doctors became very inventive. They created effective methods for self-healing and the prevention of disease by using physical exercises and other techniques for breathing and relaxation known as T'ai Chi, Tao Yoga, Chi Kung, Sexual Yoga, Kung Fu, and Meditation.

The mind, the feelings, sexuality, and the body do not usually function as a single unit. This is the major cause of disharmony within us. The essence of self-healing is to connect and fuse all layers of our being together to develop inner strength and resilience. It is in this way that the process of self-healing can be initiated. Sexuality unfolds most easily in a healthy and natural body. Physical disharmony or weakness affects sexual energy in one way or the other.

### 3. The Tao of Emotion

Emotions rule our everyday life, our relationships and our sexuality. What are emotions? From where do they arise? What do

---

[3] When the Chinese talk about *chi*, they refer to the power that initiates all the processes of life. In the Indian culture, this force is called *prana*. Western culture is not familiar with the concept of chi, therefore there is no equivalent expression.

they cause to happen within us? How do we distinguish true feelings from old wounds? Undigested and repressed feelings interfere with and distract the natural flow of love and sex. How do emotions prevent us from merging with the infinity of life? The Tao teaches the path of emotional independence and shows us how to identify emotions as a body language and to recognize the energy frequency of various emotions. We will learn how to transform negative emotions into healing energy. On the female path it is important to be rooted and feel at home in the world of feelings, so we are able to feel at home inside ourselves. Therefore women on the path must understand that it is of utmost importance to heal old wounds and digest repressed emotions.

### 4. Tao of Nutrition and Healing Herbs

Over a long lifespan we women lose our precious blood every month; that's why nutrition is so important. Where else can we draw the raw material that we need to replenish this volume of blood? Love and light cannot do that miracle alone. Some people think that menstrual bleeding is very healthy because it helps to detox the body from emotional tensions and toxins. The Taoists look at this issue at bit differently. They agree that elimination of the body's toxins is essential, but not by paying for it by draining the precious yin power of the blood. Therefore, they are constantly nourishing and strengthening the body in every way to make it strong enough to free itself from toxins.

The Tao of nutrition teaches us to choose food according to the body's requirements, to support the production of blood and energy, and to strengthen our center. The Tao of nutrition is the art to of selecting foods and herbs according to the energetic effect of yin and yang and the qualities of the five elements, so that they support our constitution and lifestyle.

### 5. The Taoist Healing Arts

The well known Eastern healing arts—acupuncture, acupressure, meridian massage, and the transmission of healing energy—all have their roots in the Tao. Sex was also used as a healing art. The legend handed down says that the Yellow

Emperor himself was initiated into the art of healing love by a young woman known as the "mystic girl" in Taoist literature.

### 6. The Tao of Sexuality

Taoists distinguish sexuality in terms of human and divine. Divine sexuality leads from self-healing to longevity, and climaxes in immortality. Human sexuality is characterized by ejaculation and menstruation, and leads to a loss of vitality, sickness, and finally ends in death. In old China, the emperor was supposed to be the only one who was authorized to practice the secret sexual rituals of "the bedchamber." He should be the only one having access to immortal power and everlasting sexual energy. Otherwise he would not be in a position to please all his many wives and concubines, and at the same time rule his empire successfully.

While making love to the emperor, it was the woman's responsibility that he should maintain his sexual power (meaning not to ejaculate) at the level of the most pleasure and excitement possible. However, for women today it is optional to take on the responsibility for her lover's sex life or not.

### 7. Taoist Skills and Fine Arts

The Taoists have developed great skills and fine arts to increase their energy level and to enhance their love life. For example, they use the power of feng shui and its symbols to invite love and happiness into their lives. The arts of physiognomy and astrology are used to find a matching partner, or to enable them to understand the one they have. There were many other precious skills they knew, such as calligraphy, martial arts, architecture, agriculture, and so on, which supported them on their path. Even though some of these skills have become known in the West, the more exotic methods are often interpreted as superstition or humbug. The best thing to do is to be creative and experiment with these methods for yourself to see if they enhance your love life or not.

### 8. The Living Tao

Sexuality is always affected by personal circumstances, the individual life style, and relationships. As an everyday guide, to allow the Tao to penetrate all aspects of their lives, Taoists use the oracle called the I-Ching.[4] With its 64 hexagrams, it symbolizes the ever-changing possibilities of human existence. The I-Ching can help us recognize and understand the different phases of our lives. Specifically in times of conflict and confusion, it offers guidance, clarity, joy, and peacefulness, so darkness, conflicts, and stagnation will be illuminated. When there is light, it is easier to find the right way.

## Women and the Tao

Because I am interweaving women's liberation with the Tao, this could give rise to the misinterpretation that the attitude toward women in China has been respectful, progressive, and supportive in the past. The Taoist attitude of life arose out of the Chinese culture. I don't want anyone to be blinded by the mystique that surrounds Eastern healing arts. In olden times, the Chinese denied that a woman had a soul, believing that only men had them. A Chinese father would only count his sons. If he had only girls, he would consider himself childless.

I have been informed that in the origins of Taoism, the status of women was a bit better, but as time progressed, not much of that respect remained. When I was reading for the first time the old Taoist scriptures about their sexual practices, I was shocked. In those scriptures, instructions were given on how to choose a good woman. The criteria were similar to those required to pick good fruit at the market, such as, "She needs to have crunchy cheeks," or, "Her skin needs to be as soft as silk." For the ambitious power-oriented gentleman, to make love to a woman, or even better to a young girl who has not given birth yet, was just a means to an end. A woman's menstrual blood and sexual secretions were considered to be the nourishing yin juices of life. The Taoists believed that the juice from the mysterious door of a woman could lead them toward

---

[4] There are several English translations of the I-Ching. If you choose to work with this oracle, find one that appeals to you.

immortality, or at least help them have a healthier and longer life. Taoist legends relate that the Yellow Emperor only reached immortality because of the "Yin-Elixir" of his thousands of concubines.

The Taoist way of exploring and cultivating sexual energy is unique, but as in all the other patriarchal traditions, it does not give much importance to women's interests. There are only a few reports rising out of Taoist literature based on women's experiences with the Tao. My favorite is called *The Immortal Sisters*, translated into English by Thomas Cleary.[5] I am sure that there were many wise women who realized the Tao. Because of their yin qualities, and also because of their inferior social status and lack of basic education, they were not in a position to pass on their experiences publicly, nor were they able to write them down.

In my work as a sexologist using the Tao, I have noticed that men and women not only have different bodies, but that they also react to methods very differently. For men, traditional Taoist practices seem completely appropriate. Men like these powerful techniques and are able to apply them in their everyday life to improve their energy and strength. But what works for men seems to take women further away from themselves. The more closely I observed this phenomenon, the more I realized that women need a completely different approach and path to reveal their potential. So I kept investigating and searching for methods to promote and strengthen the female.

Some of the old Taoist masters noticed that the female path is different from the male path. So far, so good, but how is it different? And how could it ever be possible for men to find and develop ways or methods that bring the female essence to flower? Many women I meet on the path seem so focused on and already infected with male qualities, that their female qualities are extremely hurt and wounded that it is not possible to set their female essence free within a male system. So being

*In search of the female Tao*

---

[5] Thomas Cleary, trans. *The Immortal Sisters* (Boston: Shambhala, 1989).

focused and dependent on "male" is the biggest obstacle women have to surpass.

I have spent years meditating and exploring, searching for the female Tao. For me this has been a journey full of surprises, one that keeps revealing new perspectives that open my perception as a woman. Inspired by the traditional Tao and guided by the female yin principle, and through meditating with many other women, we slowly entered the forgotten female territory, the Heavenly Palace (uterus). This is the place where the mind has no access, where logic ends, and where images and ideas dissolve: it is the door to a new dimension of womanhood.

When we work with the female Tao, it is very easy for us women to have access to our inner strength and stillness, and within a short time, profound changes in our lives take place. That the female way works for so many women speaks for itself, and the Tao shall accompany many more of us on our way. The female Tao is not a fixed concept; it just helps us begin to discover new possibilities. It is an invitation to dedicate our life to yin. Let it guide us on our individual journey so we will be ready to receive the divine, to initiate a spiritual pregnancy, to eventually give birth to the ever-shining light of love.

# Chapter 2

# YIN AND YANG

According to the ancient Taoist cosmology, wu chi, the vast open emptiness, absolute unity and oneness, divides into two aspects: yin and yang. Every form of life is a unity of these two complementary forces. These two poles belong inseparably to each other. Yin and yang are not related to each other as "either/or," but are interrelated—"as well as." Light only exists in the medium of darkness, the positive needs the negative to exist, what goes up must come down. The continuous interaction between yin and yang, one of the major natural laws that rule the eternal flow of the Tao, constitutes the original rhythm of life. Nature is always eager to maintain a balance between these two opposites.

The Taoists consider the human body as a microcosm of the universe, and so view human nature as also being ruled by the ever-changing contradictory forces of yin and yang. Yin symbolizes the female principle: condensing, taking on form, matter. Yang represents the opposite male pole: expanding, rising upward, pure energy without form or structure.

The Tao invites us to understand the interdependence of the opposites as a permanent interplay. The magnetism evolving out of that interplay produces the tension that is needed to keep the flow of energies alive. If this flow becomes stagnant,

**The Union of Opposites**

the balance is disturbed, the harmony dissolves, and this leads us toward separation, distance, and isolation.

Our relationships are also ruled by the laws of yin and yang. On one hand, we are moved by a desire to melt and share with the other, and on the other hand, we want to withdraw and find our own space and individuality. The Tao is inviting us to learn to understand and accept both of these extremes. All conflicts and problems in our relationships can be seen as an imbalance of yin and yang. As long as these two forces are struggling and fighting with each other inside of us, the inner unresolved conflict will manifest itself in our relationships, at work, and at home, preventing happiness and fulfillment.

## Defining Yin and Yang

The dualistic law of yin and yang offers a model that allows us to look at situations in a different way. By recognizing these patterns in our own lives, it is possible to understand how these patterns affect us. Table I (on page 15) will help you familiarize yourself with the various features of yin and yang. I have chosen a selection of opposites that I feel are connected and refer to sexuality.

### Dependency

Yin and yang provide each other the foundation for their existence and their development. Take a moment to look at the yin and yang symbol (at left). When you are looking at it, you will see a light dot in the dark yin section of the symbol, and a dark dot in the light yang section.

An ancient Taoist saying is: "When yin reaches its deepest point, it will change to yang." The little white dot is the seed for yang, which will unfold only in the absolute depth and stillness within, but the little white dot is just a possibility. "When yang reaches its climax, its biggest expansion, it will change into yin." We will be investigating the consequences of this interplay of yin and yang from many different angles, and examining how this interplay affects our sexuality. The Taoist model of yin and yang will be the thread that guides us in our journey through the book, and will help us to get in touch with our intrinsic nature.

Yin and yang symbol.

14

*Table 1. Yin and yang qualities.*

| Yin | Yang |
|---|---|
| Female | Male |
| Water | Fire |
| Night | Day |
| Earth | Heaven |
| Outbreath | Inbreath |
| Estrogen | Testosterone |
| Inside | Outside |
| Depth | Climax |
| Unconsciousness | Consciousness |
| Darkness | Light |
| Relaxation | Tension |
| Soft | Intense |
| Matter | Energy |
| Feelings | Mind |
| Intuition | Logic/Discipline |
| Wisdom | Knowledge |
| Resting | Moving |
| Nature | Technique |
| Cold | Hot |
| Slow | Fast |
| Receiving | Generating |
| To feel good | To be good |
| To be | To do |
| Passive | Active |
| Peaceful | Aggressive |
| Surrender | Dominating/controlling |
| Togetherness | Aloneness |
| Subjective | Objective |
| Adaptable | Determined |
| Stillness | Movement |
| Weak | Strong |

*The root of power*  It would be wrong to assume that yin is equivalent to "woman" or yang is equivalent to "man." There are women with strong yang characteristics, and there are men with a strong share of yin qualities. But the fact that a woman has female sexual characteristics shows that she is ruled by the female principle, yin. On the other hand men, with their male sexual functions, are ruled by the male yang principle.

That means men have their strengths rooted in yang and women have their strengths rooted in yin. Let's just have one more look at the symbol. If we say yin is weak and yang is strong, this is just half the truth. If we look closely at the symbol, what we notice is that yin is weak and soft on the outside, and is strong (yang) on the inside. And yang is functioning the other way around. It is strong and hard (yang) on the outside and weak and soft (yin) in the inside. This would mean that women have their strength within, and men have their power more on the outside.

*Female and male*  For years I have asked the people who attend my seminars or who come for a counseling session the same question: "What do you feel is the cause of your problem?" It is amazing how precisely and clearly women grasp the core of their problems. Intuitively, they describe the causes of sicknesses or the energetic state of their inner organs. Only when they begin to think about what they were saying do they get insecure and confused. And then they are adding: "But I do not know if this is really true." Mostly it turns out that their first impulse was right. Women are pretty good in knowing what is going on in them. Deep inside they know.

When I ask men the same question, the answer sounds mostly like this: "I have no idea." Then I will ask them to close their eyes for a moment to let the question sink in a bit deeper. But their ignorance only gets confirmed. Occasionally an idea pops up in their heads; mostly something they have heard or read which has not the slightest connection with their own situation.

It is for this reason that I love to work with women. I feel there is so much potential and possibility there, so much hope and fertility. As soon as a woman finds the courage to turn her awareness in, and is ready to move from the surface deeper inside to explore the depth of her being, she comes in contact with wisdom and strength. Which woman does not know this situation? You are together with a male friend, husband, lover, or son and you feel that there is something strange going on. His behavior is different and you ask him what is the matter. Very often we get as an answer a nearly convincing, "Nothing." Working with men is different, they seem to have a different perception, but this is not the moment to analyze male behavior and try to solve the mystery of men.

Symbolically, yin is represented by water in Taoist mythology, and yang by fire. Fire and water each have their own characteristics, and both are able to exercise power over the other. Fire can heat water until it boils and evaporates. Water has the power to control or even extinguish fire. We could not say that fire is stronger than water. But even so, yin is considered weak and yang is considered strong. Worldwide, women are thought to be the weaker sex, and men the stronger. In fact, the surface of a female body, like the skin and muscles, is softer then the male body, which, due to a higher level of testosterone, is harder and rougher.

*Strength and weakness*

One of the main characteristics of the cosmic law of yin and yang is that it is always trying to find a balance. If strength manifests itself on the outer surface, the inner becomes automatically weaker. On the other hand, if the strength gathers and manifests within, the outer layer becomes softer and weaker.

Western society is very yang oriented. It is dominated by the intellect, by fantasy, and by action, always on the run, hoping to get faster, higher, and better. Feelings and intuition are ignored or repressed, signals of the body are neglected. Mother Nature is cold-bloodedly exploited by modern technology. Our religions are very yang predominant. We pray and look up to the Almighty Father in heaven and worship Jesus and the Holy Ghost. The hope of humanity goes toward the future and into

*The yang society*

fantasy. Most people dream their lives away, hoping to achieve a goal that will make them happy in their future. "If only I find the right partner," " If he changes, then our relationship will be fulfilling," "When I have lost enough weight, then I will be beautiful," "When I have more time, then I will meditate." A thousand and one big or small ideas and fantasies absorb our attention and flow toward the outside to there and then. Being continuously absorbed somewhere else creates an inner vacuum, like a dark whole within, and there is not enough energy left to perceive the real cause of the problem. Nor will there be enough energy left for inner transformation, or a foundation to feel really good. Transformation and fulfillment never happen in dreams and fantasy. It only happens in the reality, in the pulse of the here and now.

*Let's go!*  To cope with this desperate situation seems to be easier for men than for women. Through their yang nature, men are more at home and at ease in the outside world, so they do not suffer so much through the state of inner emptiness as women. Through their yin nature, a woman's home is inside herself. If she is cut off from her roots, this will cause deep pain and frustration within her. Over the centuries women have learned to ignore their pain by cutting themselves off from their womanhood, and thereby living a superficial life. It will take generations for women to feel at home again in the depths of their being. So let's begin the journey to find the female treasures within.

*Part Two*

# THE
# INNER
# JOURNEY

# Chapter 3

# YIN—THE FEMALE PRINCIPLE

Down the ages femininity was considered something mysterious and unfathomable and was referred to as the depth of the unconscious. Words will never be able to adequately describe the essence of femininity. This is a difficulty I keep coming across and it is always painful for me. As soon as I want to put the female essence in words, it loses its vibration, strength, and depth. That's why so many women maintain silence. To me, to put in words what there are no words for, and to try to explain what cannot be explained is frustrating. However, it is so easy to experience the essence of yin when sitting in silence and meditating together with women, even for women who do not have access to their yin qualities yet. To say things that go beyond words, to touch deeper layers of our being than the mind and intellect, the Taoists have been using symbols. Symbols have the ability to touch and influence the unconscious, the place where yin is rooted.

**Deeper than Words**

Yin—female principle.

Symbol that vitalizes female sexual organs.

*Water quality*  The nature of water has been used in Taoism as a symbol to describe yin qualities. Water has no form; it is flexible and fluid. It naturally flows downward, seeking the deepest point. The power of water is its softness and its lasting nature. Water has control over fire for it has the ability to put out fire. Water is able to assimilate and store other qualities within it. And it can be changed and moved by other forces like wind and fire. If it is cold, water can cool until it freezes. Warmth can melt the ice. Fire can heat water to the boiling point until it evaporates. As you surrender to the essence of the water, you can trust its flow, which will lead you toward the hidden power of the yin in a very natural way. This is a process that will touch a place in you that reaches far deeper than words ever will reach.

## Tao for Women

Since a woman's body is ruled by the yin principle, for us women it is important that we perceive, nourish, and preserve the precious treasures of yin. Because our society is so yang oriented, areas like health, therapy, life style, and sex are ruled by this approach, and not really in tune or adjusted with female patterns and requirements. For the health and well being of a woman, we will consider female sensitivity and vulnerability, as well as the energy patterns of a woman's body. For a woman today, it is necessary to develop self-confidence so she can decide for herself what is good for her and what is not. In this confusing jungle of endless possibilities, it is helpful when a woman is able to adjust her health program, to select the right therapy, and choose the foods necessary, according to her ever-changing body symptoms, circumstances of life, and personal likes and dislikes.

*The way of self-healing*  We are living in a time of new orientation where deep-rooted change is in process. The standards and norms that once were valid are about to dissolve. Worldwide, national borders are shifting. Just compare today's map of Europe with that of ten years ago to see how changeable the situation is. Intercultural exchange is increasing, especially in America, because many different cultures are living and mixing together. We have access to an abundance of knowledge and possibilities, and it seems impossible to keep an overview. From all sides, life preservers are being thrown at us to give us a feeling of security. With a life preserver we will not drown, but we will not learn to swim on our own either.

The Tao offers tools of self-healing so you can become independent; you can be directly in contact with your own strength and wisdom. You will learn to develop your own center, or as the Taoists say, your middle. "The middle," as such, does not exist in the English language or conceptualization, as I am using it here in this book. Therefore, you might need some time to get used to the word. In China, the concept of the middle has manifested itself in many ways. For example, old China was called the Empire of the Middle. There were medical schools called the Medicine of the Middle, and in the Taoist tradition, to activate and cultivate one's own middle is the base for all there is. To find the point within, where all the ten thousand aspects of life can be merged into one is the base of self-healing. The middle is the place within where it is easiest for the spirit to penetrate and root itself in matter. The Tao is teaching you to be in your middle, and to move from there to be able to give yourself what you need. In the following pages, I will introduce you to the foundation of the Tao of self-healing.

The inner conflict and spiritual emptiness prevalent today is leading us to a point where we actually focus and identify our lives mainly with outer clichés. We look for support and for something to hold on to in material values, in relationships, status, hobbies, and so on. The main center of our attention is mostly outside ourselves. This inner absence is perhaps the major cause of our problems and it is precisely that which makes dealing with them so difficult, because if there is no one there, how can anything be solved or changed?

The first step in healing yourself is to bring your full attention inside yourself, into your own middle to build up your energy field there. Your middle is the place where it is possible

*Self-healing from the middle*

23

to merge or fuse all your different layers, your mind, feelings, body, and sexuality into one unity. If your middle is charged up with energy and awareness it becomes the place for inner alchemy, the place where you can brew your inner medicine.

*Inner medicine*

In the illustration below you can see the three main energy centers, which in Chinese are called Tan T'ien. The lower Tan T'ien is below the navel in the middle of the belly; the middle Tan T'ien is located near the heart, and the upper Tan T'ien is in the head. The lower Tan T'ien is also known as "the field of medicine" in Taoist methodology because there it is possible to collect energy to brew your own inner medicine without causing any side effects. On the other hand, to collect and store energies in the middle and the upper Tan T'ien can be very dangerous. Too much energy in the heart and in the brain can create severe problems for body and soul.

To fill up your Tan T'ien, which develops a positive energy field within, is the foundation of self-healing. The process of refining and condensing inner energies is not an instant thing; it is a yin process that is nourished best by being slow and steady and aware.

The three Tan T'ien

Most people are torn, not centered. They are not connected or rooted in their middle. In an attempt to speed up the process of centering, they start filling up their middle with mind-power, fantasy, or imagination. But a real feeling of being in the middle cannot be substituted with the mind. Thoughts can never replace a real feeling.

Years ago I attended a Taoist retreat in upstate New York, where I had the opportunity to exchange experiences with other participants. At that time I was very much interested in getting to know what the middle feels like. Most of the Americans who attended the workshop kept telling me about their inner experiences and the extraordinary sensations they were having while meditating. Wow, I was completely amazed—from psychedelic fireworks, to having orgasms with their personal star above, and so on. All those stories were so beyond my experience that it made me feel like innocent little Heidi from the Swiss Alps. Back then, my middle was nowhere; I couldn't feel it at all. And no one was able to give me convincing hints as to how to go about finding and feeling my own middle. But I was not ready to give up. I felt there must be something more to it. In all the old Taoist scriptures, I came across statements about the middle over and over. The middle seemed to be a major key; a sacred place that I felt was worth searching for.

In the following months I was fully involved with exploring my center, with the help of all the techniques available to me. I was experimenting with different breathing techniques, belly massages, Chi Kung, the power of the Moon and the Earth, you name it. Over and over again I guided my awareness into my center.

In time I started to feel my middle more and more. The more I focused there, the easier and faster it became for my body to remember. To feel the middle is one thing, but to remain there throughout the day and night is a different story. Driving a car during rush hour, making love, or going shopping while being centered is an ongoing challenge.

# Your Own Middle

*My way toward the middle*

In the beginning it is advisable to center yourself in a protected space. Lying in your bed, sitting or standing in meditation; just find a place where it works best for you. Then you can expand your centering to include various situations in your life, while at the post office, in the middle of a big argument with your mother, husband, or child. There are endless possibilities in life for us to deepen the roots in our center.

## The Secret of Self-Healing

Centering is the slow process of leaving your dreams and fantasies, and facing reality, which is the foundation of self-healing. Healing never happens in your fantasy, only in reality. The following exercise will support your process of becoming centered.

**Try This!** → **Centering**

Centering.

• Sit or stand in a relaxed upright position and close your eyes.

• Put your right hand under your navel, and the left hand on your back exactly opposite your right hand, with the palms facing each other.

• Breathe in deeply through your nose, and with the outbreath let all your energy awareness flow into your middle.

• Connect and surrender to your middle deeper and deeper until you can clearly feel your blood pulsing there.

• Allow the sensation of the pulsing to draw you deeper and deeper into finding and manifesting your middle.

To be centered at all times, do the centering exercise as often as you can, wherever you are, whatever you do. At the minimum, do it until you feel your own pulse inside very clearly. Once it has become possible for you to be centered within yourself, with or without this exercise, and you are able to generate warmth and an energy feeling in your middle (this process can easily take weeks or months), then you can pass on to the next step.

## Chi ball

- Sit or stand in a relaxed upright position and close your eyes.

- Start breathing into your center, with or without the help of your hands, as in the previous exercise on page 26, until your middle is warm and pulsing.

- Allow your awareness and chi to begin to spiral or turn in your middle.

- Stay with your awareness focused on your middle, until the energies become dense through the spiraling, until there is a locus of energy, like a ball, a chi ball.

- Experiment with how to direct the spiraling, the speed, direction, and intensity so that the best energy condenses the most. (This process is comparable to cooking a pudding. First the mass is very watery, and after stirring and heating, it thickens into a pudding.)

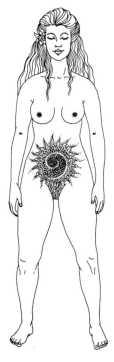

Chi ball.

Through centering you have learned to generate an energy field within, the foundation of self-healing. The art of self-healing is to charge this ocean of energy with positive vibrations, allowing the healing power to unfold. There are different ways to do that. I will introduce two possibilities:

*The essence of self-healing*

## The inner yes

← **Try This!**

- Put your whole awareness into your center, and charge it up with an inner yes. Do this until the whole middle starts to vibrate with a full-hearted yes and with a positive vibration.

## The inner smile

← **Go Deeper!**

When we talk about the inner smile, we mean the quality of love. It's the feeling you get, for example, if you see a beautiful rose, a baby, or an animal. Experiment to find the easiest way to get in touch with the fragrance of your heart, to create a posi-

27

Inner smile.

tive feeling within. Once you are connected with your positive energy source, don't let that feeling flow outside of you. Just keep the feeling inside, and as it accumulates, let that elixir flow in your middle and condense that pleasant feeling there more and more. From there, in your middle, it can nourish and heal your whole being.

• Sit or lie down, and relax. Close your eyes, and start to gently breathe deeper.

• From your inner eye, recall an image that helps you get in touch with the quality of the inner smile, until a feeling of sensual well-being begins to arise.

• Guide that pleasant feeling with your outbreath inward, and fill up your whole body and inner organs with it.

• Continue until the body and inner organs start "smiling" and feeling good.

• In the end, bring your awareness back to your center, and collect and condense this sense of well being there in order to preserve it in your middle.

Get in touch with the fragrance of your heart as much as you can, with your eyes closed, as well as with your eyes open. Take your time with it until you really feel it and are able to enjoy it. Pay attention that you connect with a real feeling, not just with a phony cliché or cloudy dream.

# Chapter 4

# THE TAO
# OF SEXUALITY

In the Tao, sexual energy is considered to be the basis of physical and spiritual health, as well as creativity and meditation. A major aim of this book is to liberate sexuality from physical, mental, and emotional dependencies, blockages, and burdens so that it can be used as a tremendous source of strength and vitality.

Aim and Potential

The sexual energy is the only force that multiplies. This potential can be used to deepen and intensify inner processes, such as self-healing and meditation. The Tao teaches us to guide sexuality consciously, to raise it up to the higher energy centers, to connect it with love and spirituality.

The potential of sexuality can only unfold in an environment of responsibility and independence. The individuality of a person, the personal history, attitude, and the entire circumstance of life manifests and influences a person's sexuality. By the way that a person lives, feels, or handles her sexuality, she can recognize the degree of emotional and physical dependence she is caught in, and the amount of misery it generates in her life.

Free and responsible

Inner emptiness and being uncentered leads to the fact that in our society, sexuality mostly happens on the surface and in the exterior. That means to connect with our sexual energy we need outer stimulation, such as a fantasy, or another person. Many of us are only confronted with our sexuality through an intimate relationship. When we are on our own, sex is often not an issue.

Since sexual energy is usually only perceived when it is aroused, only a few women are aware of the permanent presence of sexuality as an energy source. To assume sexual responsibility involves connecting to this deeper layer of our own sexual force. That source of inner strength can be available at all times, not just when it is stimulated externally. To feel our sexuality, we do not need to depend on the "right" partner, who is touching us in the "right" moment on the "right" place and who whispers tenderly in our ear, "I love you baby."

*What is sexuality?*

In the dictionary, sexuality is defined as the procedure through which reproduction happens. Sexuality is a mechanism to preserve the species. The mechanism of reproduction affects not only the physical plane, it also influences our emotions and our energy. Intercourse, conception, pregnancy, birth, and menstruation are all part of female sexuality.

*Water and fire*

Sexuality has many faces and facets, shrouded by images, myths, fantasy, feelings, dreams, and thoughts. The difficulty of dealing with sexuality is that as long as it remains sexual as such, and caught in the lower energy centers, it is an ongoing struggle between the two forces, male and female, positive and negative, tension and relaxation, striving for the harmony of water and fire, the unity of yin and yang. The wisdom of yin and yang has been used in the Tao as an important guide to unfold the treasures of sexuality.

> If one wants to work with one's life energy it is essential to know the Arts of the Bedchambers. The one who does not know the art of yin and yang won't be able to keep these two forces in harmony, therefore he will be exhausted, run down, and depleted. Only with an enormous effort will he find his inner strength.[1]

---

[1] Thomas Cleary, trans. *Vitality, Energy, Spirit* (Boston: Shambhala, 1991).

While the characteristics of water represent yin, fire symbolizes yang. Sexuality is influenced and moved by both. Water has no color or form of its own, but it can assimilate and take on different qualities, images, fantasies, feelings, and thoughts. Due to the qualities of water, sexuality manifests itself in various ways in each of us.

The water, because it is so permeable, absorbs the qualities that dominate the individual most. These qualities can arise from the conscious or the unconscious of a person. Unconscious forces, and negative emotions or ideas often rule human sexuality. Fire is responsible for the intensity and power of sexuality. Fire has the ability to intensify all qualities and aspects inside of us.

## The "Art of the Bedchamber"

In China, sexual wisdom was known as the "Art of the Bedchamber." Originally these arts were exclusively for the emperor's use. In time they found their way out to a bigger circle of chosen confidants. In old China there were about ten different schools involved with sexual practices. Even in those days, cultivating sexuality was very controversial, and it was being practiced out of many different motives.

There were schools where sexual yoga was studied to benefit health. Within certain circles of alchemists, there was hope that it was possible to achieve immortality by the proper cultivation of sexual energy. On the other hand, there were also schools where charlatans abused the Taoist sexual practices for their own pleasure or to enhance their position. Rich and powerful men were buying or stealing young girls for their sexual practices. There are also stories that in old China, female and male shamans practiced sexual yoga as part of their orgies and rites. Legend has it that sexual secrets were originally taught by women, like the "Mystic Girl" who initiated the Yellow Emperor.

*Sexual wisdom*

All the different traditions of Taoism seemed to agree upon one thing, that sexual energy is the foundation of health, creativity, and spiritual activities, and that wisely used, sexuality could be an essential enrichment and support on the spiritual path. Therefore methods were developed to connect more easily with the sexual force and to liberate its hidden powers.

The whole secret was to retain sexual energy, not to let it drain outside, but to keep it inside the body. For in that way, the body is revitalized and filled with life force. Sexual energy can nourish and strengthen the brain, the inner organs and glands, and enrich the bones. It is not commonly recognized how much energy the human body invests in replenishing its sexual reserves.

Unlike other religious traditions, Taosim does not advocate a life of celibacy. The Taoist retention of sexual energy does not mean living like a monk or a nun. The Taoists were not willing to renounce a great sex life. On the contrary, they developed methods through which they could generate even more power through making love. Sexual wisdom could be explained as the art of playing with the fire without producing any ashes or burning your fingers. To retain sexual energy, a man needs to keep the semen in and not ejaculate. For that, a man has to learn how to separate orgasm from ejaculation. Women, in general, do not lose their life force through sexual activities. The female essence is stored in the egg. Women lose their sexual energy more through menstruation, bearing children, and emotional turmoil.

**Technique and discipline**

Traditionally, Taoist sexuality was developed by men for men, therefore its approach is very technical and requires exacting discipline and an intense physical training. For the majority of men (and for the old Chinese who developed it), this might be the right approach. But in my long-standing experience as a sexologist, I have observed that physical training and energy work alone are not enough to fully integrate Taoist sexual wisdom into their lives. I can confirm that for men, a well-trained body and the use of the techniques are important requirements and a big help. A man needs enough power to be able to control his fire.

If women practice yang methods and approach their sexuality with this hard discipline and training, it does not necessarily help them get in touch with their intrinsic womanhood in a natural way. On the contrary, yang methods can bring them further and further away from their yin nature. That many women today are living their lives in a very yang-oriented way is a major cause of their sexual dissatisfaction. Techniques and discipline belong to the yang category, and in my view, they do not support the fluidity of the female water essence to surrender and flow. In fact, yang methods can easily hurt or evaporate sensitive female fluid energies.

*Liberating sexual energy*

The liberation of sexual energy is a holistic process that involves the bioenergetic, as well as the emotional, mental, and spiritual planes. To be able to experience how precious and healing sexuality can be, you need to detach it from all romantic ideas and free yourself from all emotional entanglements.

# Three Treasures

The three treasures are the "secret recipe" that transforms sexual energy. They are: Essence (ching chi), Life Force (chi), and Spirit (shen). The three treasures describe the path to refine and transform the heavy and dense sexual essence into the highest state of being. How do the three treasures influence our sexuality and what do they want to teach us?

*The essence*

Essence describes the material foundation of sexual energy (the egg cell, sperm, and embryo), which, according to traditional Chinese medicine, is mainly stored in the kidneys. The essence is like an energy reservoir of the body, as it were, a battery. By menstruating, giving birth, or ejaculating, that reservoir gets slowly exhausted and in time more and more depleted. In a lifetime, a woman's body produces up to 400,000 original egg cells, from which only between 400 and 500 will form a mature egg cell. One ejaculation contains approximately 300 million sperm cells. The egg cells, as well as the sperm cells, contain the basic foundation for a soul to start an earthly existence of life. All the

DNA and information needed for life is contained within that small beginning. For the purpose of reproduction, the body makes available only the best raw material it has to offer. The raw material the body needs to produce egg cells and sperm is taken mainly from the kidneys. But other organs, the glands, and the brain and bones are also tapped.

*Keeping ovarian power*

The first secret is to keep your essence in the body. Ovarian breathing is a technique used to draw ovarian power out of the egg cells and guide that energy back into the body. In this way you can strengthen the inner organs, the glands, the brain, and the bones. In the course of this book, I will introduce you to the technique of ovarian breathing. To produce the desired healing effect, ovarian breathing should not be practiced separately, but always as a part of a whole healing system and built up from a solid foundation. Ovarian breathing is very powerful, and it should only be practiced when the uterus and other organs have been cleared of negative emotions and toxins. Otherwise, it could produce negative side effects.

*To refine the essence*

The ching chi is more dense and coarse than chi, the life force, which is circulating in the body. Because of its density, it is heavier and more sluggish. If ching chi is returned to the body unrefined, this can affect your health in a negative way. For example, if unrefined ching chi gets into the kidneys, this can cause allergies, or if it gets into the liver, this can cause tension and a hot temper. The more refined the energy is, the easier it is for the organs and glands to absorb. The microcosmic orbit which you will be introduced to on page 59 is one of the methods for refining energies; another method that can be used is "the inner smile."

*The life force chi*

Many people wish to have more life force and vitality, but not everyone experiences life lived on a higher energy level as something positive. Through more energy, not only the nice or pleasant qualities of life are intensified, but also negative emotions become stronger, which people with a very low energy level can thereby elegantly avoid. In an energy field of higher intensity, unwanted or repressed tensions and conflicts come to the surface and ask for our attention. These unpopular guests keep coming until we are on good terms with them and we can say goodbye to them forever. The second treasure is more an art than a secret: to refine the body and the energy, and to liberate them from negative emotions. I will cover dealing with negative emotions in detail in another chapter. The third treasure is to clean the mind from distortions of the senses and from confusing thoughts. The mind should be clear and open, to provide the empty space to set free the buried spirit. The spirit needs all the space possible to become fully alive, to be able to mirror reality and be prepared for the union with the highest state of consciousness.

To deal with sexuality in a healing and transforming way needs special care, sensitivity, and time and attention. It is best to learn different methods and find out by experience which methods feel right for you, as everyone who embarks on this journey reacts a bit differently. We all have different needs and rhythms that come into play in the process of healing and balancing our sexuality. The process of refining sexual energy should always be supported with meditation and body/energy work, so we can be fully prepared to function on a higher energy level. In particular, it is important to learn the art of centering before beginning the journey to liberate and explore new dimensions through our sexuality.

*Sexual energy needs care and attention*

# Chapter 5

# THE BASIS OF A FULFILLED SEXUALITY

I am always touched when I hear what women and men expect from a sexually fulfilled life. Sexual longings often substitute for a lost religiousness. The expectations placed on sexual experience go far beyond other areas of life, even though the actual sexual moments take up very little time in people's lives. You can calculate for yourself how many minutes in a month you are sexually active or when you are feeling orgasmic and fulfilled. And compare that with the time involved doing housekeeping, making phone calls, reading, eating, working, arguing, etc.

What is sexually fulfilling is very individual for every person. It seems to me that the desire to be sexually fulfilled is often more of a longing to be saved or redeemed; it has more of a spiritual flavor than sexuality per se.

When it comes to sexuality, many people are preoccupied with what is normal. It is amazing how many men and women come to see me for counseling to find out if their sexual inclinations and feelings are normal or not. Normality means everything which corresponds with the norm, and that's not very achievable. The norm is the most reliable love killer there is. It kills aliveness, individuality, and creativity, the main ingredients that make

**Sexual Fulfillment**

*What's normal?*

37

sexuality spicy and juicy. These days, what's considered normal could easily seem perverted and sickening to you and me.

The sexual norm is constantly being created by the collective, and this process is influenced in many ways: by morality, religion, and to a large degree by sexual fantasy and violence. Today, the sexual norm is increasingly manipulated by the media for its own purposes. So what is normal? Do you really want to be normal and live a normal sexuality? Or, is it really achievable to have a normal sexuality? Or, do you want to live your sexuality and get to know what that is all about?

## *Fulfilling or discharging*

Let's stay with what's assumed as normal. According to the norm, sex is assumed to be fulfilling when lovers reach orgasm at the same time, and when the male orgasm escalates into an ejaculation. And somehow this is true, with ejaculation the actual purpose of making love, for the mission of reproduction is fulfilled, at least for a certain time. But how can a "discharging" sexuality be really fulfilling?

The distinguishing characteristics of a state of fulfillment are inner fullness and well-being. How can it be possible to achieve a state of sexual fulfillment through stimulation and triggering the body until it culminates in the discharge of the juices of life? I am not speaking about sexual satisfaction here, but about sexual fulfillment. Satisfaction and fulfillment each have a different quality to them. Sexual fulfillment embodies more yin qualities; it is more lasting, nourishing, and healing. Whereas satisfaction implies the energetic state after a lustful unloading of sexual tension, having more of an immediate or short-term effect. We all know that sexuality can be satisfied in the same way hunger can be satisfied—by taking the edge off. The legitimate question is if there is really such as thing as sexual fulfillment. If there is, then what is it? Let's begin by becoming aware of our own perceptions and ideas.

**My Diary!** ➔ Take your diary and explore the following questions.

1. What does sexual fulfillment mean to you?

2. How fulfilling is your sexuality?

3. Remember and write down a situation in your life where you really felt fulfilled. (This memory does not need to be connected with sex.)

I would like to ask you to stay with these questions for a while, to give you an opportunity to discover for yourself what sexual fulfillment is, uniquely for you.

To be sexually fulfilled does not just depend on the goodwill of the love god Eros. We ourselves can also enhance the chances to be fulfilled. It is our responsibility to create an inviting environment. There are many successful businessmen who come to see me because they want to improve (funny how they always use the word "improve") their sexual performance. These men are ready to totally invest their full energy and time in their career, that's why they have become successful in their businesses, but their sex life is poor and weak. Sex is like any other area of life. The more time people invest in it, the more will become possible. That's what I explain to these businessmen. If they are ready to invest as much in their sexuality as they do in their profession, I am sure that the quality would change for the better in a natural and easy way.

*Inviting fulfillment*

The expectation of a sexual climax is comparable to scoring a goal in world championship soccer. Just being interested won't make anybody a soccer player, much less a top scorer in the game. To play soccer one needs talent, a feeling for the ball, intense training, a good sense for teamwork and of course, some luck. In sexuality, one wants to reach the highest experiences without any preparation. Out of nowhere, after work, between the TV dinner and the next load of laundry, people want to experience orgasmic heights!

There are so many forces counteracting the development of sexual awareness or consciousness. It takes a great deal of care and willingness for a woman to recognize the deeply ingrained mechanisms and patterns that cut her off from consciously experiencing her sexuality.

*Repressed power*

Many of the old cultures and religions knew perfectly well that it is through the natural flow of sexual energy that the qualities of intelligence, independence, individuality, and power develop on their own accord. Therefore, they created a number of rituals and restrictions to keep people under control. For instance, I recently read that in Kuala Lumpur they have officially prohibited kissing. And not only that, so no one is tempted to kiss unobserved in the darkness during a movie, the lights in the theaters are now required to remain on during the showing.

Everything possible has been done by society to keep the tremendous power of women under control; both through maintaining the current structure of power using laws, morality, and religion, and by keeping women financially and emotionally dependent through their role as a mother. In this dependent state, it requires extra effort to break out of this collectively repressed situation to explore or develop new values.

If the natural flow of sexual energy is oppressed, or sex is handled in an unconscious and unnatural way, our intelligence becomes stunted and undermined. In the past, sexual wisdom has been passed on to chosen adepts under strict secrecy in China, as well as in other countries. The European witches, alchemists, and magicians also knew the secrets of sexual power. This knowledge has been kept hidden from the common people.

Over the centuries in the West in particular, under the influence of law and morality, sexuality has become taboo, and as such it has been confined to secrecy and relegated to a world of darkness. Worldwide, in one way or another, sexuality has been separated from our natural social behavior, and thereby also separated from our consciousness. Living in the shadows for so long, as it were, it has lost contact with the sunlight, without which it cannot grow and blossom into maturity. The whole collective needs to be nourished with new information. Sexuality needs more light and transparence in our society, and for this it requires the effort of each one of us.

Sexuality has been pushed out of our everyday life. How often do you hear your neighbors making love? A young woman who has been working with me for a few years reported that while she was making love with her boyfriend, giggling and moaning with pleasure, her neighbor phoned her, very angry, to ask her what they were doing. You rarely see or hear people making love, and usually one does not speak openly and naturally about one's own sex life, even with an intimate lover..

We are not fulfilled sexually because our sexuality has been cut off from the rest of our being. As children, we learned to cut conscious perception off from unwanted, unpleasant, and unknown experiences. In this way, we have fallen out of a state of oneness into a state of being torn. Large aspects of our personality are not directly connected with our conscious perception. And so we do not have the possibility to influence them. The parts of our being which are not filled with our presence and awareness are vulnerable to be manipulated and used by others. Through these unconscious parts within us, we live like marionettes that have no will of their own.

To be in the present, in the here and now, as an integrated unity is an important goal on the path of the Tao. The healing exercise for this is centering (see page 26). In the long term, it will help us reconnect with all our aspects, including our sexuality, and integrate them, so we can experience life and sex in its wholeness.

## Being Cut Off and Unfulfilled

To be able to experience sex in its fullness you need to get to know and develop all the aspects and layers of your being, and then to consciously connect them. Each part is like a brick, and many bricks will make a solid foundation from which you can build your experiences.

### 1. Incorporate the head
In the Tao, the spiritual and mental dimensions of a person are not divided from sexuality, but incorporated and integrated. The state of confusion and blindness we are continuously liv-

## Sexual Reconnection

ing in prevents us from merging with the infinite ocean of existence through our sexuality so we can experience its mysteries.

In the next chapter we will be looking at the mental aspects that distort our sexuality, such as images, fantasies, memories, patterns of behavior, etc. They all influence and limit us. The Taoist exercises train our attentiveness and awareness to clear our minds and hearts from an unnecessary burden, so we can face and receive reality.

## 2. Experiencing the body

Without a body there is no sex, without body perception, no sensual feelings are possible. Only through a body is it possible to be sexual. Having intense sexual experiences requires a healthy and harmonious body, a sensitive perception of the body's experiences, and a strongly rooted centeredness. Many sexual problems can be traced back to physical weaknesses and physical disharmony. To be disconnected from the body means not to be aware of its sensations and signals, and therefore not able to hear and understand its language. This disconnection prevents sexual energy from flowing freely and naturally.

There are different reasons to disconnect or cut off from the awareness of our body. We cut off as a means to escape from unpleasant or painful situations, as a desperate attempt to protect our inner core. For example, children or adults who have been abused or beaten, could find a way to put up with the terrible situation by cutting themselves off from their pain. As a kind of protection, they disconnect. Physical and emotional shocks and pain can interrupt the internal connection between body and mind.

Many men are proud to have an insensitive and hardened body. In order to overcome natural body sensations and sensitivity, they invest time and discipline trying to conquer the body so it becomes like steel. While doing sports, they go over the limit of pain on purpose to toughen the body, to make it insensitive and numb. Also, painkillers, sleeping pills, tranquilizers, drugs, and alcohol weaken the feeling of the body. No exercise will be able to counteract or neutralize the effect of drugs.

However, the main reason for not being in touch with the body is because we never learned to give it enough care, love, and attention. I would like to introduce two techniques that can enhance the connection between body and mind. It is best to do them early in the morning while still lying in bed.

## Connecting the head and the belly

**Healing Point!**

- Massage the two points shown below (Kidney 27) with the thumb and index finger of one hand.

- At the same time, put your other hand on your forehead.

- Stimulate the two healing points, Kidney 27, until your breath deepens and you feel your mind and body are connected.

- Bring the hand that was massaging the energy points down to the navel and start massaging the navel for a while, leaving the other hand on the forehead.

- Rest the hands on your forehead and belly, and stay like this for a while. Deepen the contact between these two areas through your breathing.

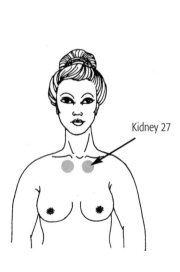

Kidney 27

Connecting the head and belly.

**Try This! →**  **Massaging the ears**

Massage and knead your outer ear strongly, both inside and outside. Pull the ears in all directions until they feel warm and alive. This also helps reconnect body and mind.

*3. Feeling the feeling*

From early childhood, we are trained to repress our true feelings. Our parents and educators used various methods and means to force us to adjust to their desires and the norms of society. The first words a child has to learn are "Thank you," "Please," and "Sorry." Boys are usually exposed to this repressive conditioning even more than girls. From our earliest years of life, repression—not showing our true feelings—becomes our life strategy. No wonder dealing with feeling is confusing, especially for those who were emotionally manipulated, abused, beaten, or rejected in childhood. To get in touch with feelings can be difficult and frightening, and it needs a lot of love, patience, and self-confidence.

When dealing with sexuality, our emotions are always the biggest obstacles we stumble upon. Breathing can help us get back in touch with repressed and unprocessed emotions.

*Breathing and feeling*

Here are two breathing techniques to start with. The goal of working with your breath is to develop an awareness of feelings while breathing, and to help the breath return to a deep and natural flow.

**Try This! →**  **Expanding your breath**

- Stand in an upright position and start to breathe deeply. Expand your chest as much as you can.

- While breathing out, make a sound for as long as you can, until the lungs are completely empty. Do not breathe in straight away, hold the breath out for a while. Let go and take a couple of "normal" breaths. Do this about 3 times.

- Bend your upper body down, keeping the knees slightly bent and the hands hanging loose. Keep this position and continue breathing deeply until the body and the breathing relax.

• Slowly come up again, and finish by centering yourself.

## Deep breathing

← **Go Deeper!**

• Lie down and close your eyes. Bring your awareness to the back of your throat.

• Begin to breathe as if sucking the air in from your throat. Your mouth remains closed. Breathe like this in a very slow rhythm, without any effort. At the beginning do not breathe in too much air, or you may get dizzy. Increase slowly.

• Breathe like this as long as it feels good.

### 4. Let the energy flow

Not everybody has the ability to feel subtle energies. But to be able to work and transform sexual energy, a high energy level as well as the ability to sense energy is needed. The energy also needs to be flowing. Many women are afraid to surrender themselves to the flow and the intensity of energy. If you start moving into your energy more and more, suddenly it will take over and all there is left for you to do is to relax and let it happen. It is usually easier to try that first by yourself, and then you can allow it if someone else is there.

Here are two methods you can use to enjoy your energy. To energize your body you can also use breathing techniques.

## Dancing

← **Try This!**

• Dancing is one of the most effective methods to bring your energy into a flow, but dance freely, without any structure or observers. It is all about feeling good, not looking good. Put on music that is full of rhythm, power, and swing. Close your eyes and just go wild. Move it all to get your energy flowing. Do that for about 20 minutes.

• Afterward, lie down on your back. Put both your hands on your center.

- Let all the released energy flow in your center and collect it there.

**Go Deeper! →**

### Kundalini meditation

The kundalini meditation is a very powerful method to bring the body's energies into a flow. There are four phases that are all done with closed eyes. It is best to get yourself a blindfold to wear during the meditation. There is also a CD for the meditation. You can purchase it through the address listed in the back of the book.

*First Phase*

Take on the position of a horsewoman, and start to shake your whole body as wildly and ecstatically as possible. Let your body be moved by vibration, shaking and moving for 15 minutes without stopping. The deeper you go into this, the more effective it will be. Menstruating women should do this phase softly.

*Second Phase*

For the next 15 minutes let your body dance as freely and intensely as possible, without stopping. Go on breathing deeply in this stage.

*Third Phase*

This is the yin phase to integrate. Stand totally still for the next 15 minutes; do not move at all (do not scratch, cough, or sway back and forth). Just stand there rooted and centered, and be aware not to move away from yourself into thoughts or space out into the world of dreams.

*Fourth Phase*

The healing phase—lie down and put both hands on your middle, to heal and balance your body and your energy from there.

# Chapter 6

# OUT OF THE HEAD

We are raised and educated in a lopsided way, as if the mind would be our only valuable reality. Other dimensions and layers of our being are all redirected toward the analyzing mind in the illusion that they can be understood in this way. Our emotions, and certainly our sexuality, cannot be lived and integrated through the intellect. This only leads to a state of confusion and tension.

In this chapter we will explore the different states of consciousness and activities of the mind. This includes your attitude toward life, your conditioning, your thinking patterns, your fantasies, your dreams, your imagination, and your spiritual power. Mind can be divided into two main categories, consciousness (which develops from the yang principle), and the unconscious (which evolves out of the yin). Most of our problems evolve out of the conflict between the conscious and unconscious aspects inside us.

We could define "conscious" as that which describes our perception and experience of thoughts, memories, imagination, sensory perception, feelings, and will. "Unconscious" can be defined as "psychic content" and processes that are not consciously perceived by the "I." The unconscious can be divided

**Conscious– Unconscious**

into two parts, the personal and the collective unconscious.

The unconscious stores everything, even that which has not been consciously experienced, registered, or digested. To enter consciously into the unknown abyss of the unconscious is to bring consciousness into the unconscious. This process is a heightening of one's inner world of awareness. With the help of the female treasures of the Tao, we learn to get in touch with the personal and collective unconscious fragments inside us that possess our sexuality. In this way it is possible to dissolve inhibiting and limiting behavior patterns and blocks.

In chapter 15 you will find exercises for your inner organs. You will learn to develop a love affair with your organs, and in time you will be able to feel the unconscious contents that have been stored within them. Feeling these contents is the first step toward dissolving or changing them.

*Heightening of awareness*

Through our yin nature, it is easy for us women to get in touch with the depths of our unconscious. To get to know these deeper layers it is necessary to be able to surrender to stillness and depth. The deeper we are able to dive into the inner self, and the more receptive and relaxed we are about it, the easier it is to feel, explore, and discover the unconscious.

There are many approaches in dealing with the unconscious. A yang-oriented approach will attempt to dominate and control yin areas of the unconscious, like feelings and sexuality, with discipline, demanding physical training and mental techniques. Our so-called holy, spiritual men, our monks or priests, are often overwhelmed by sexual desires they cannot completely control, and they wind up losing themselves in their repressed unconscious, raping a woman, or breaking their vows. The point here is that unless we develop a strong connection to the unconscious, the light of consciousness is not able to illuminate sexuality. It is possible to keep the fire of sexuality under control by the power of will, but it is very strenuous, and there is always the deep inner fear of losing control—for the inner monster can go off at any moment and explode like a bomb.

It is a very common idea that one should be able to switch off the mind while making love, to stop the ongoing chattering of thoughts, our continuous inner commenting and judging. These thoughts are just the tip of the iceberg, most of which is submerged in the unconscious. To be able to shut down the annoying inner noise, we first need to recognize the underlying patterns of behavior that feed the process of thought.

*Clarity*

To develop our sexuality, our heads need to be clear and alert. The Tao asks us to clear and empty our minds from all images and conditioning, so that we can relax and perceive reality as it is. In this way, we prepare ourselves to experience life in its original vibrancy and clarity. The continuous circling of thought prevents that clarity. This movement of thought reflects our unconscious, our conditioning, our values, our past unresolved experiences, and so forth. If you want to let go of these disturbing thoughts, you will need to be ready to sacrifice your personal ideas and dreams, and to drop all boundaries and limitations: to live a little death so there is space for the new to come into being.

We have fixed ideas about how we want our life to be, and this is true especially of our sex life! Things like how we would like our lover to behave toward us, and which are the right circumstances and conditions under which we are ready for sex. We automatically assume we know what would make us happy and fulfilled. The tragedy is that things are the way they are and not necessarily the way we want them to be, both within us and in the world surrounding us. Very rarely do the circumstances of life adjust themselves to our beliefs and dreams. So one conflict follows another because our lovers, partners, and the people we come across in our day to day lives are not really the way we want them to be, but are the way they are.

*Fixed ideas*

Reality, as it is, is sexuality's best breeding ground. Rooted in the here and now, it can begin to grow until its flowers and fragrance spread into our lives. Fixed ideas, demands, wishes, dreams, and fantasies kill your nature. They castrate your aliveness and distort reality.

## Sexual History

In order to recognize your own sexual behavior, you must be willing to understand it at its roots. There are always good reasons that sexuality is the way that it is in your life. Being loving and patient with yourself will support you to decode your own behavior. Give yourself enough time to deal with your sexual history. By doing this you might develop some compassion for yourself.

The following questionnaire will assist you in exploring your past. If it begins to feel overwhelming for you at any time, take a break and center yourself, keep on breathing, and fill yourself with positive energy, with the help of the "inner smile."

### Questionnaire

*Childhood*

- What kind of mood, spirit, or attitude toward sex was in your home when you were a child? Were your parents or educators open about sex, or more reserved and closed?
- Could you recognize the sexual relationship between your parents? How was their love life?
- How did your parents portray their intimate life to you?
- What was your reaction to that?
- Have you seen your parents and your brothers and sisters naked? And vice versa?
- How was that for you?
- Did that change at any point?
- How do you feel about showing your body today?
- How do you deal with showing your body now?
- Do you have any memories of playing any sexual games as a child?
- In your childhood, have you ever been seduced or forced to have sexual contacts from an older child or a grown up?
- At that time, did you have any unusual experiences with sex?
- How old were you when sex first entered your mind?
- Who answered your questions and how were they answered?
- According to you, how should the facts of life be explained to a child?

*Puberty*

- Compared to other girls, how was your development (breasts and menstruation): early, average, or late?
- Were you prepared for your first bleeding?
- If yes, by whom and how?
- According to your opinion, how should girls be prepared to become a woman?
- Have you been sexually pestered or abused at any time after the age of 12?
- Have you had any sexual contacts that hurt or frightened you?
- Were you brought up religiously?
- How did this affect your sexuality?

*Masturbation*

- Are you able to have an orgasm?
- If yes, how does it work best for you?
- Are you masturbating?
- If yes, when did you start?
- How did you discover it?
- Did you talk about it with anyone?
- How often do you masturbate?
- How do you like to masturbate the most?
- Do you masturbate in the presence of your partner?
- Do you have any negative feelings associated with it?
- If you have never had an orgasm, don't worry, we will get to that later. You will get some hints.

*Loving a man*

- How was your first romantic or sexual contact with a man?
- How old were you when you first had intercourse?
- Was it your own wish to have sex, or was it more somebody else's?
- How was it?
- What kind of feelings were there at the time?
- With how many men have you had a sexual relationship?
- How do you like making love?
- Do you feel fulfilled while making love?
- Do have an orgasm while making love? Always, often, seldom, never?

- Is it possible for you to make love without being in a love relationship?

### Loving a woman
- Do you feel attracted to women?
- Have you had sexual experiences with women?
- How was that for you?
- Do you consider yourself a bisexual?
- Are you a lesbian?
- If yes, do you feel okay with that?

### Unusual experiences
- Have you had unusual or exceptional sex experiences?
- With children?
- Rape?
- Sadistic and/or masochistic sex games?
- Sex with more partners or in a group?
- Prostitution?
- Others?

### Tools

- Are you using sex tools like a vibrator or love balls, etc.?
- Are you using pornographic material, like videos, photographs, or books?
- Others?

## Facing Reality

This in-depth look into your own sexual history has opened a possibility to discover deeper layers of your personality. To confront your reality is sometimes very unsettling at first, but it is the best possible initial situation for you to be in, to precipitate a change for the better. As long as your sexual reality is hidden under your desires, projections, and fears, dealing with this aspect of yourself will remain a very confusing affair.

Basically we have two possibilities to approach life. The first possibility is that we are focused and interested in discovering our reality. We choose the path of self-knowledge to get to the bottom of the mystery of life, to explore and reveal our own nature and its potential. For this adventure we need a deep longing, a natural curiosity, and enough courage to meet the unknown.

The other possibility is to create our own reality according to images and ideals—to try to become who our society, our religion, or our dreams expect us to be.

The Tao is supporting us to explore our reality to get to know ourselves, and not to waste our time and energy in building castles in the air. But as long as we remain identified with our dreams, it is difficult to distinguish between dreams and reality.

Daydreaming is a state between sleep and wakefulness. Psychoanalysts define daydreaming as a dreamlike activity of fantasy that diminishes the clarity of our consciousness. Sexuality is a very common and frequent subject of daydreaming. Research has proved that much more time is spent in sexual daydreaming then in actual sexual activity. It is interesting to note that abused children tend to daydream much more than other kids. Because they are not able to deal with their actual experience, they escape into daydreams and create a fairytale world so they are able to bear the pain. Of course, this does not mean everyone who is daydreaming has been abused.

*Daydreams*

Romantic dreams prevent many women from getting really involved in sex. Women often depend on their outer circumstances fitting with their romantic dream to find their Prince Charming, to feel happy and sexually excited. As long as sexual and sensual feelings are only arising when triggered by a certain person, in a certain way, in a very special moment, sexual fulfillment will remain a lucky shot.

*Romantic dreams*

Female sexuality has the potential of being independent, which can be a big advantage in a woman's life. A woman can feel sensual and good in any situation. If she is with a partner or not, whether the partner is understanding, insensitive, loving or perverted, a woman is capable of enriching every possible sexual

*With or without a partner*

situation with her own healing qualities. Every situation can be a new challenge to discover another unconscious part of her and a new opportunity to heal and develop it.

Therefore, women need to be permanently rooted in (and connected with) their sensual womanhood. Otherwise, sexuality with a partner remains limited and can easily attract conflicts. Many of us in the Western world are able to decide for ourselves how we want to live our life. It is our own choice whether to get married, to have many children or none, or to have sex with a woman or a man, or with many men. It is possible to have a new partner for each phase of our life and to live an independent and free life as a happy single.

*Personal energy field*
It is our own personal responsibility to live in such a way that self-healing and meditation are possible. Every action we take, our thoughts and emotions, all produce a certain vibration and contribute to our personal energy field. It is up to us if we are spreading the fragrance of joy and light in our life, or if we are a needy vacuum that attracts negative energy. In the following chapter we will get to know the Taoist energy work known as inner Chi Kung, which will support us to strengthen and refine our personal energy field. Chi Kung helps us become aware of destructive energy patterns and enables us to transform negativity into a positive vibration.

*To recognize and dissolve patterns*
The ability to recognize energy patterns that rule our daily life requires a certain amount of inner reflection and time. To only recognize these patterns intellectually won't be enough to transform them. The more light and awareness we bring into unconsciousness, the easier it will become to recognize the patterns that limit and hinder our being. And the more we live in and from our center, the more new insights and qualities can be integrated to become a constant part of our life.

# Chapter 7

# THE REALM OF SUBTLE ENERGIES

**M**any of the religious and esoteric teachings in many cultures are based on the discovery that a refined net of subtle energies spreads through each of us, connecting us to the universe. For over 4000 years, the Chinese have worked with a system of subtle energies that run through the body that are called "the veins of the dragon." These veins are better known in the West as "the meridians." The energy that streams through these channels is called "chi" or "qi." In Japan this force is known as "ki," and in India, it is known as "prana." There is no exact translation for the word "chi" in English; mostly the word "energy" has been used. But the word energy gives an incomplete and limited picture of "chi." Chi is far more then just energy. If Tao is the essence, it is manifested by chi. When we talk about chi, it is also the breeze, the vitality, and vibrancy that makes us alive.

**Chi and the Subtle Energy Centers**

The Taoists were able to use the phenomenon of subtle energies to develop a deep understanding of the functioning of body and soul. They discovered that if a body was energetically unbalanced or ill, certain points on the skin became very sensitive. There are over 300 different energy points spread out over the body and they are interconnected through the meridians.

*Energy points*

These sensitive energy points are also known as acupressure or acupuncture points, and they can be stimulated by massage, pressure, or needling. If the right points are stimulated, it helps the body return to its natural healthy flow.

The energy points are also known to be openings to the universe. The more open and porous these points are, the easier it is for the cosmic energies to flow through them. If the points or energy centers are closed or wounded, chi becomes trapped there or is diminished, and this can cause people to feel insecure or isolated. In the appendix, there is an overview of some of the points that can have a supporting and healing effect on female sexuality.

*Energy centers*   The energy points are distinct from the energy centers, places where different meridians cross and flow together. In these places, your energy field becomes more dense and stronger. These energy centers are the major openings to the outside world, where it is possible to assimilate or to lose chi. It is also interesting to note that it is through these energy centers that other people can easily be manipulated.

*Energy work*   One of the main purposes of energy work or Chi Kung is to bring the human body in harmony with the universe. Learning how to bring sexuality in tune with the whole is also an essential part of the inner Chi Kung. Being able to feel the flow of subtle energies and then guide them through all the energy centers is the basis of Taoist energy work. The microcosmic orbit, which you will learn in this chapter, is one of the basic tools used to transform and heal your sexuality.

Energy, which is non-substantial, belongs to the yang principle, even though it can be very soft and tender. And dense material substance belongs to the yin principle. A healthy body (yin) is able to attract and absorb energy or vitality (yang). The healthier and stronger a body is, the more energy it can absorb and store.

*Women and energy work*   Because of their yang nature, it is not possible for most men to merge and surrender to the vast open emptiness of the Tao, nirvana, or however you want to call it. Men first need to generate a high level of energy to break through the protective, isolating yang shield on the outside, which protects the tender, vulnerable, and receptive yin inside a man. Only in this way is it possible for them to merge with the whole.

Since the yin principle works just the other way around, we women must start from a totally different base. Contrary to men, it is important for a woman to only generate as much energy as she is able to integrate and absorb in her chi-ball and into her silence. If a woman starts to surrender her body to the male principle, and her energy becomes too extroverted and dominant, her female essence evaporates and this prevents her from getting in touch with her true nature. The female energy source reveals itself only through yin. Yin, also known as Mother Earth, has the ability to receive and absorb the heavenly yang.

A weak body can hold little energy. Women with a blood deficiency, for example, can only keep a limited amount of energy. Therefore, women with weak constitutions, with depleted organs and bones for instance, need to be careful not to trigger an unnecessary surplus of energy in their body by

Yin holds yang.

Weak yin cannot hold yang.

exercising, being emotional, or having intense sex. For these women, excess energy is an unhealthy condition that could only further weaken their yin essence. Remember that too much fire (yang) will evaporate the water (yin).

**Important Hints!**

Symptoms or side effects may occur when there is a surplus of energy and heat in the body.

*Possible side-effects of energy work:*
- Restlessness
- Sleeping problems
- Intense dreams
- Stress
- Hot flashes
- Emotional imbalance
- Impatience
- Irritability
- Heavy menstrual bleeding
- Fear
- Strong heart palpitation
- A stitch or pain in the chest
- The feeling, after an intense experience, of falling into a hole

If you are suffering from some of the symptoms mentioned here, you need to begin to build up your physical base. Start by eating good food that will increase the substance and volume of blood. It is important to make sure you get enough sleep, and ideally, support your body with traditional Chinese herbs, carefully chosen by an expert in Chinese medicine. The stronger your body becomes, the higher your energy level can become. Finally, it is important to practice the centering exercises. The more rooted and centered within you are, the more you can keep a high energy level.

# The Microcosmic Orbit

When the two energy channels, Ren Mai and Du Mai, are joined together, and the chi is able to flow in a circle through the whole body, this is called "the microcosmic orbit." The microcosmic orbit interconnects important energy points and energy centers. The Ren Mai channel, also known as the "Directing Vessel," belongs to the yin, and the Du Mai channel, which is also called "Governing Vessel," is a part of the yang principle. If chi is flowing freely within the microcosmic orbit, the whole body gets nourished and harmonized by it. Guiding chi consciously through these channels will refine and purify it. So the microcosmic orbit can be used to adjust other energies, such as sexual energy, to our own energy system. It is a very helpful tool for meditators, lovers, and healers.

*Women and the microcosmic orbit*

I have noticed that many women do not like to practice the microcosmic orbit. Nevertheless, I consider opening the microcosmic orbit essential training for women. The art of energy work includes intuitively triggering and provoking a sensational flow of energy, and letting that tide of energy take you wherever it may. This is just one of the possibilities of energy work. To consciously guide your energy—and to be able to condense and integrate it—is another possibility. And without having developed both aspects, your approach will be incomplete, and energy work may not be effective. The first step, before opening the microcosmic orbit, is learning to center yourself and to collect and store energy in your middle.

*The microcosmic orbit and its points*

The interconnected energy flow between the following energy centers forms the microcosmic orbit.

1. *Navel:* Here you start and end the microcosmic orbit

2. *Heavenly Palace:* The sexual center of a woman. It is located about one hand below the navel, level with the uterus.

3. *Perineum:* The "Door of Life and Death" is located between vagina and anus and is like a collecting pool of yin energies. Through this door the life force can easily leak out of the body.

*4. Sacrum / Coccyx:* The Taoists call the eight holes of the sacrum the "Eight Doors or Caves of Immortality." If they are blocked, it is not possible for sexual energy to rise and unite with the higher energy centers and consciousness.

*5. Kidney Point / Ming Meng:* The "Door of Life" is opposite the navel and supplies the kidneys and sexual organs.

*6. Adrenal Glands:* This point is located opposite the solar plexus at the level of the adrenal glands.

*7. Point between the Shoulder Blades:* This point, located opposite the heart center, stores old pain and diseases to relieve the heart. The heart can also be eased from emotion and heat through this point.

*8. Neck Point:* This point corresponds with the seventh cervical vertebra and is a very delicate passage within the microcosmic orbit, which needs special attention. If this center is blocked, the energy cannot flow up and chooses the way of least resistance and flows out through the hands. Bodyworkers need to take special care here.

*9. Medulla Point:* The "Jade Pillow" regulates the breath and is part of the cranial pump, through which the brain is supplied with chi and cerebrospinal fluid. The cranial pump can be activated by pulling in the chin slightly. In this position the neck can expand and becomes more permeable.

*10. The Crown Point:* Is located in the middle of the top of the head and is connected with the pineal gland. This center helps us see our life from a higher perspective so we can develop ourselves.

*11. The Third Eye:* Is located in the center of the forehead, slightly above the eyebrows. Glide your finger over the forehead; you won't miss this point. It is connected with the pituitary gland.

*12. The Palate Point:* Also known as the "Heavenly Pond." At this point Ren Mai and Du Mai, the yin and yang forces flow together. To connect these two energy vessels, place your tongue behind your upper teeth. Be aware to keep your mouth closed as often as possible, as in this way, the energies can flow in a closed circle, which protects you from many unwanted energies that can otherwise enter your system. While speaking, we lose a lot of our strength via an open mouth.

*13. Throat Point:* Is located a bit below the thyroid and should not be stimulated too strongly. It is a very sensitive point that easily overreacts.

*14. The Heart Center:* Is controlled by the thymus gland. For self-healing, it is the most important center, where love, peace, and compassion can unfold.

*15. The Solar Plexus:* Is located in the upper belly area between the ribs and the navel. From this center the aura develops. Repressed emotions, self-control, and difficulties with power can cause an unpleasant feeling of tension in this center.

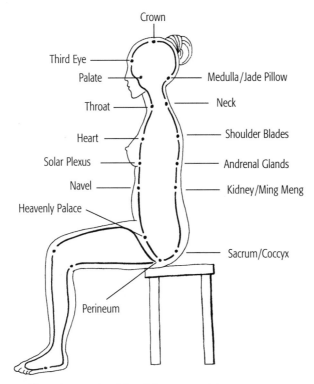

The microcosmic orbit and its energy points.

*Opening the microcosmic orbit*

Before you start experimenting with the microcosmic orbit, I would like to give you some more basic information. The purpose of practicing the microcosmic orbit is to open and activate all the different centers and to connect them through the two channels. It will take some time to be able to really feel the points. I come across many people who are practicing the microcosmic orbit only in their imagination, which is not how it should be done. Like this, the essence of it is missed. To prevent this from happening, practice the centering exercise until you really feel it without any doubt at all. Once you are able to do that, it will be easy to open the points of microcosmic orbit and guide energy through them. As long you are asking yourself, "Do I feel the right thing?" or "How is this supposed to feel?"—you have not experienced it yet. But as soon you have really experienced it, you will know how it feels to be in contact with it.

*Getting to know the points*

Take your time to connect with all the points—one after the other—until you are experiencing the quality of each individual one. Be creative to get in touch with them and try every possible means: use your hands, your breathing, as well as your ability to feel. Circle or spiral with your awareness around each point until it becomes alive. Bring your awareness, with the help of your breath, from one point to the next one. In the beginning you can also use the palms of your hands to touch each point as you come to it. This will help stimulate the points and guide the energy flow.

For many women, the microcosmic orbit naturally flows the opposite way around than it does for men. That is, it flows up the front and down the back. Still, there are two reasons why we practice the energy flow as it has traditionally been taught. First, as the heart center is blocked for most women, from all the disappointment and pain it has experienced, sending even more energy toward the heart can have a negative effect. It can produce symptoms like pain in the chest, stress, irritability; all of the symptoms of too much energy or heat that are listed on page 58. Secondly, the opening of the microcosmic orbit is a kind of a training to learn how to guide your energy flow consciously. It is not about generating intense sensations.

## Microcosmic orbit                                      ← **Try This!**

- Sit on your chair, upright and relaxed, without leaning on it. Close your eyes and let your whole awareness flow to your center.

- As soon as you feel truly connected with it, bring your attention and hands to the navel. Surrender to the navel.

- Begin to circle or spiral with your inner sense of feeling around your navel from within, until you feel that the point is becoming alive.

- With your outbreath, bring the quality and the feeling of that point down to your Heavenly Palace. Start activating that center with the help of your breath, circling there with your awareness or inner sense of feeling until you are able to feel this point coming alive as well.

- Go on to the next point in the sequence.

- When you have reached the crown, bring the tip of your tongue up to your palate, just behind the front teeth. This is the way to interconnect Ren Mai and Du Mai so the circle is closed. And then guide the energy flow through the third eye downward to the throat center and continue as described.

- When you have reached the navel again, bring all the energy back to your center and collect it there until it becomes dense.

To guide the energy flow downward, it works best to use your outbreath, and to bring the energy flow upward, you can use the inbreath, as if you were sucking it up with a straw.

The more you practice the microcosmic orbit, the more porous your energy centers and channels will become. Once the blockages are dissolved, it is possible to complete the circle with one breath. But there is no hurry to be so proficient with it, just go step by step. The centers are not just energetically blocked, but also mentally and emotionally give them the time they need to be able to open up. This process cannot be forced, so again, take your time with it.

**Sexual Centers**

Sexual energy is regulated by the interplay of different areas of the body called sexual centers. When these centers are blocked or wounded, sexual energy gets stuck there and cannot flow anywhere else. To be able to let sexuality spread through out your whole body, so it can connect with the higher energy centers, it needs to be liberated. Give yourself time to explore the different sexual centers of your body.

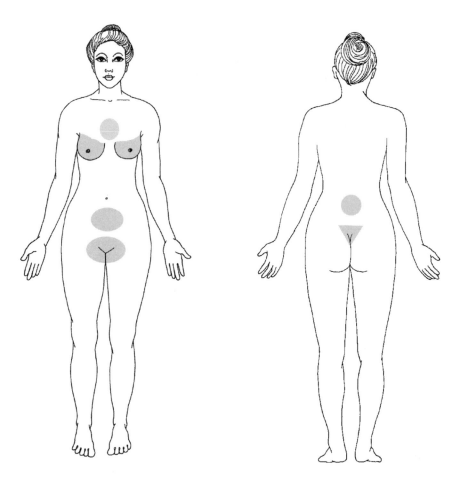

The sexual centers.

The Ming Meng (shown in illustration on page 64 right) is called the "Door of Life" or the "Door of Vitality" and is considered the well of sexual energy. The door of life is the well of water (yin) and fire (yang) and is the residence of the Ocean of Essence. The Ming Meng guides our sexual functions, and is located opposite the navel. The fire of the Ming Meng is warming the uterus and it rules fertility, menstruation, and sexual activities. Water gives fire a material foundation. Listed below are three methods to strengthen the Ming Meng..

*Ming Meng*

## Ming Meng breathing

← **Try This!**

- Stand in an upright position.

- Close your eyes and mouth, and guide your awareness down to the Ming Meng until you feel it. The quality of the Ming Meng is very deep, tender, and soft.

- Breathe in deeply through the Ming Meng.

- While breathing out, let the energy stream from the Ming Meng into your kidneys.

- Do this breathing as softly, quietly, and deeply as possible.

## Kidney cleansing

- Sit upright on your chair and close your eyes.

- Connect with your kidneys.

- Take enough time to feel what weakens or burdens your kidneys.

- While breathing in, let the upper part of your body start gently leaning forward. Cross your hands in front of your knees.

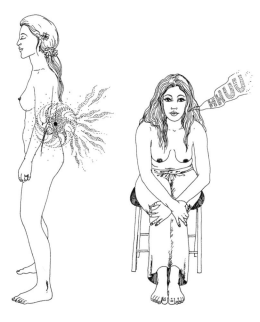

Ming Meng breathing.          Kidney cleansing.

- Clean and unburden your kidneys with the sound "Huuuuu." While you are making this sound, pull in your stomach a bit so that the kidneys get some pressure.

- Repeat as many times as you like, but give yourself a pause of stillness after every breath.

### Kidney breathing

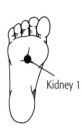

Kidney 1

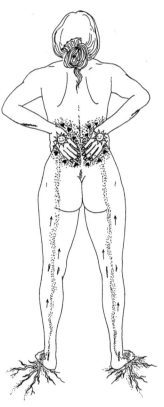

Kidney breathing.

- Stand again in an upright position, feet parallel, and a shoulder width apart.

- Lay your palms on both your kidneys.

- Bring your awareness down to the soles of your feet to connect with the acupressure point Kidney I, also known as the "Bubbling Well," until you feel this point pulsing.

- While breathing in, draw earth power up through that point, and while breathing out, fill the kidneys with that healing force.

- Kidney breathing is very deep, soft, and tender, just like Ming Meng breathing.

It is also very nice to do this exercise out in nature.

The vertebral column supports the body and protects the spinal cord. All the impulses of the nervous system of the body are relayed through the spinal cord; therefore, the spine is also related to sexuality. The more flexible a spine is, the easier the sexual energy can flow. Back problems can cause sexual problems. A strong and healthy back can easily deal with your sexual energy. There are many methods available today for strengthening your back, supporting it to find its natural flexibility again, like osteopathy or craniosacral balancing. A skilled professional can help you get your back in shape again.

*The spine*

# Chapter 8

# ENERGY PATTERNS RULING FEMALE SEXUALITY

T|he well of a woman's sexuality lies in her innermost core. It arises from a place of silence and is rooted in the depth of her being. The main part of a woman's sexual organs is completely invisible from without. This is opposite to men, who have their sexual organs hanging outside their bodies. Since female sexuality is ruled by the yin principle, a woman's treasures are hidden within. Our sexual organs are located in a protected space, imbedded in our lap. To be able to take on the biological responsibility of female sexuality, a woman's body is able to open up to receive the male sperm, and to provide space for new life to grow inside.

*Yin: the Foundation of Female Sexuality*

Strong inside and weak outside is the pattern that the yin principle embodies. It is a woman's responsibility to develop and live her inner and outer life in a balanced way. For many women, it only becomes possible to surrender to (and enjoy the sensuality and vulnerability of) their sexuality when they are connected with their inner strengths.

The yin archetype, being soft and open toward the outside, enables a woman to live her life in deep communion with the outside world. She has the ability to absorb and feel her surroundings. For a woman, it is a necessity to be connected with

*Strong inside, weak outside*

Strong inside—
weak outside.

69

her sensitivity and ability to feel, in order to have a precise perception of the situations and atmosphere around her. Through her inner strength, a woman is able to influence and neutralize negative situations and emotions before they become destructive or hurtful to her.

*Openness*  To be open and receptive are yin qualities. These are the prerequisites to experience the potential of womanhood. To be open is not limited just to sex; it is a feminine approach to life. To be open means to let yourself be touched and inspired by life, to be able to receive and take in the capabilities, ideas, energies, feelings, and moods of others. To be open means to be able to welcome what life is offering you.

Being open, surrendering and receiving while making love, makes women even more vulnerable. That's why we need to learn how to deal with this highly sensitive yin state, and being centered through our centering exercise is one of the most helpful tools for this.

*Vulnerability*  I have not come across a woman who has never been hurt in her life. In connection with sex, our vulnerability is even deeper, and can leave profound wounds behind. So, either we need to learn it or leave it. For women who want to explore their sexuality, the art of self-healing is an essential tool to learn. A woman who is rooted in her middle will be able to deal with her vulnerability in a more creative way. To me, our vulnerability is more like a capacity to allow life to touch us in a delicate way, in a place deep inside of us, rather than something that implies a disadvantage or a liability. It completely depends on the inner state a woman embodies. If she carries a positive vibration or mood within, we call it love and compassion. If life touches a negative ground within her, it is interpreted as being wounded or hurt.

## More Energy Patterns

"Strong outside and weak inside" corresponds to yang. Yang energy is radiating to protect the weak and tender within. When ruled by the yang principle, sexuality takes on qualities that make us extroverted, exciting, energetic, and fiery. Because yang energy always remains on the surface, yang-oriented sex has no healing or nourishing effect on women. It is not that we are unable to cope with yang sexuality; as women, we are very adaptable and can have lots of fun with it. But we are not able to reveal our potential through yang behavior. Taoist sexuality is the art of being able to root highly explosive yang energies in the deep silent abyss of yin.

Strong outside–
weak inside.

### Weak inside, weak outside

Unfortunately, we see this alarming state more and more often these days. The body is neither protected by an outer yang shield, nor is it able to influence effects entering from the outside in a healing way. In this state, people easily become a medium for the collective unconscious to function through them. They are absorbing the world around them without any filtering. For a woman in this state, it is neither possible for her to really open up, nor is she capable of drawing a line. For this woman, as long as she is in this state, it is better not to have sex. Such a woman needs to build up her energy field within herself so she can sense her own needs and limits again.

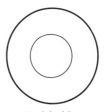

Weak inside–
weak outside.

It is very common these days for men and women in a state of inner deficiency to try to compensate for it in any way possible. To escape the dark hole or abyss inside of them, they attempt to squeeze the juice out of an empty life, just to feel sexually aroused for a few moments. This behavior pattern becomes addictive; it repeats itself again and again. Some of the techniques that are being used to provoke this sexual intensity are very abusive, from fantasizing and pornographic material to perverted sex involving power games, which often spiral out of control without any consideration for others.

Strong inside–
strong outside.

To see such a power pack in nature is very rare. In any case, this will be an exception.

### Strong inside, strong outside

*From yin to yang*

Yin sexuality is ruled by the qualities of water. It is emotional, deep, soft, quiet, relaxed, nourishing, and healing. Yang-oriented sexuality is ruled by fire. It is intense, climax-oriented, rough, exciting, and intense. Only the unity of these opposites becomes a whole. The Tao of female sexuality supports women to develop their yin qualities. Developing a solid rooting in yin qualities, which are the foundation of yang, makes it possible for women to move more freely into yang areas without losing themselves.

*Part Three*

# OUR
# BODY—
# HEALTHY
# AND NATURAL

# Chapter 9

# HARMONY WITHIN THE BODY

Energy, air, healing exercises, and love are important ingredients that maintain our well-being and health. But the body also needs good quality raw material to maintain its proper functioning. These essential nutrients are drawn from foods. The different tastes, colors, energetic and thermal functions of foods all directly influence the body. That means that all eating disorders and bad eating or drinking habits affect our sexuality to a significant degree.

**How Nutrition Influences Health and Sex**

Who does not know the saying, "You are what you eat"? The more natural foods you give your body, the more naturally it can function. The modern treatment and handling of foods add countless numbers of chemical substances to what we normally ingest today. This places strain on the body. How should it be able to identify and digest all these man-made chemicals? The remnants of hormones, penicillin, pesticides, flavor enhancers, artificial colors, and preservatives all tend to remain unprocessed within the body.

**Natural Foods**

The consequences that chemically treated and gene-manipulated foods have on the human organism should not be underestimated. For instance, recent studies have shown that due to hormonal additives we have ingested from the food we eat, girls today grow faster and taller, and also have fuller breasts. Manufacturers of bras had to start producing more of the larger sizes than ten years ago. This is just one example of how additives can influence the body.

The body does not know how to process unnatural chemical substances; therefore they are being left behind in the intestines, in the joints, bones, organs, and in the tissues. This chronic state of poisoning can provoke unpredictable physical and emotional strain, and also sexual reactions.

## Yin and Yang of Nutrition

The Taoists understand that all food and drink has a thermal effect on our organism, and nutrition can be looked at from the perspective of yin and yang. All food, drink, and herbs have been categorized as either "cold," "refreshing," "neutral," "warming" or "hot." This has nothing to do with whether the foods are eaten cold or warmed up, but on how the foods affect the balance of yin and yang within us. Let's look at how the thermal consequences of our foods can influence sexuality.

## Undernourished women

When leafing through fashion magazines and looking around Western cities, you'll see lots of skinny, undernourished women and girls. In the restaurants, you see them sipping their diet sodas and ordering salads with low fat dressing. Dressed up, these women might look very fashionable, but underneath there is often only an unsightly skeleton covered with a wafer-thin layer of skin.

In youth our inner reservoir is still filled. The organs, glands, and bones contain enough reserves, and it is possible to live on those resources for a few years. But if our emergency reserve gets depleted, one starts to slowly consume oneself. I am not talking about women who are from their body type naturally slim; they eat as much as they want and do not gain weight. I am addressing those women who are obsessed with their figure and torture themselves to be able to fit into a plastic, thin ideal. In the Western world, many women are very conscious of their intake of calories, consuming mainly low calorie foods. Most of the low calorie foods contain little energy and have a cooling effect on the body.

Since a woman is ruled by the yin principle, it is natural that her body is rounder and has a fuller mass than a man's body usually does. The stronger the yin quality is within a woman, the more yang energy it can assimilate. That a woman fights to eliminate her curves by all possible means is an indication of how little she loves and respects her yin nature. Today, the beauty ideal we promote is very yang—being tall, skinny, and full of muscles— and that ideal can only be achieved at the cost of the female essence.

*Body substance and energy*

To be round does not mean that you are overweight! These are two different things. To be overweight is also an imbalance. It can occur out of a yang deficiency, a lack of movement and activity, or from a lack of enough yang-oriented sex. It can also be the result of bad eating habits, if one is eating too much food at once, or eating foods that create dampness and cold within the body.

This book is not about beauty, but about female sexuality. Female sexuality does not depend on an outer image of beauty, but upon the aliveness, well being and joy of a woman. The Tao of nutrition will help you choose foods that enhance and maintain your female essence. For many women, learning to eat properly is an important step toward enjoying sexuality more.

What is considered to be right or wrong nutrition can easily lead to an endless discussion. I do not want to burden you with new theories and rules, but I would like to pass on some essential information that has already helped many women. Nutrition should not get complicated, so let's keep it as simple as possible. For a woman over 30, to maintain a strong and healthy body, a properly cooked meal at least twice a day, including soups and vegetables, is a must. Organically grown meat can give physical strength. The meals should be as varied as possible, seasoned according to your own taste.

*The right foods*

*Feeling cold*   Many women feel cold all the time because they eat foods that have a cooling effect on their system. In general, these women need an endless amount of time to arouse their sexual energy. In the summer when it is hot outside, they can still manage somehow, but in a long and cold winter, especially if their partner does not have enough fire himself, how is it possible to melt the ice and get the water boiling?

*The following symptoms indicate "cold" in your body:*

- A strong sensitivity toward cold
- Cold feet and hands
- Dislike of or aversion to cold weather, cold drinks, or taking a cold bath
- General slowness or inactivity
- Being very emotional or pessimistic
- Lots of light colored urine
- Pale complexion
- Cramps while menstruating
- No sexual desire

**My Diary!**    Make a list of all the foods in your regular diet. Most of us have a rather limited variety within our eating habits, so don't worry, there are not so many. Then check all your foods with the help of the following chart (Table 2 on pages 79–81) and identify their thermal effect, so you can find out how thermally balanced your nutrition is.

**Important Hint!**
→   If there is too much cold in your body, be careful not to try to counteract it by only eating warming and hot foods. Remember: too much fire evaporates water. The precious yin elements of your body, such as your blood, will only be weakened by the consumption of hot foods. So it is best in your case to select foods from the neutral and slightly warming section.

*Too much heat in the body can cause the following symptoms:*

- Edginess
- Restlessness
- Impatience
- Insomnia
- Dark urine
- Heavy menstrual bleeding
- Strong hot flashes (for women in menopause)

*Table 2. Food Chart.*

| Foods | Cold | Refreshing | Neutral | Warming | Hot |
|---|---|---|---|---|---|
| **Vegetables** | Algae | Cabbages | Celery | Fennel | |
| | Iceberg | Eggplant | Tomatoes | Spring | |
| | lettuce | Cauliflower | Zucchini | onions | |
| | Endive | Broccoli | Avocado | Leeks | |
| | Green salad | Mushrooms | String beans | Horseradish | |
| | Cress | Pickles | Green peas | Carrots | |
| | Dandelion | Cucumbers | Potatoes | Sweet | |
| | root | Radish | Kohlrabi | potatoes | |
| | Asparagus | Sauerkraut | Brussels | Onions | |
| | | | sprouts | | |
| | | | Beets | | |
| **Grains and Legumes** | | Adzuki | Yeast | Amaranth | |
| | | beans | Millet | Buckwheat | |
| | | Spelt | Chickpeas | Oats | |
| | | Peas | Lentils | Sago | |
| | | Yellow | Corn | Sweet rice | |
| | | soybeans | Flour | | |
| | | Barley | Rice | | |
| | | | Rye | | |
| | | | Red soybeans | | |
| | | | Sourdough | | |
| | | | bread | | |
| | | | Black | | |
| | | | soybeans | | |
| | | | Pole beans | | |
| | | | Wheat | | |

*Table 2. Food Chart (continued).*

| Foods | Cold | Refreshing | Neutral | Warming | Hot |
|---|---|---|---|---|---|
| **Fruit** | Bananas | Unripe fruit | Pineapple | Apricots | |
| | Kiwi | Berries | Dates | Strawberries | |
| | Rhubarb | Apples | Figs | Mango | |
| | Watermelon | Pears | Honey | Papaya | |
| | | Black | melon | Cherries | |
| | | raspberries | Plums | Grapes | |
| | | Blueberries | | | |
| | | Raspberries | | | |
| | | Currants | | | |
| | | Oranges | | | |
| | | Grapefruit | | | |
| | | Cranberries | | | |
| | | Sour | | | |
| | | cherries | | | |
| | | Lemons | | | |
| **Dairy Products** | | Cows milk | Ricotta | Hard cheese | |
| | | Yogurt | cheese | Camembert | |
| | | Sour cream | Butter | cheese | |
| | | Sour milk | Eggs | Goat cheese | |
| | | | Cheese | Goat's milk | |
| | | | Cream | | |
| **Nuts** | Sunflower | Cashews | Peanuts | Chestnuts | |
| | seeds | | Hazelnuts | Coconut | |
| | | | Almonds | milk | |
| | | | Sesame | Pine nuts | |
| | | | seeds | Walnuts | |

*Table 2. Food Chart (continued).*

| Foods | Cold | Refreshing | Neutral | Warming | Hot |
|---|---|---|---|---|---|
| **Meat and Fish** | Duck<br>Caviar<br>Crab<br>Squid | Rabbit<br>Pork | Veal<br>Carp<br>Beef | Eel<br>Pheasant<br>Trout<br>Chicken<br>Venison<br>Lobster<br>Salmon<br>Mussels<br>Shrimps<br>Anchovies<br>Tuna<br>Wild boar | Lamb<br>Goat |
| **Spices** | Cold-pressed oils<br>Salt<br>Soy sauce | Tarragon | Honey<br>Malt<br>Sugar cane<br>Saffron<br>Licorice | Basil<br>Dill<br>Vinegar<br>Ginger<br>Cacao<br>Garlic<br>Oregano<br>Rosemary<br>Mustard<br>Thyme<br>Vanilla | Chili<br>Fennel<br>Nutmeg<br>Cloves<br>Pepper<br>Cinnamon |

## Food and Sexuality

*Raw foods and whole grain products:*

To digest raw foods as well as whole grain products is too much of an effort for many women's bodies. As an indication of it, women feel washed out and tired rather than vital and erotic after eating them.

*Milk products:*

Milk products are a food for babies, and tend to have a sleepy effect on sexuality because they produce dampness and mucus in the body. The subtle energy channels get clogged and the tender energy flow of a woman easily gets thick and stagnant.

*Sweets:*

Sweets also produce dampness in the body. Too much dampness suffocates female sexuality and makes the body feel heavy and dull.

*Drinks:*

Pure water has a detoxifying effect on the body, therefore it is important for our wellbeing to supply the body with enough fresh, pure water. Like no other liquid, it helps absorb different substances from the body and transport them out of it. There is no substitute for pure filtered and energized water. You should be aware that almost all alcoholic beverages contain chemical substances.

**My Diary!** → Make a list of the different things you drink during the day, so you have an overview of your drinking habits. And then check their impact according to the following chart (Table 3).

*Healing herbs*

Brewing love potions and creating recipes to strengthen sexual potency has become a special art in China, and studying healing herbs has always been a major focus of Taoist tradition. With the help of secret potions, Taoist alchemists down the ages hoped to find the stone of wisdom through their sexual power.

Still today, the gel of a stag horn, ginseng root, or the penis of a seal are ingredients of Chinese herbal medicine. Also, the

*Table 3. Beverage Chart.*

| Cold | Refreshing | Neutral | Warm | Hot |
|---|---|---|---|---|
| Green tea | Champagne | Chamomile tea | Honey wine | Fennel tea |
| Stout beer | Fruit juice | Malt beer | Ginger tea | Hot spiced |
| Pilsner beer | Vegetable juice | Cornsilk tea | Coffee | wine |
| Black tea | Grain coffee | Licorice tea | Dry red wine | Schnapps |
| | Rosehip tea | Water | Grape juice | Whiskey |
| | Peppermint tea | | Sweet wine | Vodka |
| | Soy milk | | | Yogi tea |
| | Dry white | | | Cinnamon tea |
| | wine | | | |
| | Wheat beer | | | |

human placenta has been used as an important remedy for women. In some parts of China it is still the custom that mothers, after giving birth, eat their baby's placenta so that they recover faster. (Cows do it when they are allowed to give birth naturally.)

It is a great gift that Taoist gynecology, with its immense wisdom of healing herbs, has been preserved and is still available to us. To be able to choose the right herbs is a skill that requires years of study, and is well beyond the scope of this book. But there are many skilled people practicing traditional Chinese medicine, so I am sure you can find someone who can create the right healing herbal mixture for you.

# The Five Elements

Besides the concept of yin and yang, the theory of the five elements is another important tool in Taoist sexology and health care. The five elements—wood, fire, earth, metal, and water—can help us more deeply understand the way the body functions.

In the following chapter we will be looking at the main substances of the body, the inner organs and their equivalents according to the five elements from the perspective of those

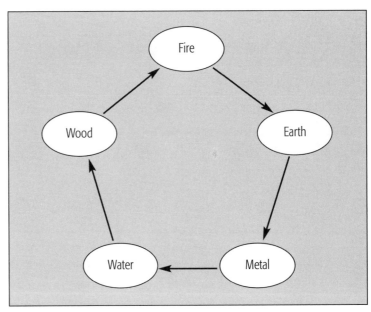

The five elements.

aspects that influence our sexuality the most. You will also learn some healing points and receive a few practical hints to balance and strengthen your inner organs so that different sexual functions are enhanced.

*Fullness and emptiness of the inner organs*

Chinese medicine sometimes refers to a state of fullness, meaning there is "too much" energy, heat, or dampness in one of the organs, or in a larger part of the body. Stagnation can also cause a state of fullness. On the contrary, emptiness is considered a state of deficiency: of energy, blood, or warmth. Fullness is a yang characteristic, and emptiness is a yin characteristic.

**Wood Element**

Wood energy is innovative and vibrant, gives inspiration, and is creative. Growth, movement, and regeneration characterize wood qualities, which are manifested in spring. In sexuality, wood is responsible for energy, vigor, change, and sexual excitement. It promotes the flow of sexual energy. Wood energy is extroverted, erratic, and full of drive. The wood element loves and lives for superficial playful flirtations and love affairs. The organs that correspond to the wood element are the liver and gallbladder.

*Wood*

- Yin organ: liver
- Yang organ: gallbladder
- Sense organ: eyes
- Body fluid: tears
- Body parts: muscles, tendons, nerves, and nails
- Fragrance: sour
- Root of energy: chi
- Energy movement: upward
- Color: green
- Direction: east
- Healing sound: *schschsch*

*Liver*

The yin organ of the wood element is the liver.

*General functions of the liver are:*
- moves chi
- promotes a harmonious flow of emotions
- processes impressions
- reduces stress
- gives the body its tone and needed tension

*Functions of the liver during menstruation:*
- stores blood
- moves blood
- stimulates and harmonizes the uterus
- provides a harmonious flow of energy

*Liver fullness*

**Liver stagnation**

Blocked chi, as well as blood and dampness, can lead to liver stagnation and can cause the following *general symptoms:*
- Epigastric tensions and pain
- Depression, melancholy, moodiness

*Menstruation:*
- PMS with a feeling of being irritated and edgy, rapid mood swings
- A feeling of tension in breathing and in the throat

- Irregular menstruation
- Lumpy menstrual blood
- Cramps

*Sexuality:*
- Sexual energy is inhibited and not really flowing
- Suddenly the sexual flow gets stuck and stops

**Healing Points!**

- Gallbladder 34 regulates liver chi
- Liver 3 regulates liver chi and blood
- Spleen-Pancreas 10 regulates blood

**Hints for Healing!**

- Activities involving movement, such as dancing and kundalini meditation
- Softly massage and tap the liver with a loose fist
- Creative activities, such as painting or making music
- Cleansing and detoxification of the liver in the springtime
- Relaxation to relieve stress and digest emotions

### Liver Heat

*General Symptoms:*
- Irritability
- Being tense, restless, restless sleep, insomnia
- Bitter taste in the mouth
- Dizziness
- Hot flashes
- Myoma

*Sexuality:*
- Sexually excitable but only superficial satisfaction is possible
- Lust for masturbation
- To have an orgasm can cool down liver heat

*Menstruation:*
- Early menstruation, short cycle
- Heavy bleeding

- Liver 2 diminishes liver fire
- Gallbladder 20 calms liver fire

**Healing Points!**

- Do relaxing exercises on a regular basis to ease the emotions
- Avoid greasy and hot foods, coffee, alcohol, and cigarettes

**Practical Hints!**
←

Liver heat is a yang condition that in the long term can be best balanced by promoting yin qualities.

### Dampness and heat in liver
*General Symptoms:*
- Vaginal itching
- Smelly discharge, fungus, or herpes
- A yellow, sticky coating on the tongue
- Strong, perhaps uncontrollable anger

*Menstruation:*
- Heavy bleeding with intense odor

*Sexuality:*
- The sexual energy can be very rough and heavy and easily gets stuck in the lower energy centers

- Gallbladder 34 moves stagnant chi and removes dampness

**Healing Points!**

- Avoid raw foods, dairy products, sweets, alcohol, and meat
- Meditation and sensitivity training

**Practical Hints!**

### Liver blood deficiency
*General Symptoms:*
- Dizziness
- Waking up at night
- Night sweat
- Blurry vision and dry eyes
- Brittle nails
- Bad memory

*Liver emptiness*

- The feeling of meaninglessness
- Stress

*Menstruation:*
- Weak or no bleeding
- Pale blood

*Sexuality:*
- Sexual excitement can cause an unpleasant feeling or pain
- Little or no sexual interest

**Healing Points!**
→

- Stomach 36 and Spleen-Pancreas 6 promote the formation of blood

**Hints for Healing!**
→

- Reduce stress and activities
- Promote the formation of blood with appropriate diet and herbs
- Enough, but not too much, movement
- Healing sound for the liver: *schschschschsch*

## Fire Element

Fire is the emperor of the body; it radiates warmth, love, and joy. Fire brings light and clarity. It always expands and strives upward. Fire stands for communication and development. It creates passionate sexuality, the desire to dominate, and forms the urge to reach a climax. It stimulates and excites the body, and is responsible for intensity. Fire governs all mental and spiritual activities, sexual fantasies, and desire. The organs ruled by fire are the heart and small intestine.

*Fire*

- Yin organ: heart
- Yang organ: small intestine
- Sensual organ: tongue (language)
- Body fluid: sweat
- Body parts: face and blood vessels
- Odor: burnt
- Root of energy: warmth
- Energy movement: expansion
- Direction: south
- Healing sound: *haaaaaa*

The yin organ of the fire element is the heart.

*Heart*

*General Functions:*
- It governs all mental and emotional activities of the consciousness like memory, thinking, sleeping, dreaming
- It grounds and hosts the spirit, so it can cool down and relax
- The heart governs the blood
- The heart changes nutritional chi into blood
- It promotes blood circulation

**Heart Heat**

*Heart fullness*

*General Symptoms:*
- Psychic restlessness
- Agitation
- Insomnia
- Feeling hot
- Fast and endless talking
- Lack of concentration
- Strong palpitation of the heart
- Unclear thinking
- Red tip of the tongue

*Menstruation:*
- Early menstruation
- Heavy bleeding

*Sexuality:*
- Sexually driven, very excited, but not able to enjoy sex deeply
- Stimulates sexual activities and fantasies

- Heart 8 clears heart fire
- Ren Mai 15 calms the spirit and reduces heat

**Healing Points!**
←

- Bitter taste can reduce heat (like wormwood)
- No alcohol, but in exceptional cases, a real bitter Guinness beer
- No hot and greasy foods or meat

**Practical Hints!**

- No vitamins and minerals. Be aware that vitamins and minerals are very powerful and can create extra heat and energy, especially in a sensitive body, and therefore can easily intensify a condition of fullness.
- Reduce stimulating activities, including TV
- A good acupuncture and herbal treatment is helpful
- Cold water foot bath
- Relaxation
- Strengthen yin

## Heart emptiness

### Heart blood—deficiency

*General Symptoms:*

- Unable to define one's own space
- Lack of concentration while thinking
- An indefinable feeling of unwellness or uneasyness
- Forgetfulness
- Being nervous and jumpy
- Strong heart palpitation, state of anxiety, panic
- Disturbed sleep
- Small things are too much
- Traumatic experience or shock can cause a state of heart blood deficiency

*Menstruation:*

- Late menstruation
- Little or no bleeding

*Sexuality:*

- Because a heart blood deficiency can cause one to feel fragile and oversensitive, affected women are easily overwhelmed by yang energy and male excitement
- Becoming dependent, not able to find one's own space
- Little or no sexual desire at all
- Instead of sexual desire, there is more a feeling of wanting to be close and to feel the warmth of the heart, needing attention, security, and affection

**Healing Points!**
→

- Heart 7 tones up the heart, promotes yin of the heart, and is calming to the spirit

- Take it slow and easy
- Sleep and rest a lot (the best is alone in a bed)
- Protect yourself from stress and negativity
- Eat really well, cooked meals three times a day
- Get massages with lots of good oils
- Meditate
- Get the help of a Chinese doctor
- Healing heart sound: *haaaaaaaaaaaaaaaa*

**Hints for Healing!**

The earth element is the queen of the middle. Out of her center she is balancing her environment and promotes inner and outer peace. Transformation and integration are her qualities, enabling us to realize our ideas and to live according to our convictions. The earth element helps the body absorb essential nutrients and process them. The late summer is the earth season, the time of maturity and harvest. A strong earth quality within makes it possible to live a responsible sexuality from our own center. Women with weak or empty earth are easily manipulated and used. The organs that correspond to the earth element are the spleen and stomach.

## Earth Element

*Earth*

- Yin organ: spleen
- Yang organ: stomach
- Sensual organ: lips
- Function: tasting
- Body fluid: saliva
- Body parts: flesh, tissue, and limbs
- Odor: fragrant
- Root of energy: The power of the middle
- Movement: balancing
- Color: yellow
- Direction: center
- Healing sound: *chuuuuuuuu*

*Spleen*    The yin earth organ is the spleen.

*General Functions:*
- Transformation and integration
- Nourishes muscles and limbs
- Controls the upward movement of chi
- Keeps organs in position
- Governs the ability to concentrate and think
- Learning and memorizing
- Maintains the blood in the vessels

*Spleen*    **Spleen dampness**

*fullness*    *General Symptoms:*
- Feeling heavy and sluggish
- No thirst or desire to drink
- Feeling easily full and nauseated
- Dull and drowsy head
- Smelly discharge and stools
- Water retention in the lower part of the body

*Sexuality:*
- The tender energy flow of a woman drowns in the swamp of the spleen and the sexual fire is put out

**Healing Points!**
→
- Spleen-Pancreas 9 drains dampness out of the lower body part
- Spleen-Pancreas 6 removes dampness

**Hints for Healing!**
→
- Living from your middle
- Centering and rooting
- Eating regularly
- Do not take in sugar, raw foods, dairy products, and alcohol for a minimum of two months
- Certain vitamins, drugs, or hormones can produce dampness in your body

*Spleen*    **Blood and chi deficiency**

*emptiness*    *General Symptoms:*
- Feeling lazy, tired, and dull

- Pale and wan complexion
- Weak limbs
- Soft stools or diarrhea
- Sagging of organs
- Hemorrhoids and varicose veins
- Feeling tired after meals
- Uncontrollable craving for sweets
- Empty-headedness
- Not being able to concentrate or focus
- Difficulties learning

*Menstruation:*
- In the initial state the bleeding can be very heavy and then stop
- Smeary light color and watery bleeding during the day

*Sexuality:*
- Too lazy and lethargic to even think about sex

- Spleen-Pancreas 6 strengthens spleen chi
- Ren Mai 6 strengthens and raises spleen chi in case of sagging or prolapse of inner organs
- Spleen-Pancreas 1 counteracts excessive bleeding

**Healing Points!**

- Eat regularly in a peaceful and quiet atmosphere
- Avoid raw foods and juices, full grain products, sweets, and alcohol
- Do not eat too much at once
- Reduce mental activities, such as learning and working with the computer

**Hints for Healing!**

Because the stomach has an essential function as the only yang organ, it will be looked at a bit closer. The stomach is the root of the five yin organs and the main nutritional source of the body. It does not matter how ill a person has fallen and how strong the symptoms are; as long as the stomach is strong and healthy, the prognosis is good.

*Stomach*

*Stomach fullness*

**Stomach heat**

*General Symptoms:*
- Bad breath
- Bleeding gums
- Stomach acidity or nausea
- Constant feeling of being hungry
- Psychic imbalance, restlessness, insomnia
- Desire to drink cold beverages

**Healing Points!**
→

**Hints for Healing!**
→

- Stomach 45 clears stomach heat and calms the spirit

- Avoid irritants, such as caffeine, tobacco, alcohol, tablets, and chemical nutrition additives (like e-factors)
- Eat regularly in quiet surroundings, and eat slowly, chewing your food well
- Eat only small portions
- Avoid greasy, hot, and spicy foods
- Eat lots of cooling vegetables and fruits (cooked)

# Metal Element

In regard to our sexuality, the metal element takes care of our protection and defense system, and provides us with our animal instinct. The organs ruled by the metal element are the lungs and colon.

*Metal*

- Yin organ: lungs
- Yang organ: colon
- Sensual organ: nose
- Body fluid: blood, mucus, lymph, sweat
- Odor: pungent
- Root of energy: blood and juices
- Movement: downward and condensing
- Color: white
- Direction: west
- Healing sound: *ssssssssss*

The yin metal organ is the lung.

*Lung*

*General Functions:*
- The lung is also called the master of chi and breathing; "heavenly chi" (air) is breathed in and "impure chi" breathed out to vitalize the body
- The lung controls the skin and hair

*General Symptoms:*
- Stiffness of the spine, neck, and structure
- Chronic problems with the sinuses
- Shortness of breath
- Cough with mucus

- Lung 1 clears mucus and reduces cough

- Avoid sweets and dairy products
- Go to the forest and nature and take in fresh air as often as you can; avoid polluted or smoky air

*Lung fullness*

**Healing Points!**

**Hints for Healing!**
←

**Blood and chi deficiency**
*General Symptoms:*
- Being tired and without any energy
- Pale complexion
- Weak voice
- Prone to colds and flu
- Weak resistance
- No perspective or future
- Despondency
- Sadness
- Ungratefulness

*Sexuality:*
- Too little energy for sex

- Lung 9 tones the lung chi

- Take in fresh air
- Inhalation

*Lung emptiness*

**Healing Points!**

**Hints for Healing!**

- Enough sleep
- Breathing exercise to enhance the volume of the lungs
- A little bit of aerobics, once a day
- Avoid air conditioning
- Avoid smoking and polluted air
- Healing sound: *sssssssssssssssssss*

## Water Element

The water element is the most yin element there is. Water represents the end of a cycle and at the same time the foundation of the new. The qualities that belong to the water element are to absorb, store, and preserve. The kidneys belong to the water element and are considered to be the roots of life. Female sexuality rises out of the depths of the water.

### Water

- Yin organ: kidney
- Yang organ: bladder
- Sensual organ: ears
- Body fluid: sexual fluids
- Body parts: bones, marrow, brain, teeth, knees, feet, and lumbar vertebra
- Odor: rotten
- Energy root: substance
- Energy movement: inward
- Color: dark blue, black
- Season: winter
- Direction: north
- Healing sound: *chuuuuuu*

### Kidneys

The yin water organs are the kidneys.

*General Functions:*
- Kidneys are the mother of reproduction
- Kidneys govern pregnancy and birth
- Kidneys preserve life force

- Kidneys produce and nourish bones, marrow, and the brain
- Kidneys control lower body openings

*Sexuality:*
- Kidneys are the root of female sexuality

The right and the left kidney are assigned different functions. The left kidney is considered to be the actual kidney, whereas the right kidney is seen as the door of vitality. Kidney yin provides material substance and is the well of all yin energies in the body, as well as the foundation of kidney yang. Kidney yang is also called kidney fire, and is the well of yang energy for the whole body.

*Please note:*
Kidney fullness is very rare, so it is not included here.

### Kidney yin deficiency
*General Symptoms:*
- Dark urine
- Night sweats
- Dizziness
- Red cheeks
- Dry skin
- Forgetfulness
- Increased thirst, especially toward evening
- Back problems, or bone problems
- Osteoporosis
- Hair loss
- Hot flashes
- Restlessness
- Red tongue without coating
- Incontinence
- Miscarriage

*Menstruation:*
- Long cycle
- Smear bleeding after cycle
- Bright red and watery blood

*Kidney yin emptiness*

*Sexuality:*

- The body lacks the physical substance to surrender and let go
- Easily excitable, but feels very washed out or bad after sex
- Often too excited to be able to have an orgasm
- There is no contentment and fulfillment
- A kidney yin deficiency is very common for women in menopause
- Fear of letting go and surrendering, as well as going deep

**Healing Points!**

- Kidney 1 nourishes kidney yin

**Hints for Healing!**

- Lots of rest, go to bed before midnight
- Reduce activities and social life
- Avoid stress completely
- Good healthy food to build up your substance
- Make love only very gently and lovingly
- Chinese herbal treatment is highly recommended
- Only a little physical sport or activity
- Meditation
- Centering and inner smile

*Kidney yang emptiness*

**Kidney yang deficiency**
*General Symptoms:*

- Extremely tired and exhausted
- Depression
- No will power
- No desire to go out
- Light colored urine in large quantities; weak urine flow
- Incontinence
- Chronic vaginal discharge
- Feeling cold, aversion toward cold
- Backache
- Weak legs, especially knees

- Infertility
- Edema of the legs

*Menstruation:*
- Late menstruation
- Extended bleeding

*Sexuality:*
- No sexual interest

- Ren Mai 4 strengthens kidney yang

**Healing Points!**
←

- Kidney breathing
- Warming and massaging the kidneys
- No sexual activities
- Avoid cold, also cold water
- Check your diet
- Soft exercises
- Kidney healing sound: *chuuuuuuuu*

**Hints for Healing!**
←

The bones are the deepest and densest part of the body. Because of their pronounced yin qualities, they have a strong capacity to preserve. We preserve not only energies and minerals in the bones, but also information and memories.

*Bones*

The body preserves the substantial essence in the marrow, the important foundation of the sexual force.

*Marrow*

# Chapter 10

# THE FEMALE BODY

**Blood**

For every woman, because of the blood lost each month through menstruation, blood plays a very central role in her life. The blood influences and determines the quality of a woman's life, her health, and her state of well being. The quality and quantity of blood is the material foundation of female sexuality. In the Taoist understanding, blood is also considered to be the material home of spiritual forces. It is the host of the soul and is predetermined for each individual. In old China, blood has been called "the red juice of Mother Earth," and represents yin qualities that give life to all things.

*Nourishing blood and juices*

Because of its spiritual and magical power, to preserve and strengthen the blood is a central issue in Taoist health care and meditation practices for women. Blood and other body fluids have the same source, and depend on and influence each other. All other clear and unclear body fluids which lubricate the skin, mucous membranes, the joints, brain, bone marrow, eyes, ears, nose, and mouth are known as yin fluids: saliva, sweat, mucus, gastric juices, lymph fluids, sexual fluids, urine, bile, and so forth.

The blood is weakened by an excessive release of body fluids as in profuse sweating (in a sauna, for instance), vomiting, or diarrhea. The essence (ching chi), the substance of the body (organs and bones) and menstruation are produced from a surplus of blood.

### How blood is made

- The raw material needed for blood production is mainly drawn from nutrition.
- Chi gives the stimulus to promote transformation of the raw material.
- The stomach takes in food and passes it on to the spleen, where the pure parts are drawn from nutrients and liquids.
- The lungs move the nutritional chi to the heart, where it is transformed into blood.
- For building blood, the kidneys contribute an essence that has been stored in the bone marrow.
- The fire element gives blood its red color.
- The liver stores the blood.

*General function of the blood:*

- Blood provides the physical foundation of female sexuality.
- It provides the material foundation for the spirit, therefore it is also called the carrier of the soul.
- Blood is the mother of chi; weak blood means weak chi.
- Blood nourishes and lubricates body tissue.

*Empty blood*   ### Blood deficiency
*General Symptoms:*

- Tiredness
- Pale complexion
- Forgetfulness
- Sleep disorders (insomnia)
- Blurry vision
- Nervousness
- Palpitation
- Anxiety

*Symptoms of Chronic Blood Deficiency:*

- Dryness of the body (dry skin, brittle hair and nails)
- Weakened sense of individuality
- Difficulties taking or defining one's own space
- Emotional imbalance; for example, easily breaking into tears
- Not able to handle stress

*Menstruation:*

- Dull pain at the end or just after the period
- Not much bleeding

*Sexuality:*

- The juice of life and an inner fullness, the physical foundation enabling one to enjoy sexuality to the maximum, are missing

- Ren Mai 4 nourishes the blood and uterus, and at the same time calms the mind.
- Stomach 36 and Spleen 6 tone blood and chi.

**Healing Points!**
←

- Foods to build up substance
- Herbal treatments
- Reduce stress and activities
- Enough peace and sleep
- Avoid sweating
- Enough fresh air

**Hints for Healing!**
←

### Blood heat

Too much heat in the body can overheat the internal organs as well as the blood. Blood heat can arise when the heat has entered a deeper layer of the body. Mostly, blood heat manifests from a chronic set of conditions and develops over time. To be in a state of blood heat is usually unpleasant and difficult for the person affected, because it always invokes strong emotions. To clear blood heat from the body takes time and needs proper treatment tailored to address the inner and outer conflicts which are at the root of the situation.

*Blood fullness*

*General Symptoms of Blood Heat:*
- Feeling of heat
- Dry mouth
- Thirst
- Skin diseases
- Restlessness leading to extreme anxiety
- Impulsiveness and strong emotional outbursts
- Insomnia
- Manic or psychotic behavior
- Dark urine
- Constipation

*Menstruation:*
- Sudden and heavy bleeding
- Bright red or dark red blood
- Early menstruation
- Smear bleeding after menstruation

*Sexuality:*
- The body is under a lot of tension and can easily be sexually excited
- Sexual excitement can easily over-stimulate, preventing orgasm
- Having an orgasm can cool and balance the body energies for awhile

**Healing Points!**

- Spleen 6 cools and moves blood
- Kidney 2 cools and clears heat
- Liver 2 cools blood

**Hints for Healing!**

- Avoid alcohol, drugs, and nicotine
- A treatment utilizing Chinese herbs and acupuncture is absolutely necessary
- Learn how to deal with emotions
- Find ways to relax
- Avoid additional stress and tension
- Clear conflicts with others
- Avoid hot, spicy, and fried foods
- Avoid foods and beverages that contain preservatives or other chemicals

The breasts are considered to be the symbol of womanhood. And no matter if they are big or small, for many women they are the most sensitive sexual center. While writing the English version of this book, I was surprised that there are no other words in the English dictionary for the female breasts, as there are in German. This I find very significant.

It is from the breasts that most people have gotten their first meal. That breasts are able to produce milk to nourish a baby shows their potential very clearly. For the health and well-being of a woman, the breasts are an important source of nourishing and healing qualities, which should not be underestimated. In this chapter I will introduce exercises that can help you get in touch with the magical power of your breasts.

# Breasts

Breasts.

The rate of breast cancer is rising steadily. Among women between 35 and 54 years of age, breast cancer is the leading cause of death. The breasts of far too many women are being amputated. Scientists do not fully understand why so many breasts are falling ill in this day and age. Perhaps we can contribute something helpful by looking at the situation from a more feminine perspective.

Breasts are very sensitive, soft, and tender. Many small blood vessels, nerve cells, milk glands, and lymph vessels build a complex system inside the breasts, which need to be treated carefully and lovingly.

*In the Taoist tradition the following hints for the well-being of breasts have been passed on:*

- Do not hurt the breasts by biting, pinching, or strong sucking (this is not valid for the nursing period, when the nipples are less sensitive).
- While making love, do not over-stimulate the breasts.
- Avoid nicotine, coffee, and alcohol as much as possible.
- Avoid chemical nutritional additives, and fertilizers, pesticides, hormones, preservatives, and flavor enhancers completely.

## *Suffering breasts*

Suffering breasts.

**105**

• For your personal hygiene, use only natural products. According to Taoist medicine, a feeling of "pulling" in the breasts, little knots, or even cancer are always somehow connected to the liver. The liver's important task is to move chi and blood within the body. If the liver is not able to do that properly, it is advisable to see a good Chinese doctor to support the liver with acupuncture and the right Chinese herbs. Also, a self-healing exercise for the liver can help. Scientists have agreed on the following points as high risk factors for breast cancer:

• Hormonal changes (early menarche, late menopause, hormone therapy, such as taking estrogen)
• Hereditary disposition
• Exposure to radiation, such as x-rays
• Overweight

## Getting to know your breasts

Take as much time as you need to get to know your breasts. The following questions will support you while getting in touch with them and investigating how you relate to them:

1. What do your breasts mean to you?

2. How do you relate to them?

3. How do they feel?

4. Do you like your breasts?

5. How do they react when touched?

6. Do you touch and caress them yourself?

7. Do you like it when someone else is touching, stroking, or playing with your breasts?

8. Do you like it when your breasts are being sucked?

9. How do people react to your breasts?

**← Watch Out!**

*To get in touch with your breasts:*

- Only work with your breasts as long as you feel good doing it. If you start to become restless or feel hot, stop the exercise and bring all the energy down into your middle, and do the centering exercise, and the inner smile exercise until you feel good and relaxed again.

- Women suffering from breast diseases release all the burden and negativity they have been carrying within through the disease. Take your time until you really connect with your breasts and feel them. Very tenderly fill them with the fragrance of your heart.

- Having a sharp pain in your breasts, thorax, or heart can be an indication of too much heat or stagnation there. If this is the case, do not focus more energy in this area with an exercise like breast breathing. It is better to cool and empty the breasts to release and clear the heat. Here is a helpful exercise to dissipate excess heat:

## Cooling sound

**← Try This!**

- Assume the horsewoman position (see page 125)

- While breathing in, bring both arms up from beside your body, over your head (see top left figure on page 108)

- Twist your palms so they are facing the earth, with the right hand on top of the left (see top right figure on page 108)

- With the outbreath and the sound "Heeeeee," glide your hands slowly down in front of your body, combing the heat down from your upper body into your legs. Let the heat or restlessness flow through your legs and release it into the earth.

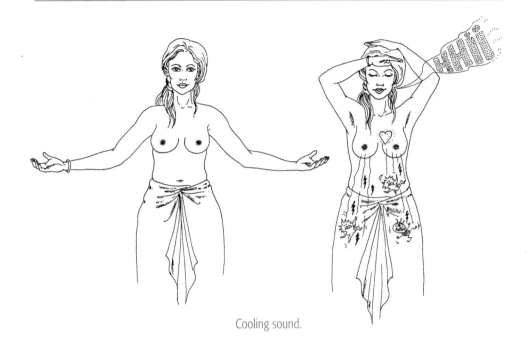

Cooling sound.

**Try This!** →  I do not want to say much about the possible effects of the following exercises. To reveal the hidden secrets of the breasts, a peaceful and quiet state, and enough time to be, is all that's required. Just give the exercises a try, and let your breasts surprise you with their feelings and energies.

### Happy breasts

No matter how you get in touch with your breasts, feel them, let them breathe and be happy.

Breast awareness.

## Unburden your breasts

When a heart is full of negative emotions, like sadness, pain, and desperation, it can store or repress these painful feelings in the breasts. Purifying and unburdening the breasts can also ease the burden of the heart.

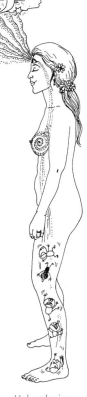

- Take on the position of a horsewoman and close your eyes.

- Start by breathing in golden light from the universe through your third eye point. (The third eye is an energy point located on the forehead in a small indentation. It is a very powerful opening to absorb divine energies from the universe.) Let the golden light flow into your breasts and fill them up.

- With the outbreath, guide all the heaviness and negativity out from your breasts and down toward your feet. You can use your hands to stroke the unwanted energies from your breasts down to your feet, letting the energy pass from your feet into the earth.

Unburdening your breasts.

## Breast breathing

- Stand in the horsewoman position (see page 125) and close your eyes.

Breast breathing.

- Get in touch with your breasts using your breathing until you feel their tenderness and openness clearly.

- Gently and slowly begin to breathe through the buds or nipples of the breasts until you feel a slight sucking sensation.

- Start filling your breasts up in this way until they are getting really firm.

- Put your hands on top of your breasts and enjoy them, feeling them pulsing and becoming more and more alive.

- Smile into them to fill them up with the fragrance of your heart. Go on breathing into them slower and deeper, until the breasts are so full that their energy is overflowing and spreading throughout your whole body.

**Try This!** → **Breast massage**

This is an exercise that belongs to the daily routine in a woman's life. Use a natural oil which feels good to you to massage the breasts. At the moment I am using a very nice ayurvedic oil mixed with a sesame oil base which feels so nourishing, my breasts are loving it.

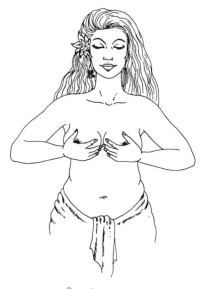

Breast massage.

- Use enough oil. It is also very nice to use slightly warm oil, and start by massaging your breasts in circles. Don't go too fast, but take your time to feel and enjoy the massage.

- Change directions once in a while and sense if the two directions feel any different. The movement from the middle of the chest upward and outward has a more expanding effect; the other way around has the opposite—a more concentrating and collecting effect.

You can provoke different sensations depending on whether or not you are massaging softly or more intensely, slow or fast, in big circles or just around the buds. Have fun exploring and surrendering to your breasts.

## The secrets within the breasts          ← Try This!

- Sit up so your back is relaxed, yet straight, and close your eyes.

- Massage your breasts until they are energized.

- Sit silently and bring your whole awareness into your breasts and fill them up with a loving quality; breathe slowly and deeply.

- For at least 10 minutes, fill your breasts with the mantra Aum (pronounced OHM).

- Afterward, sit quietly and deepen your breathing. Surrender more and more to your breasts, until they begin to release their treasures.

- Lie down and center yourself for another 10 minutes.

There is a direct internal connection between the breasts, heart, and sexual organs. According to Taoist medicine, there are two meridians responsible for that connection, the Bao Mai and the Chong Mai. The connection between the breasts and the uterus is most obvious during menstruation, pregnancy, and when you are breast feeding. Some of the traditional sex-

*Breasts and the sexual organs*

111

ual practices of the Tao, like the deer exercise, are based on that internal connection.

*Limp (flabby) breasts*

The breasts are not made of muscles, but out of a combination of fatty and connective tissue. To maintain firmness, it is not possible to train breasts like muscles. The consistency of breast tissue is best influenced via the spleen, since the spleen is responsible for nourishing connective tissue. Therefore, it is good to pay attention to nutrition. Avoid sweets, raw foods, and dairy products as much as possible.

*Healthy breasts*

**Hints for Healing!**
→

- Loving treatment. Don't allow your breasts to be treated in an unloving way, like biting or pinching them, unless you really like it.
- Develop an affectionate relationship with your breasts and increase your awareness of them.
- Breasts like daylight and fresh air, but not too much (not more than 15 minutes of direct exposure to the Sun).
- A slightly cold shower, brushing your breasts regularly with a body brush, and massaging your breasts with an appropriate oil will enhance the blood circulation and keep your breasts vibrant and healthy.

**Healing Points!**
→

- Stomach 18 harmonizes the breasts.

**Recipe for breast oil**

It can be very nice to create your own breast massage oil. Almond oil can be used as a base and you can add your choice of essential oils to this base. Use about 30 drops of essential oil in a base of 2 tablespoons of vegetable oil. Here is a very popular recipe of essential oils to create your own breast potion:

- Lemongrass strengthens tissue
- Geranium develops breasts
- Fenugreek stimulates glands in breasts
- Rose awakens deep feelings

Breast oil.

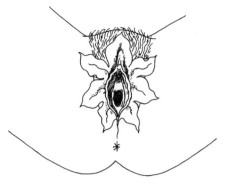

The Fragrant Rose.

## The Sexual Organs

The names the Taoists created for the genitals are very beautiful and poetic, like the Fragrant Rose, Lotus Flower, the Jade Gate, or the Golden Gorge. Let yourself be inspired by this tradition and baptize your sexual organs with a name that suits them.

*The Fragrant Rose*

The female sexual organs serve reproduction; they produce eggs. They can receive the jade shaft (penis) and generate pleasure that can climax in a yin tide (the female orgasm). They can open up the Inner Gate (uterine orifice) and receive the semen. They provide a protected space to the fertilized egg so it can grow and develop until the new being is ready to be born.

The big lips of the vulva are bulges made out of plenty of fatty tissue. On the outside they are covered with hair. Inside they are covered with delicate skin. Many sebaceous glands lead into this area to keep the skin smooth and slippery.

*The Heavenly Field*

The small lips of the vulva are thin creases within the big lips, next to the entrance of the vagina, and surrounding the clitoris. They are smaller then the big ones, but they can also protrude. There are some tribes in Africa where it is considered a sign of beauty to have "big small lips of the vulva." In these tribes the women enlarge the small lips with weights. Naturally, the lips also enlarge when a woman is sexually aroused.

*The Red Pearls*

The clitoris is named the Precious Pearl, and it is much bigger than you can see from the outside. It is endowed with a complex system of sensual organs. They supply the "Yin Bean"

*The Precious Pearl*

(another name for the clitoris) with its sensitivity, which makes it so special and precious. When it is aroused, it enlarges and hardens with the help of the erectile tissue.

In some countries, the female genitals are still circumcised. The clitoris is either cut or burned out, and sometimes the lips are also either cut or sewn together. This is usually done without any anesthesia.

The genitals of each woman look very different. When I was 19 and studying nursing, I discovered this while working in a clinic for urology. It was my job every morning (so I would learn quickly) to insert a urine catheter into about six different women. In the beginning it was difficult because the structure of each of the women's genitals was so different. I had to search and search to find the right entrance for the catheter. That was a very difficult task. I would like to invite you to take a hand mirror and start to look at all the details of your rose flower.

**Try This!** → **Look at me**

- Choose a quiet space where no one can disturb you and have a hand mirror ready.

- Sit down in a comfortable position, put your knees up, and spread your legs as much as possible without strain.

- Place the mirror between your legs at an angle, so that you can easily see your rose bud.

- While looking, breathe slowly and deeply. With your fingers, you can slightly spread the lips so you can see more.

- Observe the thoughts and feelings that pass by while looking and breathing.

- Do this for about 15 minutes, and when you are finished, lie down and center yourself again.

- Write down your experiences in your journal.

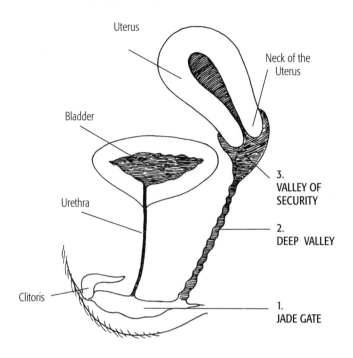

Uterus

Neck of the Uterus

Bladder

Urethra

Clitoris

3.
VALLEY OF SECURITY

2.
DEEP VALLEY

1.
JADE GATE

The three sections of the vaginal channel.

## The pulse of the rose flower

← **Go Deeper!**

- Lie down and bring your awareness and breathing down to your lips and into the clitoris.

- Start smiling into your outer genitals until they are smiling back to you.

- Allow yourself to feel deeper and deeper until you get in touch with the pulse there.

- As you continue to lie there, feel the rose flower pulsing, expanding and contracting, and becoming more and more alive.

The opening of the vagina is originally more or less closed by a thin layer of skin called the hymen. The thickness and elasticity of the hymen can vary. It usually cannot stretch enough to allow a jade shaft to enter the vagina without ripping it. The first sexual encounter usually rips the hymen, which causes a little bleeding and leaves fringed shreds of tissue.

*The hymen*

**The vaginal channel**

The actual birth channel is in general about 3 to 4 inches (10 to 11 centimeters) long, very elastic and spacious. Its walls contain no glands, and it is covered by a thick, spongy mucous membrane.

**The G-spot**

On both sides where the hymen is attached are the openings of the Bartholin's glands, which produce a lubricating secretion. Insert your finger into the vagina and glide along the upper edge to find and feel the two glands. In this area you also will find the G-spot, which swells when sexually aroused. The G-spot is able to produce and ejaculate a clear secretion, the Yin Flood, also known as female ejaculation.

**Vaginal channel reflexology**

Various positions for making love have been developed to stimulate the reflex zones of the vagina. During love play, with or without a partner, all the areas should be activated evenly, rather than just one zone being stimulated. An exercise using the energy egg, which you will be introduced to later in this book, can be helpful for that. Vibrators can also be a wonderful tool to stimulate the different zones separately.

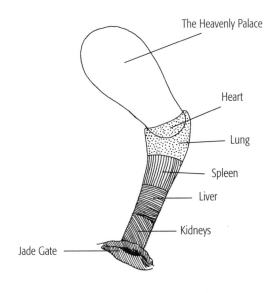

The Heavenly Palace

Heart

Lung

Spleen

Liver

Kidneys

Jade Gate

Reflexology of the female genitals.

*Irritated and dry vagina*
Possible causes:

- Chronic state of yin deficiency (blood deficiency)
- Low estrogen level
- Weak lungs
- Medicines that dry out the mucous membrane
- Smoking

Due to a decrease in the level of estrogen, women after menopause tend to have a very dry vagina, which can be painful while making love. There are creams available that contain lactic acid bacteria, and these can be applied directly into the vagina, supporting the mucous membranes to produce lubrication.

- Do not wear synthetic underwear.
- Wash your clothes with mild, allergy free soap, and avoid perfume or strong herbal essences in your soap.
- Do not use tampons. Use natural sponges or natural unbleached sanitary napkins, which you can find in health food stores.

**Hints for Healing!**
←

The vaginal channel ends at the neck of the uterus, in the lower third of the uterus, and it reaches up to the uterine orifice. In the Tao, this very delicate and sensitive area is called the Inner Gate. I know some women who are able to control this Inner Gate, which actually enables them to keep menstrual blood in the uterus as long as they wish, opening the gate to allow the blood to flow out consciously. It is possible to train the Inner Gate, much like training the bladder or the colon. The advantage of not needing tampons or sanitary napkins is obvious. In addition, the uterus is strengthened and nourished by the blood maintained inside.

*Neck of the uterus*

Some women have the idea that the muscles of the uterine orifice cannot be consciously influenced, and that it only opens with lots of pain during the birthing process. At this point, I can only talk from my own experience and refer to the experiences of my female Taoist friends. I myself cannot close it completely; sometimes it works more, sometimes less. But I can move the muscle, stimulating the uterus, out of which arises a very deep sensual feeling. Experiment for yourself and find out what is possible in your own body. Our experience in working together shows that it is much easier for younger women to learn.

*Pain while making love*

Even though the vagina is very elastic, there are women who suffer a lot of pain while being penetrated. This can have different causes:

- If the liver is weak, sexual excitement can become painful.

- Sagging of the uterus, bladder, or colon can cause pain while making love. Try different positions to find the best one for you.

- Making love can be painful if you are not sufficiently sexually aroused before penetration.

- The penis can be too long for that vagina. Every woman is built differently, and if the "turtle head," the tip of the penis, is entering the Inner Gate, this can be very stimulating for men, but very painful for women. It is best to avoid stimulating the uterine neck because this can cause inflammation, and provoke other diseases and disorders. There are plastic rings available, which can be put over the penis, so

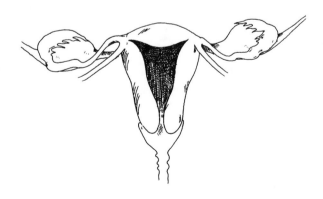

Uterus and ovaries.

that it cannot enter the vagina so deeply. You can find such products in sex shops. Consult with the salesperson there to make sure you are getting the right thing that will serve the purpose.

Experiment with different positions. When lying on your back, try putting a pillow under your pelvis. This might help.

The experience of pain while being penetrated can also have psychological causes. In this case, it is recommended that you consult a qualified therapist. It is important that you find someone you trust.

At the uterine orifice the uterus is connected to the vagina. The uterus is pear-shaped, very muscular, and weighs 3 to 4 ounces in an average adult woman. Before menstruating it is engorged with blood, and so it is a bit heavier at this time. During pregnancy that weight increases about ten times. The main mass of the uterus is a thick layer of smooth muscles. From within, the muscles are covered by a mucous membrane.

*Heavenly Palace: the uterus*

Having a uterus makes it possible for women to menstruate, and to receive male semen into the protective environment of the womb, where an embryo can grow into a new life. The uterus is an incredible phenomenon, having a language of its own. A person able to understand this language is able to know much about a woman's state of health. The language of the uterus reveals itself through menstruation and vaginal discharge. You have learned the main symptoms in chapter 9, in the section about the five elements. A skilled Chinese doctor is actually able to diagnose your body through the way you are menstruating! Therefore, a long-term observation of your menstruation is required. It can be very helpful to write down all the signals the uterus is offering.

*The language of the uterus*

It would be good to get a special notebook, a menstruation book, just to note all your observations about your period. The following criteria are meaningful to watch:

← **My Diary!**

- Length of the cycle?
- Length of the bleeding?
- How is the bleeding? Slight, normal, heavy, smeary?
- How is the blood flowing?
- What is the color of the blood?
- Is it painful? If yes, when? Before, at the beginning, during, or after menstruating?
- How is the pain? Cramps? Dull or sharp?
- How do you feel emotionally? Before, during, and after?
- Do you suffer from PMS?
- Is your cycle in tune with the lunar cycle, or does it have its own rhythm?

Diseases of the uterus can be seen as an SOS call from our femininity, which is crying for our attention. Because the uterus is playing such an important and essential role in a woman's life, I will dedicate two more chapters of this book to the Heavenly Palace.

*Heavenly Funnel— fallopian tubes*

The fallopian tubes are on average about 4 to 6 inches long. The beginning is shaped like a funnel and narrows toward the uterus. The inside is lined with a shimmer epithelium. Its secretion helps the egg move—with the help of the contractions of the fallopian tube muscles—down into the uterus.

*Hidden Treasure— ovaries*

The ovaries are about the size of a walnut. They produce the hormones needed for reproduction. The main task of the ovaries is to develop about four or five hundred mature egg cells out of the 100,000 pre-egg cells that are stored from birth in every ovary, and prepare them to be fertilized each month.

# Chapter 11

# STRENGTHENING THE WOMB

In this chapter I would like to introduce you to several exercises to strengthen your womb area. I am of the opinion that exercising is not necessarily a healthy activity. It depends on who is doing the exercise, for what purpose, and how it is being done. Some techniques are cleansing, some are relaxing, other exercises will loosen you up, while others are more energizing or increase your sensitivity. Just be aware that exercises have different effects. Not all problems can be solved by exercising. This idea is especially valid for women. Usually, I don't make general recommendations about exercises, such as, "Do this exercise 20 times." To me, exercising is getting to know yourself better, and developing a feeling for what is right for you and what isn't. It is not about fitting yourself into a structure, a technique, or an ideal of how you "should" be. It is all about getting a feel for your own body and experimenting with new things.

I often get phone calls from women who would like to attend my seminars, but who are concerned that they will not be able to keep a discipline or continue to train regularly.

**Exercises that Make Sense**

*Women and discipline*

Consequently, they worry that they might not really gain any benefit from the seminar if they attend. I always tell them that if a woman is not able to train with discipline, it is a sign that her femininity is still intact! To strengthen the body according to the yin principle does not mean we have to withstand a rigorous physical training designed to enforce control on the body. The feminine aspect reacts very strongly to yang-oriented behaviors and attitudes, such as discipline, technique, and control. And in fact, female energy is strengthened the most in a natural state of surrender and letting go. The most important thing for women to remember is that female energy is best nourished out of a state of well-being, not "well-doing." So it is a must for women to feel good and sensual while doing any exercise or workout, otherwise the benefit will be limited and uncertain.

Sometimes I go to the gym and I'm always surprised at what I see there: stepping is very popular these days, and I see women on the stepper forever, it seems. Stepping is very boring. I tried it myself. If you watch closely, no one seems to really like it. So while stepping, people read magazines or books, watch TV, or men watch women doing their exercises. In this way, exercise does not help one to get in touch with one's own nature, but takes you further and further away from it.

All exercises have a different effect on each individual body, and this effect cannot be predicted. So it is a very important point to remain connected with yourself and your feelings while exercising, so you always know what's going on inside your body. While experimenting with and exploring your body, make sure a sensual feeling of well-being is the foundation of each exercise.

- *Menstruation*: Only exercise as long as it doesn't increase the bleeding. Don't work with the ovaries or the womb area while menstruating.

- *Pregnancy*: Pregnancy is not the right moment for you to experiment with your body and start working with your energy. It is a time to relax and enjoy.

- *Coil*: Women wearing a coil should exercise in a very sensitive and gentle way.

- *Myoma*: A myoma always develops out of an excess, therefore exercises that bring more energy into the area, like the egg exercise, are not recommended, as they can increase the problem. It is recommended to increase the energy flow of the body by working on your liver and to cool, empty, and clear the uterus. Chinese medicine, using herbs and acupuncture, is very effective in treating problems like this.

- *Cancer and other diseases:* Please consult a doctor.

*How to start*

The exercises presented in this chapter do not need any prerequisite. You can try them even if you have not opened the microcosmic orbit yet. How long and how often you do them is entirely up to your own experience. Find out what works best for you and leave out any exercises or experiments that don't make you feel good.

To begin, be aware of what you want to achieve by exercising. This is especially true for women who do not feel healthy. Choose exercises that you like doing, and that can strengthen your weakness. Nothing kills your motivation to work on your body more than not getting a good response from something you don't like doing in the first place. Only a few women are able to effectively work out of a motivation of the mind that dictates a "should" or a "must." So remember: having fun and feeling good while exercising is the best inspiration for women to explore themselves deeper and deeper.

Choose a suitable place and time, where it is possible to do your experiments without much effort or preparation. My two favorite places are my bed and the bathroom, and my favorite time seems to be as early in the morning as I wake up.

*Basics*   The two basic ingredients of self-healing, centering yourself, and getting in touch with the fragrance of your heart, you know already. Everything else is based on that. Working with your body and your energy always affects your whole personal energy field, and this process can be easily compared with an operation. An operation always ends with sewing up the cut again; then the body needs a resting period to heal and readjust. So make it a habit to begin and end each activity or meditation by centering. Centering is neither imagination nor thought, but an art of being, which will help you integrate your experiences so something new can grow inside. When centering yourself, always find a good position, where the upper body is in an upright position, so the back is straight and the energy can flow easy, no matter whether you are sitting, standing, or lying down.

**Try This! →**   **Sitting on a chair**

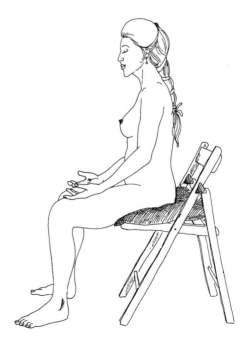

Sitting on a chair.

124

- Sit upright on the edge of the chair so that the vertebra are straight and your shoulders are relaxed.

- Pull back the chin slightly, in exactly that position you usually avoid because you do not want to get a double chin, so that your neck can expand and your head is sitting straight.

- Your feet should be placed a shoulder-width apart, firmly on the ground, with the legs gently opened.

- Make it a habit to sit up straight, allowing your center to "hold" your balance, instead of leaning on the back of the chair.

### Sitting on the floor

← **Try This!**

Sitting crossed-legged on the floor is not a comfortable position for some women. It is easier if you put one or two pillows under your pelvis or use a special meditation cushion. The more you get used to sitting on the floor the easier it becomes. The stronger your middle becomes, the easier it is to sit up straight.

### The horsewoman position

← **Try This!**

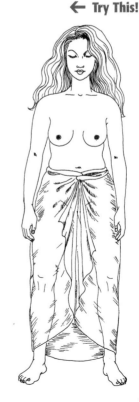

- Stand in a upright position.

- Put the feet parallel, a shoulder-width apart.

- Relax the toes (do not curl them).

- The knees are softly bent and the thighs are open (as if sitting on a horse).

- The vertebra are in a straight line.

- Find a position for your pelvis where your energy is not cut off. Make sure you do not stand with a hollow back and that your behind is not sticking out.

- Allow your body to relax into this position.

The horsewoman position.

**Breathing**

There are many different breathing techniques, so let's keep it simple. Unless it says to breathe differently for a particular exercise, do the exercises with a natural, slow and deep breathing through the nose. The inbreath is the yang phase, active and intense; it is used to draw in energy. The outbreath is the yin phase, a passive letting go, or receiving and storing the energy.

**Go Deeper! →**

## The art of centering

You can be centered wherever you are and in whatever you do. In the beginning, use the help of your hands to get in touch with your middle more easily. Once you have gained enough experience to know what this feels like, you can continue the centering without your hands.

• Place one hand touching your belly just below the navel, with the other hand on your back, just opposite the hand in front. The palms of your hands face each other. The magnetism present between your hands helps you keep your awareness there.

• Surrender more and more to the middle, deeper and deeper, until you can clearly feel your blood pulsing there.

• The pulsing helps you to stay in your middle and feel the middle.

• Allow the breathing to become deeper and the body to relax and become soft and open on the outside, so all the strength can flow within and gather there.

Art of centering.

• In the depths of your being, all the different layers of yourself can be merged and united as one.

**Strengthening Exercises**

*Closing the gates*

An important part of inner energy work is learning to close all the gates or openings of the body. Women often feel weak or exhausted because their gates remain unconsciously open, allowing all the energies of the body to flow out. And in addition to that, the inside of the body remains unprotected and exposed to negative influences!

126

In this inner energy work, we distinguish between the upper and the lower gates. The eyes, ears, mouth, and nose are called the upper gates. During meditation and while practicing the exercises, you should close your eyes and mouth and turn all your senses toward the inside—looking, hearing, tasting, smelling, and feeling inside yourself. When we talk about the lower gates, we refer to the vagina, urethra, anus, and perineum, a very important energy point.

At this point I would like to give some special attention to the lower gates. In working with female sexual energy, it is of utmost importance to be able to close the lower gates properly. Otherwise, unrefined sexual energy and yin energies are continuously leaking out, their dense and heavy water qualities carrying them in search of the lowest point. To be able to open and close your gates consciously gives you the possibility to protect your insides, when necessary. To open and close your gates is the first step toward strengthening the womb.

*The lower gates*

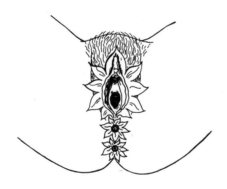

The lower gates.

The energy center that is located at the perineum, an energy point between the anus and the vagina, is called the door of life and death or "the meeting of the yin." To transform sexual energy, the condition of this point is pivotal, either guiding the sexual energy upward to the divine, or allowing sexual energy to leak from the body. You should take enough time to be able to

*The door of life and death*

feel and connect with this point, distinct from the other lower gates. This point can have a strong healing effect, and can be activated by either pressing or massaging it. It will strengthen the female genitals, the lower gates as such, and help regulate menstruation and clear the mind.

Train this point until you are able to influence it even while having an orgasm. This usually will take some time. Women who have had an incision at the perineum while giving birth need to give special attention to this point.

**Try This! →**

### Activating the perineum

- With the help of your finger, locate and feel your perineum. You can also sit on a hard rubber ball to activate the point, so you are able to feel it better.

- Once you can feel it, begin to breathe in through the perineum until you feel a slight suction there.

Do this as much as possible, but remain relaxed in it. It is important not to tense up.

*The love muscle*

The strength of the lower abdomen also depends on the tonus and flexibility of the "love muscle," the pubococcygeus muscle, also known as the PC muscle. It passes through the whole base of the pelvis, interconnecting the sexual organs, anus, buttocks, and legs. It controls the vagina, urethra, and the anus. It is called the love muscle because it is able to give us women pleasure, and in addition, it is also very important for our health.

**Try This! →**

### Playing with the love muscle

- Sit or stand and close your eyes.

- With your inbreath, begin to suck the muscle at the entrance of the vagina slightly inward, so you get a little tonus on it. In the beginning, you can use a finger to localize the muscle a little easier.

- Hold your breath and tonus for a bit, and then slowly let go and breathe out, and with the outbreath let the energy gather in the vagina, filling the love muscle with vibrant energy.

### Opening and closing the three gates                    ← **Go Deeper!**
Try now to alternate the opening and closing of the three gates (vagina, anus, and perineum). First very slow and then try to do it a bit faster.

### Vaginal pump                                            ← **Go Deeper!**

- You can best activate the vaginal pump in a sitting or standing position.

- Close your eyes and bring your awareness down into your vagina. While breathing in, breathe in through your vagina as you suck your vagina slightly upward, drawing energy from the earth up into your body.

- Hold the breath and the tension as long as it is easy and comfortable.

- With the outbreath, let go and let all the energies, filled with the fragrance of your heart, fill your vagina and uterus or any other part of the body you like.

- Make sure that the tensioning and relaxing of the muscles are in balance.

- Do this first with your eyes closed, and then after awhile, try it with your eyes open.

### Loosening your pelvis (standing position)               ← **Try This!**

- Take on the position of the horsewoman; let your arms hang loose and center yourself.

- Start shaking your pelvis as wildly as possible until the pelvis is moving by itself and deep tensions and blockages start to dissolve.

- Keep your mouth slightly open and breathe through your mouth. If sounds want to come out, just let it happen.

- To end the exercise, use your hands to center yourself again, until all the energies that were released are guided and condensed into your middle.

**Go Deeper!** → **Loosening your pelvis (prone position)**

- Lie on a mat if the floor feels too hard for you, but don't put a pillow under your head, so your head remains aligned with your back.

- Leaving your feet flat on the ground, pull your knees up so your legs are bent.

- Open your legs and pelvis as far as it feels comfortable.

- Lift up your pelvis as high as possible and let it fall down again.

- Start doing this movement faster and faster until the pelvis has found its own rhythm.

- Keep breathing through your open mouth, and let any sounds that want to come out happen.

- Just surrender to the movement of the pelvis and enjoy it.

- At the end, take time to center yourself again and collect the energies that have been stirred up in your middle.

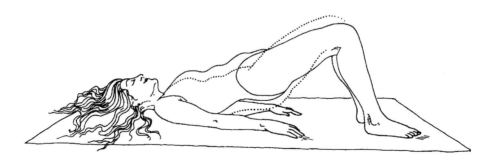

Loosening the pelvis.

## Vitalizing the belly

← **Try This!**

- Assume the position of the horse-woman.

- Put both hands on your navel and start massaging in a spiral away from your navel until the spiral is as big as it can spread over the whole body.

- When the spiral has reached its biggest point, change direction of the massage and let the spiral get smaller again until it has reached its smallest point at the navel.

- Continue doing this as energetically as possible, always changing the direction and size of the spiral, until your belly feels warm and alive.

- Center yourself to end the exercise properly.

Vitalizing the belly.

## Pulsing the vagina

← **Try This!**

- You can do this exercise standing or lying down.

- Lie down comfortably, relax, and bring your whole awareness into your vagina.

- Start smiling lovingly into it until the vagina starts to breathe on its own.

- Breathe slowly and very deeply, so you feel the vagina pulsing.

- Just lie there and allow your vagina to feel happy and alive.

## Pulsing of the womb area

← **Go Deeper!**

- Once you feel the vagina pulsing, start to expand the pulse and allow the whole lower abdomen to pulse deeper and deeper.

**Energy egg**    In the traditional Tao, the energy egg, which is made out of semiprecious stone, has been used to strengthen the vagina. I became familiar with the jade eggs through the work of Mantak Chia. These jade eggs were exclusively used to energize and train the sexual organs. But the possibilities of the energy egg reach far beyond that. Over the last ten years, I have been experimenting with the eggs myself, and with all the other women who attend my seminars, and it is amazing how many ways you can use this egg. We continue to explore the different healing effects different stones can have on our bodies. And by now, among the women I know, the energy egg has become a very popular aid to clear and empty the uterus from all kinds of negativity, as well as providing protection to the uterus. We will go into this more deeply in the chapter about the uterus.

**What you**    Choose a mineral egg that attracts you. Don't choose one just
**need**    because you think it's good for you, out of what you have read

Energy egg.

about the effects of certain healing stones. Allow your intuition to choose it. The egg should not be treated chemically, and it should have a whole drilled through it, so you can easily attach a piece of string or dental floss to it. This enables you to pull the egg out from your vagina any time, as you would with a tampon. The eggs can be ordered from the address listed in the author information on page 311. Usually we have energy eggs of rose quartz, jade, milky jade, and black stone in stock.

As a preparation to work with the egg, you need to put the egg in water and boil it for about ten minutes. Be careful that the egg does not jump up and down in the pan, as it could break. Just let it sit in the bottom of the pan and simmer. Remember to give it enough time to cool off. It depends on how sensitive you are, as to how often you need to simmer the egg, or if you can just wash it with hot water. Do not use soap or a disinfecting solution, as this can irritate your vaginal flora.

132

Only do this egg exercise very gently. It should not create any heat within the body. If you are nervous or jumpy, please wait with the egg exercise until you are relaxed and are able to center yourself within. The microcosmic orbit is another tool you can use to balance your energies at the end of the exercise.

### Egg exercise

Working with the energy egg is very intimate, so only do it if it feels good to you. Never force yourself to do it.

- Assume the position of the horsewoman.

- Take enough time to connect with your center.

- Fold your hands and put them in front of your heart, and then smile into your heart until you feel its fragrance. Let that feeling spread gently into your breasts.

- Put both hands on your breasts and start massaging them gently until you feel connected with your rose flower.

- With the outbreath, let the warm feeling from your heart and breath flow down into your vagina. You can massage the whole area gently, your whole pelvis, your lips, the precious pearl, until the flower opens and you can easily insert the egg. (This is easiest to do in a squatting position.)

- Put the egg in your vagina with your finger, as deep as possible.

- Take on the position of the horsewoman again and just stand there. Feel the egg and hold it in with your muscles.

- For women who have been cut while giving birth, just holding the egg in can be very challenging. But don't be disappointed if you can't hold the egg and it slips out. Take your time, and massage the old wound to heal and strengthen the area over and over again, until the damaged muscles become alive again.

- Now you can go to the next step. With the outbreath, start to push the egg downward, and before you reach the point (of no return), pull it up again with the inbreath. A helpful hint: keep your panties on during work with the egg.

- To finish, center yourself again, so your roots within become stronger and stronger.

# Chapter 12

# IN TUNE WITH NATURE

Attuning our sexuality with the rhythms of nature is an important aspect of a Taoist lifestyle. The female cycle of ovulation and menstruation is ruled by the phases of the Moon. In this chapter, you will become acquainted with methods to help merge with the forces of nature, to become more in harmony and one with it. It can be very helpful for women to learn to harmonize and surrender their monthly cycle to the Moon. There are many suggestions presented to help make your everyday life more natural and in tune with the rhythms of nature.

*The Rhythm of Nature*

The more you move away from your own nature and your natural state of being, the more complicated and unsatisfactory your sexuality will be. The biggest obstacles preventing you from living a more natural life include your own laziness, and an uncaring or irresponsible attitude toward yourself.

The destruction of our natural environment, supposedly in the service of technological progress, is painful and unacceptable. Naturalness belongs to the yin principle; technique and science belong to the opposite pole, the yang. It is a distinctly female responsibility to love, nurture, and heal, so that technique and science are rooted in—and able to grow out of—a positive and caring foundation.

*Naturally or technically*

**With the Moon** The female cycle is in tune with the phases of the Moon. Many women ovulate on the Full Moon and start menstruation on the New Moon. This cycle is known as the White Moon cycle. The White Moon represents the material creation cycle and is also called "the cycle of the good mother." But there are also many women whose cycle is reversed; they menstruate when the Moon is full and ovulate on the New Moon. This cycle, known as the Red Moon Cycle, is also called "the cycle of the wise woman." The women of the Red Moon Cycle are claimed to use their sexual energy not for reproduction, as the women of the white cycle, but for their spiritual growth. It is very common for women to swing between these two cycles during their lives, so there is no need to judge either of them in any way.

Because of an unnatural and yang-predominant lifestyle, many women are alienated from their natural rhythm. It is possible for us to become realigned with our rhythm through living in an environment with a natural day and night rhythm. In this, it is important to clearly separate light and darkness. Blindfolds and earplugs cannot be used as a complete substitute for darkness and silence. You should make sure that at night your bedroom is so dark that you cannot see anything at all. You should eliminate from your sleeping room any source of light, like the LED display of an alarm clock, for instance, so that you spend your night in absolute darkness.

Then, on the nights before, during, and one to two nights after the Full Moon, open the curtains and shutters so the Moonlight is able to enter your room. If you are living in a city and the artificial lighting from the street is too strong and prevents you from sleeping, a little lamp beside your bed with a very soft tender light (15 to 25 watt) will work in the same way. This method will induce your ovulation and helps to get your cycle back in harmony with the rhythm of the Moon.

Depending on which cycle you are closer to, you can do the same procedure with the lamp at New Moon, to adjust your rhythm to the Red Moon Cycle. Continue until your cycle is adjusted again. I should also mention that this method of adjusting the monthly cycle does not work for women who are taking hormones.

## Toxins

We not only absorb poisons through our foods, as we discussed in chapter 9; poisons threaten us from various sources. They can be found in many medicines, in the air, in smoke, in unnatural construction materials, such as chemical paint, treated floors or woods, and in products for cleaning our homes or washing our clothes.

### Drugs and medicine

Many of the medical drugs in use today produce strong side effects, and yet scientists and doctors remain unwilling to look in other directions to find new ways for healing. Thanks to the powerful lobby of the pharmaceutical industry, their financial interests have gained a de facto priority over health and human issues. To put it bluntly, only sick people are beneficial to the pharmaceutical industry, so as a consequence, there is no real effort made to help people toward a state of well-being and independence. Western medicine is mainly geared around controlling the symptoms of an illness, rather than finding the root of the problem. With the help of chemical substances, symptoms are repressed deeper into the body, so on the surface they are no longer felt.

A long list of drugs are medically known to be lust killers. Nevertheless, doctors go on prescribing medicines that weaken the libido to their patients out of ignorance or indifference. Also, many hormone treatments leave traces behind, often with consequences that are unknown up to now.

### Air

Fresh and pure air is an important source of energy. In our modern world, this crucial necessity is becoming more and more of a luxury. The air is freshest outside in the woods or meadows, and taking walks, or jogging in nature, as well as practicing breath exercises are important to a natural life style. Occasionally, it is good to just put on a dress without wearing a panty underneath when you take a walk (when it is not too cold outside) to allow your intimate flower to get some fresh air and sun. Ten minutes of direct sunlight is enough, but not more than that. It is also very nice once in a while to sit naked on the ground.

*Smoking*

Smoking is a burden to your organism, especially to your lungs. The lungs govern the instinctual energy balance of the body. The more the organism is loaded with toxins, the less energy it can absorb. The inbreath not only absorbs oxygen from the air, but it also supplies the body with cosmic energy or prana. I do not see anything negative when a healthy person once in while consciously smokes a cigarette or a pipe. However, the regular consumption of tobacco that exceeds three cigarettes a day can be very harmful to the yin substance of the lungs. To stop smoking is a conscious decision for positive and natural living.

**Detoxing and Cleansing**

In most people's bodies, toxins build up over time, as our bodies are not designed by nature to easily eliminate them. Toxins can be stored in nearly every part of the body, in every cell, in all the organs and joints, and even in the bones and marrow. A regular program of detoxification is necessary to maintain health and well-being. There are many different methods to eliminate toxins and cleanse the body. To free the body from toxins is physically very demanding, and there is no need to fast at the same time. Especially when a woman feels weak or ill, or has a yin deficiency, fasting combined with an intense regimen of internal cleansing can be too much for the system to handle. So remember to proceed at a pace that feels okay to you and that while "detoxing," the body needs lots of rest.

*Cleansing the colon*

The large intestine can easily get overloaded and constipated. Because of the shape of the colon, which includes many twists and turns, toxins and processed foods tend to get trapped in pockets in the colon. This weakens the body and prevents the proper functioning of a whole range of body systems. Foods that produce mucus, such as sweets and dairy products, develop into a sticky mass when trapped in the colon, and over the years harden into stone-like deposits that congest the colon and prevent it from functioning as it should.

- Include enough fiber in your diet.
- Once a week, have your last meal at 4 p.m. and the first meal the next day around noon. During this time, drink only pure or filtered water. This will occasionally give your body a longer period to detoxify to clear the digestive tract.
- Have a colonic or a deep enema at least twice a year.
- Do a thorough colon cleansing at least once a year. The best time for that is in the spring. Herbal supplements for this purpose can be found in any health food store.

- Large Intestine 4, Stomach 36 and 6

**Hints for Healing!**
←

**Healing Points!**
←

 **Try This!**

### Detoxing the skin

When I was a young girl, my grandmother gave me a body brush for my daily skin care. She told me to brush my whole body with hundreds of strokes, always toward the head, to promote blood circulation and detoxification of the skin. The brush should not be too soft.

While detoxing your body, always make sure to rest enough and to drink enough pure water.

**Important Hint!**
←

### Detoxing the joints

Get some strong and densely woven material to sew a bag that you can fill up with mung beans. A similar variety of beans will do just as well. Then sew it completely closed. With your beanbag, you tap all of your joints. This promotes the detoxification of the skin.

 **Try This!**

Detoxing joints
with a bean bag.

**Try This! →**   **Cleansing the internal organs**

- Assume the position of the horsewoman (page 125).

- Tighten up your abdominal wall and start gently tapping your internal organs with a loose fist, or with your little bean bag. Tap the liver, gallbladder, stomach, small and large intestine, bladder, uterus, lungs (leave out the heart), and then move around to your back to tap your kidneys.

- To intensify the cleansing, you can do some of the healing sounds you have already learned as you tap or massage the organs. While detoxifying, the liver needs special attention and care.

## Tuning In to Nature

The following exercises and recommendations will help you to merge and connect with the different forces of nature.

**Try This! →**   **Connecting with Mother Earth**

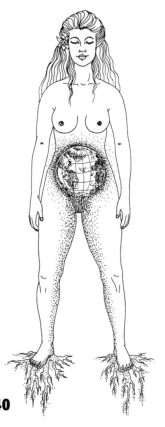

- Take on the position of the horsewoman and close your eyes.

- Bring your awareness into your feet until your breathing becomes deep and relaxed, and you are feeling the pulse in your soles.

- Tuning into the pulse helps your feet become translucent and open to the earth, so that the earth becomes a part of you, the earth becomes your roots.

- Breathe in the energy of the earth through your vagina and your perineum to bring it into your whole body.

- With the outbreath, fill and expand the earth energy in your middle until you meld with the earth, carrying the earth within.

Connecting with Mother Earth.

## Kindle your inner fire

← **Go Deeper!**

- Sit comfortably, but upright, in front of a fire or candle, and gaze with your third eye and your navel into the flame.

- Keep breathing into your center until your inner fire is lit there.

- Close your eyes and just sit. Feel and enjoy your inner flame.

## The cosmic pulse

← **Go Deeper!**

- Stand in the position of the horsewoman, preferably outside in nature.

- Bring your awareness to the following points at the same time:

    - The bubbling well on your soles (Kidney 1)

    - The perineum

    - The crown

- Remain standing with eyes closed, deeply connected with these points. Breathe slowly and deeply until the cosmic pulse begins to enter these points, and your whole body pulses with the cosmic vibration.

## Receiving the heavenly light

← **Go Deeper!**

- This experiment can be done either sitting, standing, or lying down.

- Close your eyes and bring your middle finger to your forehead to touch your third eye.

- Hold it there until it slowly begins to pulse.

- Then remove your hand and start breathing in through your third eye to activate and open it.

Receiving heavenly light.

- As soon as you are feeling the opening, go through your spiritual eye to the Sun and even further, where it is all light, and you can perceive the Heavenly Light.

- Keep breathing into your third eye, bringing the Heavenly Light into your body and filling your center with that fluid brightness until it starts shining.

**Try This!** → **Looking for your own star**

- On a clear night, sit outside or at your open window.

- Close your eyes and start breathing very quietly and deeply.

- Bring your awareness to your pituitary gland and let her guide you to your personal star. Your eyes remain closed. Keep breathing and feel the quality of your star.

- In the end, put your hands on your center and bring the star, with the help of your breathing, into your center. And then let the star energy spread from your middle all over your body.

Looking for your own star.

## Moonshine shower

← **Go Deeper!**

To shower in the moonlight means to let the silver light flow over and through your body, to heal and nourish you. It is most effective to do on a night when the Moon is increasing to Full Moon.

- On a clear night, sit outside in the moonshine and close your eyes.

- Start breathing and allow your body to become soft and receptive.

- While breathing in, let the silver moonlight flow into your body through each pore, to purify each cell and fill them up with the nourishing yin power of the Moon.

Moonshine shower.

# Chapter 13

# SENSUALITY

The sense organs are the windows through which we are able to perceive our environment. Through the nervous system, they transmit impulses to the brain, and hence, help to shape the reality each person creates for themselves. The eyes are stimulated by visual images, the ears through sound and vibration, the nose by odors, and the mouth by taste. The skin reacts to temperature and touch. When I use the word sensuality here, I refer to all the sense organs.

**The Senses and their Organs**

Sensuality and sexuality are an inseparable pair. Most people's sexuality is controlled by sensory stimulus. Sensuality is always a reaction of the body. When people are cut off from their feelings, sensuality is a common substitute, and for many, the only possibility to perceive themselves. For example, some people are always eating or nibbling on something so they are able to feel themselves through their sense of taste. Sensuality is also a popular substitute for energy. People with a low energy level can get very hooked on sensual stimulation to compensate their inner emptiness, especially in sex.

In our modern world, people are so disconnected from themselves, and live on such a low energetic level, that they have to stimulate their sense organs with all the means possible to manage enough intensity to be able to have sex.

*Connecting the sensual organs*

Some people are cut off from conscious perception of the senses. The following techniques will help you reconnect your eyes and ears with your whole being.

**Try This!** → **Connecting the eyes**

- Sit in an upright but relaxed position with your eyes open.

- Slowly start circling your eyes, making the circle as big as possible, until you feel a tension or blockage. Stop circling and fix your eyes at that point, and keep on breathing.

- At the same time, start massaging your navel with one hand and the Kidney 27 point with the other hand.

- Massage the points until the tension dissolves. Then go on circling your eyes until you find the next tension and do as above until your eyes are totally relaxed.

**Try This!** → **Connecting the ears**

- Massage your outer ears from the top to the bottom on the outside and the inside.

- At the same time massage your navel or energy point Kidney 27.

**Cleansing and Calming Sensual Organs**

Sensual organs that are over-stimulated are a burden to the nervous system and distort our perception. Take time to reconnect with them and calm them as needed. The more you are in contact with them, the easier it becomes to sense when they need a break.

*Nose*

The nose, or to be a bit more precise, the olfactory cells, play a particular role in our sexuality. The olfactory nerve relays its sensing of fragrance directly, without any detour, into the limbic center. This area of the brain has an important role in our sexual and emotional behavior, as well as in memory. It stimulates the hypothalamus and the pituitary gland, and affects the production of hormones.

A deep cleansing of the nose affects more than the body—it also has a deep clearing effect at the emotional level. I use two methods to clean my nose: lukewarm water and a little salt, or natural sesame oil.

## Cleansing the nose

← **Try This!**

- The best time to do this is at bedtime.

- You need a dropper and warm sesame oil. Put the little oil bottle into hot water until the oil is warm.

- Lie down on your back and pour a few drops of oil in the right nostril. Close your left nostril and breathe in strongly with the right to get the oil as deeply in as you can.

- Repeat the same procedure with the other nostril.

- If you need to sneeze, wait a bit first.

- Remain prone with closed eyes for another half an hour.

*Sensual fragrances*

The pheromones, your own sexual fragrance, is your most sensual and effective perfume. They are found in your sweat, saliva, urine, and especially in your vagina, and are there to attract sexual partners. And it is not only in humans that this happens. The love life of animals is ruled by this phenomenon as well. On my walks with my little macho dog Tuffy, I see this every day. He gets so excited and involved, endlessly smelling other dogs, and to me, watching all this, it remains a mystery. Taking too many showers or baths, or using perfumes, can diminish the power of your natural body odor. Before having a date with a potential lover, it is far more effective to put some of your vaginal secretion on your earlobe, rather than lessen your chances by applying perfumes like Chanel or Opium, which only destroy the seductive effect of your own pheromones.

Natural fragrances from flowers, barks, or resin can also provoke sensual feelings. To apply and activate these substances, there are many different methods, like incense, oils, and fragrance lamps. Here in Switzerland, fragrant pillows filled with hemp are very popular at the moment.

**Watch Out!** →

It is recommended that you consciously choose your fragrances and use them according to your intention. To expose yourself continuously to smells and to choose them unconsciously can provoke emotional reactions and confusion. Smells always affect your emotions, and over-stimulation will not necessarily enhance your love life, but could easily spoil it.

*Sensual fragrances*
- Patchouli
- Jasmine
- Ylang Ylang
- Rose
- Benzoin
- Bergamot
- Hyacinth
- Marjoram
- Vanilla
- Rosemary

By the way, the higher the level of estrogen in the body, the more sensitive the olfactory organs.

*Eyes*   The eyes are interconnected with and nourished by the liver. The stronger the liver, the better for the eyes. The more relaxed the eyes, the better for the liver. Things like too much work in front of a computer monitor or watching TV or other media that leave strong visual impressions, not only weaken the eyes, but also the liver and the whole nervous system. To take proper care of your eyes and give them what they need benefits your whole body.

**Hints for Healing!**
→

- Close your eyes as much as you can to give them a break.

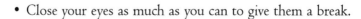

- With your warmed up palms, cover your closed eyes, breathe deeply, and feel your hands and eyes pulsing so they can relax.

- Massage the area around your eyes and do eye exercises.

- Do not read in artificial lighting.

- Be aware of chemicals in your makeup. It is better to use only natural products.

- Frequently look or gaze into absolute darkness.

- Smile into your eyes until they are smiling back at you.

- Eye care with natural sesame oil, as below.

## Eye care                                            ← Try This!

*For dry and itchy eyes*

- Before going to bed, put some drops of slightly warm natural sesame oil into your eyes. This is very relaxing for them.

*Red and tired eyes*

- Wash your eyes once a week (or more) with natural rosewater. Make yourself eye compresses with cool cucumber slices from the health food store, or with fresh leaves and herbs.

*To please the eyes*

- Find pictures you really like: an erotic picture, an untouched countryside, a house, a great pair of buns, a kitten, your favorite cake, a Buddha, whatever is pleasing to your eyes.

- Just look at the picture, breathe deeply and quietly, and let the picture affect you, whatever way that may be.

- You can also experiment with the way different colors affect you.

*Ears*

Since the ears are the opening to the kidneys, strong stimulation from noise, continuous background music, or even traffic noise can weaken the ears and kidneys, and therefore also affect your sexual energy. Noise is considered to be yang quality, while stillness is yin.

149

**Hints for Healing!**

- Give yourself as much silence and stillness as possible. As an aid, you might want to use earplugs.

- As often as you can, listen to the sound of silence.

- Wherever you are, you can close your eyes for a moment and just listen to all the sounds surrounding you, in the supermarket, in the forest, or in your office, for instance.

- Only put on radio, TV or music when you are really listening to it.

- With your lover, you can gently blow or whisper in each others ears.

**Try This!** → **Ear care**

- In the morning, put a bit of sesame oil on your ear and rub it in softly.

- Clean your ears about three to four times a year with ear candles, or let someone do it to you.

- Give your ears a good massage once in awhile.

*Sense of taste*    The mouth and tongue enable us to experience the sensual feeling of delight through eating and drinking. For a gourmet, his sense of taste is the door to sensuality. Expanding the joy of eating and drinking over many hours is often at the cost of a fulfilled sexuality. In fact, many people try to compensate unfulfilled sexuality through eating.

*Skin*    The skin is supplied and nourished by the lungs. The condition of the skin is also strongly connected to the quality of the blood. The skin has many sensory cells that pass on all kinds of information referring to temperature, pain, pressure, and touch to the central nervous system.

The skin is a very sensitive and sensual organ that can give us much joy and pleasure. The love hormone oxytocin is stimulated by touching the skin and pours out into the bloodstream, promoting a feeling of loving tenderness within. The skin also spreads the sexual fragrances, the pheromones.

- Use natural products for body care, cleaning, and laundry.
- Wear loose clothes made out of natural fabrics, especially the ones you wear directly on your skin.
- Use natural bedding and mattresses.
- Take regular steam baths (not saunas, which deplete yin).
- Massages (self massage and partner massage)
- Oil baths
- Air baths without clothes
- In winter, go once a week to a solarium.
- Do not take more then 20 minutes of direct sun a day.
- Detoxify your skin by brushing and tapping it regularly.

**Hints for Healing!**

It is very nice to mix your own body oil. Suitable oils to use as a base are almond, coconut, or wheat oil, for example. Choose the essential oils you would like to add to the base oil. Mix 6 to 8 drops of essential oil with about 2 tablespoons of your base oil, and shake well before use. The oils will have a stronger effect if you brush your skin before or right after applying the oil.

*Body oil for the sensual woman*

### Essential oils to enhance estrogen production

- Rose
- Angelica
- Geranium
- Thyme
- Vanilla
- Sage
- Coriander
- Hop
- Oregano
- Roman chamomile

**← Try This!**

*For dry skin:*

As a base, use sesame oil and add a few drops of

- Geranium
- Rose
- Jasmine

*For mature skin:*

Mix:

- 4 parts jojoba oil
- 4 parts calendula oil
- 1 part wheat oil

*For cellulite:*

As a base, use hazelnut or lemon oil and add from the essential oils below:

- Cypress
- Thyme
- Lemon
- Juniper
- Oregano
- Celery
- Rosemary
- Lemon grass

## From Sensuality to Transcendence

One of the essential aims of the Tao is the conscious perception of sexuality. When we stimulate the senses, we activate the production of love hormones, which tends to cause a wonderful state of rapture that clouds our awareness.

### The high of the senses

Sensuality can never be the expression of spirituality. We should not confuse sensual ecstasy with spiritual ecstasy. Sensuality as a "high" of the senses remains far below the possibility of the Tao. For women, sensuality is a natural state of our being, our everyday life. Hence, for women, sensuality can become the foundation of a path of transcendence. Through our senses, it is possible for our body to feel well-being and joy. For many women, sensuality seems to be a natural and reliable foundation used to build a positive energy field within.

*Transcendence*

Our image of reality is very personal and subjective. By projecting our inner images, experiences, and dreams into the outer world, we create our own world around us, which for the most part does not correspond with reality at all. When the surface of our illusory world of images, beliefs, and dreams is scratched or destroyed, this can be a very painful experience. It is also an opportunity for healing. Falling from the cozy, dreamy cloud and landing flat on our faces on the ground of reality is always a bit of a shock!

Mystics through the ages have been investigating how to get in touch with reality without depending on the unreliable and subjective way that reality is distorted through our senses. The direct contact, which does not depend on the senses, is called the transcendent. Many meditation techniques have been developed to serve one purpose: to help us enter the word of reality by leaving all dreams and beliefs behind. The following meditation technique has been practiced over many centuries, not just in the Tao, but also in other systems.

## Turn the senses within

← **Try This!**

• Sit in an upright and comfortable position and close your eyes.

Turn the senses within.

- Breathe slowly and deeply until your energy field in the middle is activated and you are feeling relaxed and connected.

- Turn all your senses inside.

- Look inside with your eyes.

- Smell inside with your nose.

- Hear inside with your ears.

- Taste your insides.

- Feel inside.

- Stay at least ten minutes in this inner state.

As a help, you can use a blindfold and earplugs. Next time you feel sexual, turn inward and let your sexual energy flow inside.

# Part Four

# NEW
# DIMENSIONS
# OF
# WOMANHOOD

# Chapter 14

# FEELINGS

Sexuality brings up intense and contradictory feelings. On one hand, the longing for a romantic and profound love affair is awakened, but on the other, we may become hopelessly entangled in emotional dramas that, in the end, can become very destructive. Unconscious patterns and repressed feelings cause these dramas, which prevent us from experiencing unlimited love. Only if we are able to understand the interplay of sex and emotion and to free our repressed emotions will it become possible to let our life force flow freely and ecstatically.

**Imprisoned Feelings and Old Wounds**

While emotional experience is unlimited, our rationality—the opposite pole—tries to set limits to keep the balance. Mind and feeling are often very contradictory. In our yang-oriented society, the qualities of the mind are valued more than feelings. From early childhood, we are trained to control and repress our feelings far more than needed.

*Emotional and rational*

The consequences are that our feelings, which are repressed into the unconscious, begin to develop a momentum of their own from the darkness of our being. Most people feel they have no say when it comes to emotions and are forced to surrender to them, or try with all their energy to avoid them.

Emotions touch a very deep layer within and help us feel alive. Emotions are a doorway to our unconscious, enabling us to penetrate the deeper layers of our being with the light of awareness. Emotions can be either yin quality—and more introverted, such as fear and sadness—or they can be of a more extroverted yang quality—such as anger. Even so, the world of feelings in general is categorized as yin. Emotions and feelings challenge us to go to the depths to find our roots.

*The Tao of emotion* Working with sexual issues and psychiatric patients for over twenty years, day in and day out I am confronted or involved with highly explosive emotional situations. It has been of great importance to find a useful model or system to help me cope with that, so I could understand and influence situations positively and constructively. In the Tao of emotion, I have found a reliable tool. The Tao challenges us to unconditionally assume full responsibility for our emotions. This can feel merciless at times, but nevertheless, it opens an opportunity for significant transformation in our lives. Here is a living example.

*Being fully responsible* Your lover comes by with a unique present for you. He is charming and kisses you gently, and a bit later, you are in bed making love. He is affectionate and thoughtful, and for you, time stops. Then he becomes restless and looks at his watch and says he needs to talk to you. He tells you that this has been the last time, because he has fallen in love with somebody else. He gets up, puts on his clothes, and walks out the door. (This story is not invented; I know several women who have experienced such a situation.)

Because this situation does not correspond with our personal reality of hopes and dreams, we are desperately trying to find a way to maintain our belief system. But no matter how horrible we feel about what happened, how many girlfriends we call, or how many good strategies we come up with to manipulate him or take revenge, we want to be able to cancel what has happened. The Tao challenges us to not close off, fight, or react, but to allow transformation to happen—exactly in moments like this. This is the right moment to look for the mechanism that is hidden behind your usual behavior. So no matter what happens, just stay open, be watchful, and allow your water essence to continue to flow.

Old and unfinished wounds, of which we are unaware, are activated in certain, mostly unexpected or unwanted situations. They are painful and ask for our attention until we have completely healed them and set them free. This process looks initially unpleasant and exhausting, because it is a new way, and you will have to let go of old patterns. But next time an unexpected situation opens an old wound, remember that this is your chance to grow and get to know deeper layers of your personality. If you manage to avoid them once more, it will not lead you anywhere. On the contrary, if you ignore them again, they engrave themselves even deeper into your unconscious and become more persistent and deceptive, and only a more extreme situation can break through to this same depth the next time.

*Take a look behind the scenes*

It is the moment to use your self-healing power to clear, strengthen, and heal layer after layer of your unconscious. Feelings of sadness, anger, and jealousy are always an indication of your unhealed wounds and limitations. And they show us clearly that we are not yet connected with our inner well of strength.

In difficult moments, the Tao offers us a possibility to expand our scope of experience through inner revolution and transformation. Life is on our side in that it keeps creating situations over and over again in the hope that we take the chance to choose the way of a responsible woman, and break out of our habitual role as victim.

When it comes to understanding feelings, it is of great advantage to be a woman. Through our yin nature, we women are more at home in the world of feelings than men are. And from their natural yin state, women are able to move in a more carefree and easy way in the world of feelings.

*Women and feelings*

A yang-oriented lifestyle and social belief system have cut women off from their feelings and their depth. This makes us feel very insecure. The inner weakness and emptiness that results from being cut off from our inner depth is often compensated with a superficial yang-oriented life style.

Feeling has its source in the female nature. It is a female responsibility to incorporate feelings in our life and our actions. If women do not restore the depth and aliveness of feeling, who else will do it? Men have far more difficulty getting in touch with deep feelings, and often this only happens through a woman who is connected with her own nature.

## Love and Sexuality

As long as happiness and unhappiness, or love and hate, remain simply a reaction to affection and recognition, we live in a dependency that leaves us open to be manipulated and used. If he loves me, I am in heaven; but if he suddenly loves someone else, heaven abruptly dissolves into hell. We continuously vacillate up and down between being loved and being ignored, being popular and then rejected. Like a marionette strung from emotion, we are pulled up, and allowed to fall into pieces again. The Tao supports you to cut through the endless cycle of emotions and to develop a feeling of love within yourself, regardless what others think of you, or if they love you or not.

## *Love—the highest feeling!*

Love and compassion are the highest expression of feeling we have. Christianity, which has deeply influenced our culture, is responsible for the fact that love and compassion are often mixed up with hypocrisy and falseness. On Sunday, you go to the church and pray "God is love." But hate and unhappiness rule every other day. The schizophrenic split from the Sunday humbleness out of which you donate to compensate for the rest of the week is a great foundation for feeding sexual perversion. And believe me, I know what I am talking about. With my work, I am confronted with it day in and day out.

Over the centuries, the Catholic Church has considered masturbation a sin. Only a short while ago, under Pope John Paul II,
it was reevaluated and now it is considered only a "weakness."
As long as religions burdened with guilt preach a negative attitude toward sexuality, it will not be possible to become more
loving and caring about our bodies. Out of the dependency religions create, they keep praying to "Our Father": "lead us not
into temptation, but deliver us from evil."

*Lead us not into temptation*

The Tao can help us experience heaven on earth. It contin-
ues to lead us to temptations, to confront us with our shadow
sides and our so-called "evil," so we get to know it. We can
become friends with it and no longer have to fight and repress
the shadow. The Tao challenges us to face our fears, our wounds,
our resistance, to take them by the hand and sing and dance
them into the light. The Tao is not a religion but a helpful tool
on the way to realize our convictions.

Sex is not a feeling, but sexuality can amplify feelings that are
already there. Unluckily, not just the positive ones are enhanced,
for negative and undigested emotions can also be reactivated
through sex. They arise from the depths, where they have been
slumbering all their lives. They interfere with our life until they
are digested and dissolved. It is possible to live your entire life
with repressed feelings. In most areas of life, it doesn't make any
difference if you are real or phony. Since the majority of people are not honest, nobody will notice if you are a part of the
club. But when it comes to sex, it will manifest very clearly if
you are not authentic, or to what degree love and sex are connected within you. Even when you have learned to play the perfect act as sexy as you can be, and men really love you for it, you
will still have to face your truth, and know exactly and very
clearly where you are with it.

*Sex and feeling*

Being able to experience great love and great sex is one of the
most sought after dreams, but only a very few are able to actually live it. The yin part of sexuality (water) is open and recep-

*Love and sex*

tive. Water always absorbs the strongest aspects within a person, whether thoughts or emotions, or even the divine. As a consequence, sexuality is often overloaded or polluted by repressed negative emotions that are intensified by the yang part of sex, the fire energy that arouses sex. This explains how neuroses, fear, insecurity, power games, pain, and fantasies control our sex lives. A person who has never learned to grow a feeling of deep love within themselves, does not really feel good inside. As long as it is more important to be loved than to truly love and accept someone else, love and sex will not be able to dance and celebrate hand in hand, but will remain separated and isolated by a deep abyss.

*Taking care of love*

When we are freshly in love, love and excitement are connected with sexual energy. Love is like a very precious plant and needs care, so it can grow deep roots inside and blossom outside. I do not know any exercise to create love. But we can clear our body from all the old garbage and negativity to create a positive energy field that will invite and attract love.

The place in the body where love likes to be is in the heart. But many hearts are in a state of desolation, too many hearts are wounded, broken, frozen, or full of disappointment, distrust, and pain. In such an environment, there is no place for love to grow. It is our task to empty, clean, and strengthen the heart to create a space for love, peace, and stillness to come and stay. The following exercise can support you.

**Try This! →**   **Unburden the heart**

- Sit in an upright but comfortable position. Put one hand on your heart and the other on your forehead so your forehead is covered with your hand.

- Start breathing in through your slightly open mouth, and expand your chest as much as possible. Stay connected with your heart until you are in touch with the feelings in your heart.

Unburden the heart.

- While breathing out, softly fill your heart with the healing sound "Haaaaa" to strengthen it so it will have the energy to set itself free.

- After a while, allow all the heaviness from your heart to flow down to your feet and into the ground, guided by your out-breath.

- Put your whole awareness into your heart. Clean it layer by layer, and support it with the inner smile.

- Ask your heart what stress or burden it is carrying inside, without stopping the breathing. Images or thoughts may come up; just let that happen and continue breathing, and empty your heart more and more.

- In the end, fill your heart with a true inner smile.

Do this exercise only as long as you feel good about it. Don't overdo it. Healing the yin does not happen from one day to another. It is a slow and ongoing process.

## Dealing with Feelings

Even though dealing with emotions is far more difficult than learning how to read and write, it is not an issue that is explored in our schools. The violence that keeps happening in schools may be a sign that it's time to look in a new direction. But let's first investigate in our own way how we are dealing with our emotions. There are many ways to deal with them once they are activated. Emotions can be:

- Felt
- Expressed
- Repressed or cut off
- Blamed on someone else
- Verbalized or talked about
- Analyzed
- Judged
- Killed
- Nourished
- Exaggerated
- Manipulated

**My Diary! →** Find out what your patterns are and how you are dealing with your emotions. How do you respond to the emotions of other people?

*Feelings are to feel* The mind exists to think, and feelings are here to feel. The mind is not able to feel, and feeling is not able to think. But we keep mixing these two different layers, and making everything confusing and complicated. Feelings can never clearly or logically be put into words, even if you analyze them for hours. You cannot grasp or understand a feeling with thoughts, but by thinking about it, you can repress or control it. Feeling always wants to be felt—to be lived.

*Intuition, wisdom, and intelligence* If we follow emotion into the depths of our being, we reach the hidden well of intuition, the place of unlimited wisdom, the key to female intelligence. The water of the well is polluted and troubled by all the repressed emotions it contains. To purify that water so it becomes clear and transparent requires a deep cleansing process and a new orientation.

Emotions can also express mental blocks and personal limitations. If you want to break through these layers, you must be persistent and determined. This liberation requires lots of physical substance. Women who are feeling weak or ill will want to strengthen their body before beginning to deal with the dark side. The goal is to get to know the dark side so we can establish a love relationship with it.

# Chapter 15

# EXPLORING DEPTHS

The yang principle is driven to shine in the sunlight—it wants to present its strength and celebrate its highlights to the world. The other side of the coin is manifested by yin. The yang flight onto the stage of life is rooted, nourished, and controlled by the depth of yin. These essential yin qualities are imprisoned and weakened by tremendous fears. To be able to explore the depths of our being, we need to recognize and face the deep fear within that prevents us from expanding our inner world. The fear of yin has many different faces:

- Fear of the unknown depth
- Fear of inner emptiness
- Fear of one's own weakness
- Fear to feel
- Fear to be left alone
- Fear of losing control
- Fear of stillness
- Fear of death
- Fear of life

We have all developed deceptive and yet reliable strategies to avoid coming in contact with our unpredictable "dark side," where the seed of female strength is hidden.

**My Diary!** → It is not uncommon for people to suppress or hide their fears and weaknesses, the shadow side, and their true feelings. You must take time to investigate and write down the strategies that you normally use to avoid coming in contact with or showing these aspects of yourself—in general or in connection with your sexuality.

## Emotional Pollution

In the emotional realm, emptiness is classified as yin and fullness as yang. Out of a fear of emptiness, we tend to saturate our lives emotionally as well as materially, filling them with all kinds of objects, ideas, memories, and people. To have a boyfriend, a husband, a big circle of friends, a big family, and many friends seems to prove that we are loved and worth something. Out of a fear of loneliness and emptiness, we maintain relationships with people we don't really like, and with whom we have nothing in common but that tremendous fear of our inner emptiness. We fill up our lives with dates, appointments, parties, hobbies, activity, small talk, entertainment, girl friends, and endless phone calls. In this way, we feel socially in good hands, accepted and secure.

**My Diary!** → Take as much time as needed to make a list of all the people with whom you have connections, whether they are close relationships or casual acquaintances, to find out what they really mean to you and what they are adding to your life. Make a list of your friends and relatives and examine the quality of the relationships you have with them thoroughly and honestly. For each person write a few sentences. There is no need to judge. Just find out if the quality of the relationship is positive or negative.

While you discover that certain relationships may be a burden, you're now ready to see that there are many other ways you can burden yourself with negative emotions. You will probably ask what this has to do with sexuality? The answer is: a whole lot. All these unwanted "guests" in your emotional world determine your inner climate, your basic state of feeling, which is amplified through sex. The more pure your inner water, the more clearly it can reflect reality. With honesty and awareness, you can decide which quality will characterize your life.

*TV and movies:*

I am always moved when I see how addicted people are to entertainment, how focused they are in filling their lives up with so much stupidity and garbage. Movies and entertainment create strong emotions by making an illusion appear real. In the process, we are filled with feelings and influenced by unreal events that have nothing to do with our real life at all. Even if the movie we see is completely fictitious, we have something to talk about with our friends to fill the time. This is a way of life in our modern world, and if this is what you want, there is nothing wrong with it. Just be aware how deeply it affects you in every possible way.

Do not underestimate the consequences that TV and other media have on you. After every evening of TV, take enough time to digest the things you have seen and absorbed. And only watch TV when you are in a good mood, when you are awake and attentive and connected with yourself. While watching TV, be aware. Sit in an upright position and close your mouth and your vagina to protect your inner self, and keep breathing. In this way you can deepen the contact with yourself even while watching TV.

*Reading:*

Choose your reading material carefully. To read the daily newspaper and absorb all the grief and sorrow of the world is not every woman's cup of tea, especially first thing in the morning. Reading affects you more than you realize. It strengthens your fantasy and imagination but prevents you from being in the here and now. Choose books that support you on your path.

*Crowds:*

A crowd is always a concentration of emotions. A sensitive and open yin woman almost automatically absorbs rougher energies like a sponge, and often suffers much through it. Being in a

*More causes of emotional pollution*

crowd and shining with inner absence is an open invitation for all the energies around to enter a sensitive woman's body. In moments like this, make sure you stay centered and that you keep your mouth and vagina closed. Fill your inside with the healing fragrance of the heart. Many women I know are using the energy egg as a protection in situations like this.

### Sex:

If you are absent-minded or not feeling joyful while having sex, it is an open invitation for negativity. We will explore this more in chapter 22.

### Chemical substances:

Chemical substances and treated foods can be a major cause for negative emotions. Alcohol, cigarettes, and drugs can have the same effect. Prepare your food as lovingly as possible and eat only in a kind environment.

*Tranquilizers* A very common method to repress emotions is through tranquilizers. Doctors very generously prescribe pills for relaxation, sleep, and to calm emotional people down, even though they know that real problems are not solved in this way. On the contrary, the problems only get bigger. Many people are addicted to these pills, and to break such a habit is difficult and painful. I cannot recall anymore how many people I have accompanied on their withdrawal from drugs. It is so arduous that only a few find their way out of the vicious cycle that addiction creates. One should be especially careful with tranquilizers. They should not be taken for more than two weeks. The best is to abstain completely from these kinds of medicines and face reality. Only in facing reality can you solve and digest difficult situations.

Elisabeth Kübler-Ross is internationally known for her work with people who are facing death. In her research, she found that getting over the death of a loved one took much longer for people given medication to ease their pain and sadness, than for those who experienced their sadness and pain. With medication, you only push the pain deeper into the unconscious, so you are not able to feel it, even if it is there.

Every emotion has a favorite place in the body where it likes to hang out and where it is best nourished. Corresponding with the five elements, each emotion governs an organ. A specific emotion has the power to weaken its corresponding organ; the reverse is also true; a weak organ manifests itself in its related emotion. Emotions can be the language of an organ. It is possible to influence emotions via the organs to defuse the tension of a stressful situation and vice versa.

*Where emotions like to be*

Table 4 below provides an overview of the connection between emotions and organs as an inspiration for your own investigation. Be aware that a list is a list and you are you, and that this list does not necessarily correspond to your experience! Do not try to fit yourself into the chart, but rather use the information given to help you to find out where emotions are hiding in your body. This might be in a totally different place

*Table 4. Emotions, organs, and corresponding elements.*

| Emotions | Element | Element | Element | Element | Element |
|---|---|---|---|---|---|
| Organs | Wood | Fire | Earth | Metal | Water |
| Yin organ | Liver | Heart | Spleen | Lungs | Kidneys |
| Yang organ | Gallbladder | Small Intestine | Stomach | Large Intestine | Bladder |
| Sense organ | Eyes | Tongue | Mouth | Nose | Ears |
| Body odor | Sour | Burnt | Sweet | Pungent | Rotten |
| Voice | Screaming | Laughing | Singing | Crying | Moaning |
| Positive qualities | Creative Tolerant | Peaceful Witty | Self-confidence Integrity | Selfless Reliable | Wise Charismatic |
| Positive action | Friendly | Optimistic | Straight | Courageous | Willpower |
| Negative yin emotions | Frustration Depression | Sadness Insecurity | Brooding Worried | Hopelessness Cowardly | Fear Pessimistic |
| Negative yang emotions | Anger Moodiness | Arrogance Desire | Fanaticism Compulsive | Egoism Dependency | Power-hungry Paranoia |

than the chart indicates. In all the books I have come across, the charts differ from each other. Don't let that confuse you. It shows how unique and individual life is, and that it is never possible to squeeze a human being into any system. But let the chart inspire you to explore new possibilities. Next time an emotion stirs inside of you, sit down and breathe into it until you feel exactly where it is located.

## Dealing with Our Dark Side

Every emotion has its own energy frequency, its own smell, and its own character. There are emotions that you feel close to and can identify with, and others that are a bit scary to you. Repressed emotion from old unfinished life situations can be like a boil or an abscess. It can suddenly burst, releasing pus everywhere inside you. The principle with old emotions is the same. Suddenly, a deeply hidden feeling can burst, and the unpleasant feeling infects you like a virus and spreads in your body. The vibration of such an emotion always differs from your regular life energy. It is usually much more dense and heavy.

According to Chinese medicine, about 80 percent of all physical and mental illnesses develop out of unrefined and unprocessed emotions, which are hiding somewhere in the body and waiting for a chance to come alive again in whatever way possible. It is recommended that you take the time to clean and empty your body from all hidden emotions.

### *Organ cleansing*

The exercise to cleanse your organs is a helpful tool to get in touch with those hidden guests. Especially for women in the healing profession, this exercise can be a help to prevent negativity from entering your body.

**Watch Out!** →

You can only influence your organs when you are able to really feel them and have established a deep connection and love affair with them. If you are doing the exercise only in your mind, this will prevent you from establishing deeper contact. The issue here is to be real, and if you do not feel your organs, you do not feel them. Go on searching until you find a way to feel them. If you do not feel them, and pretend you do, this is phony and will not help you. You will only get further and further away from yourself.

## Emotions in real life

← **Try This!**

• Next time you are caught up in an emotional situation, grasp the opportunity and right away begin to breathe into your center.

• Breathe very slowly and begin to feel where the emotion is located in your body (even if around you everything is turning upside down).

• As soon as you have found the place, or maybe by now the feeling has spread all over your body, start smiling or laughing into the place to fill the organ with a positive vibration.

• If you are not able to transform it all, let the leftovers flow out of your body through your feet, until the organ feels light again.

*Boundaries*

Inner absence and inner conflicts make us prone to be influenced by our surroundings. Because women by nature are energetically very open, this requires a special alertness while dealing with emotional or insensitive people. Develop a consciousness for what you are taking in and absorbing, and if the frequency of the entering energy does not correspond with your personal energy field, you can immediately adjust it with the power of your heart, healing sounds, or the microcosmic orbit. In this context I would like to introduce another tool which has been very helpful in the times I worked in emergency psychiatry, a pretty emotionally overloaded scene.

In a place like this it is impossible to avoid negative emotions. And being there all day or all night long, every so often you are caught up in a very tense situation. Many of the patients who were admitted were brought in by the police. So they mostly did not come because they wanted to, and for them it was a very emotional situation to find themselves being locked up in the psychiatric ward. The atmosphere in there was often highly explosive, with extremely tense people totally overwhelmed by their emotions, yelling and screaming. If you approach a person in a state like this to argue and to explain— good luck! In situations like this, I just stood there very discreetly and centered myself and started clearing my energy field, especially my liver, to maintain my positive energy field within. Usually, after some time passed, the whole situation defused on its own. Of course I did not tell anyone. If you are working in psychiatry and talk about things like this, you don't get much understanding. I experimented with these things for years and I was amazed how powerful they were, and that they not only affected me, but also the people around me.

**Try This! →**  **Finishing your day**

- Before you go to sleep, take some time to finish your day and clear things up. Become aware of anything that remains unfinished, and if it feels liberating to you, write it all down in your diary so you do not need to hold on to it overnight. This small ritual from India is quite helpful: before going to sleep, shower your feet with cold water, to wash all the burdens away.

**Try This! →**  **Blue light shower**

Blue light has a cleaning and cooling effect. Buy yourself a blue colored light bulb and insert it into your lamp, so the exercise doesn't become too intellectual.

- Sit down under the blue light and let it flow through your whole body so that your system is cleaned and harmonized.

- Do it until the blue light has also filled up your center, and then condense the blue light until a small blue light pearl develops.

- Let that little blue pearl flow through your body until your body is filled with blue light and the light overflows into your aura.

- After that go to bed.

The following exercise was one of my favorites at the time I worked in psychiatry. Each evening I came home with many impressions of suffering, injustice, and pain. Many situations were difficult to digest. Because I could not use my boyfriend as an outlet for my undigested stories from psychiatry all the time, I often did the following gibberish exercise.

### Gibberish exercise

**← Try This!**

- This exercise can be done alone in your room with a blindfold. This is, of course, the most effective, but you can try it also while cleaning, cooking, or with the people you live with. Instead of real words, speak gibberish, nonsense words without any meaning.

- Do it for about 15 minutes and just allow it to happen. Do not let your mind interfere.

- In the end, lie down for a few minutes, center yourself, and relax.

**← Watch Out!**

Negative emotions are always an indication of a weakness inside of us, no matter what or who has provoked it. They reveal old wounds that are not healed yet. They can also be an expression or an indication of a limitation in your personality that wants to be freed from restricting ideas and beliefs.

## Transforming Negative Emotions

The art of living the Tao is to be able to change negativity into life force. Your middle, just above the uterus, is like a compost pile where you can put all the unwanted garbage. Through charging the energy field there, the middle becomes warm and the transformation process can be initiated. If you pour your love into that process, a new quality can arise.

Especially through sex, we come in contact with a whole range of unpleasant feelings, like shame, jealousy, inferiority,

175

fear, and so on. Sex provides us with lots of opportunities to practice the Tao of emotion. There is always a possibility to experience a deeper layer of the unconscious, to be able to heal, and to say goodbye to another wound. Take the next exercise as a help to change your negative energies into life force.

**Try This! →**

### Allow emotions and feel them

- This is best to do when you are emotional.

- Close your eyes and feel where the feeling is arising from, and what it feels like. Meanwhile, keep breathing deeply and gently.

- Stay in touch with the feeling, and with each outbreath, allow yourself to go into it more and more.

- Put your hand on the place where you feel it most and start smiling into that dark unknown.

- With each outbreath go even deeper into it. Remain alert and keep on pouring your love into that place.

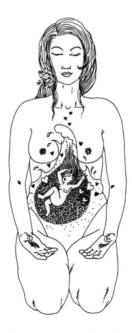

Allow emotions and feel them.

- Let your light of awareness flow into that area, until this old wound or memory melts away with the help of the power of your heart.

## Transforming emotions

← **Try This!**

This technique is used by the Taoists to transform negative emotions into life force. It is best to practice it in a situation that is emotionally charged. Do it in a sitting or standing position, and in the beginning with closed eyes.

- Turn within to feel from where the feeling is arising. Do not think about it, but feel it. Breathe quietly and naturally.

- Let all the energy of the emotion flow into your center.

- Stay centered and charge your center more and more until it gets warm.

- With the light of your awareness and your heart, start spiraling in the center to refine the energy there more and more, until the middle starts radiating light.

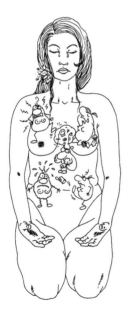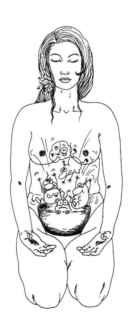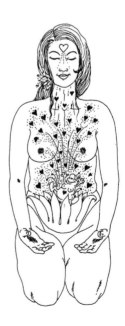

Feeling emotion.　　　　Centering emotion.　　　　Transforming emotion.

- Remain seated and feel how your middle pulses and spreads that healing light all over your body.

## No Instant Recipe but Some Wisdom

There is no instant recipe for dealing with emotions, but here are some hints that can be helpful. Even if someone else is triggering an emotional state in you, it is always your emotion and only you are responsible for it. And there is never ever a reason, or a right or wrong, that can free you from that responsibility, even if many other people are sharing the negative emotion or opinion with you.

### The way of feelings

There are always some women who get the impression that the Tao of emotion is against expressing feelings. To express feelings is a wonderful gift, but when they are put into words, they lose their power and pureness. This also happens when you are using your feelings to manipulate others. Or you may be one of those women who, as soon as you feel a feeling, express it and get rid of it as fast as you can. You can express feelings and dump them on somebody else, and make them feel responsible for it by making them feel guilty. But this is not the same as being deeply in contact with what you feel.

### Feeling the feeling

It is possible to keep your feelings to yourself and just be deeply in contact with them, which can be very healing, as long as you do not use them to nourish dreams or sentimental thoughts, staying in the actual feeling and not drifting off into a dreamy state. To allow a deep inner feeling, let life touch you deeply and just feel that. There is no need to put it in words and talk it out. This can create a tremendous energy field within. But only do that if you can maintain an inner energy flow, if the energy does not get stuck. To keep the energy flowing, the microcosmic orbit can be a big help. Also dancing will get your energy flowing. Transformation only happens through a natural flow, never out of a repression to avoid dealing with your everyday problems.

In transforming emotions, there is no shortcut. And these techniques won't help you if you are trying to avoid clearing up relationships or trying to escape a confrontation. You may also need to learn to show your feelings, or tell someone what you think or what you want.

You have to be really alert in order to avoid becoming identified with emotions and old traumas that are caused or triggered by sex. So it is better to first start healing your emotions in your everyday life, and when you have had your first "successes" in self-healing and centering yourself in emotional situations, then you can begin to deal with your sexual wounds.

*Trauma*

Women who have had traumatic sexual experiences, such as rape, abuse, or other unloving sexual experiences, need to be extremely patient and loving with themselves. Do not push your self-healing process. Remember, female qualities should not be pushed or forced, this is against their nature. The female never heals from one day to the next; it is a slow and steady process. So it is better to learn to enjoy it, each step of it.

As you explore your sexuality, the moment will come again when you suddenly encounter that big black abyss. Maybe this will be triggered while having sex or in some other situation. And the original tremendous fear and pain you have deep inside you catches up with you once more, and you feel paralyzed. This is the moment to remember the Tao. When suddenly you are lying there totally disconnected, not able to relate, surrounded by that cloud. The controlling mind is taking over and forbids you to feel any feelings. This is the time to go on breathing and to center yourself, to connect with your heart and to allow the body to relax again. Centering is the key. If it does not work the first time, keep trying until you are able to influence yourself even in such an unpleasant state.

I do not want to play down the severity of such a problem. In fact, I know many women by now who have overcome the worst memories of their lives with this strategy. For many it has become possible in this way to cut through their old patterns. But for all of us, the way of liberating our sexuality from old energy patterns and bad memories is only possible step by step, taking each step on the path at our own pace.

*Aloneness* Being alone and in stillness is the best medicine to learn how to distinguish old and new feelings, true feelings from false ones, your own feelings from somebody else's feelings. Years ago, I started to include two days of silence in my seminars so women would have the opportunity to explore a deeper layer of themselves. And for nearly all the women, once they penetrated their initial fear, it was the most healing time they ever experienced. The important insights always arise from the depths, from the deep silent place within.

Arrange as much free and empty space in between your normal day to day activities as you can, so that your inner depth has the opportunity to reveal itself, and so you are able to hear and receive it.

# Chapter 16

# THE UTERUS: A WOMAN'S SEXUAL CENTER

To many women, the idea that the uterus influences female sexuality is very surprising. According to my experience, the uterus is a woman's main sexual center and a very powerful energy source, and by now, many other women have shared this experience with me. Its potential reaches far beyond giving birth to children, but most women have not developed an awareness of their uterus. In the Taoist

## The Hidden Source of Power

The uterus—the female source of energy.

tradition, the uterus is called the Heavenly Palace, and for a woman, it can be a Door to Heaven or a Door to Hell. For most women, our most female organ has a miserable existence.

The uterus absorbs not only personal experiences but also lots of information from the collective. And its receptivity is unlimited, especially in a low energy state. In this way, ignorance and unconsciousness is passed on, unaltered, from one generation to the next. Through the uterus, women have the power to feed each new being with light and love, but as long as it remains overwhelmed and in stress, there is not much hope for a better world.

The uterus is the main place in a woman's body where years of negative emotions tend to collect and are stored, poisoning the whole organism from within. Illnesses of the womb, such as menstrual disorders, vaginal discharge, myoma, or cancer are manifestations of this inner poisoning. From a medical point of view, these diseases are considered to be normal. On the other hand, being unhappy, negative, and pessimistic is an expression of how disconnected women are from their feminine potential. In Germany, the uterus of every third woman is surgically removed, and in the USA, the percentage is probably about the same.

To liberate and re-establish the feminine in us, there is no way around healing the uterus. It is still a mystery to me why the uterus, in all the efforts of women's liberation, has been completely ignored. I have not found a single book on it yet, and we are living in the 21st century!

I would like to invite you on a journey back to your roots. To liberate the power of the uterus, we need to clear and heal all its different layers. The female process, by its nature, takes time, so it is better to enjoy it. Don't be discouraged if you don't get in touch with the powers of your uterus instantly. In many ways, the female in our society is in a pretty desolate state, so in liberating the hidden treasures, we are swimming against the stream. It will probably take centuries to collectively restore the feminine so it can reveal its true capacity.

This chapter is also useful for women who have had their uterus removed. The operation has removed the ill part of the body, but the energy patterns and the emotions, which were the original root of the problem, still remain. Many women do not feel better after their uterus is removed for this reason.

The uterus has many names and many different faces. In the Chinese tradition it has been called "The Sea of Blood," "The Chamber of Blood," "The Protected Palace," or the "The Heavenly Palace." The uterus can move, and in ancient times was considered to be an independent creature. It was compared with a wild animal, one that opens its mouth (uterine orifice) at the peak of lust to eat the semen. The movement of the uterus is connected with an indescribable feeling that floods the whole body.

## The Uterus has Many Faces

Sensuality is the natural state of the uterus, and it can be a place of great warmth and security. But if it is not in a positive mood, vibrating with life, it can be very threatening for women. We will disconnect ourselves from it and unconsciously do everything possible to avoid coming in contact with it. In this low energy state, the uterus becomes a vacuum for the collective, absorbing negativity like a sponge. It becomes completely charged with all kinds of undefined unpleasant feelings and emotions.

*The uterus and sexuality*

To avoid feeling all that, many women cut themselves off from their uterus completely, and live a shallow, superficial life. Either they dedicate their life and sexuality to the yang principle, or start pretending to feel feminine and orgasmic, or they avoid having sexual contacts at all. But there are also women who are naturally able to burn negativity in their sexual ecstasy. It is possible with the power of the heart to burn or heal the negative.

But the most common attempt to fill an empty uterus so that it becomes alive is the ever-popular method of getting pregnant. An unhappy uterus is one of the main unconscious motives to get pregnant and have a baby.

*To become a mother— yes or no*

Pregnancy and being a mother is for many women the only way to bring fulfillment and meaning in their life and sexuality. Without doubt, a mother's life is very busy and full, but being filled up and needed is not quite the same as being fulfilled. Most mothers are too occupied with their responsibilities to have a chance to liberate themselves from their conditioning, and will seldom experience other dimensions of womanhood. They simply do not have any energy left for it.

To become a mother or not is a question that a woman is confronted with as long she is menstruating, in one way or another. Earth is already overpopulated, and millions of children are starving on our planet, so from this perspective there is no urgency to bring more children into the world. The time is right to find new possibilities and ways to live as a woman. It is okay to dedicate one's life to explore new dimensions of womanhood. But the dream of having a family is so deeply rooted in us that only a few women are able to move in a different direction in their lives.

As a woman, I know perfectly well about the instinctive desire to have a baby, which manifests itself not only in the mind, but also in the body. As a little girl my only interest was in playing with my dolls and with little animals, and my main goal was to have as many kids as possible. But at age 21, I began to realize the meaning of wanting a baby, and I decided to dedicate my life to explore new ways of being a woman. Even so, the issue wasn't resolved at all yet. It was just the beginning of a long drawn out process that was not always easy. I spent lots of time exploring my uterus. Not in my wildest dreams would I have imagined where that would lead me. I didn't expect to be rewarded with such a precious gift.

I do not have the intention to criticize or attack mothers. Rather, I would like to encourage you to get in touch with deeper layers of your personality, whether you are a mother or not. I would like to inspire you to find out what really moves you. It is not about criticizing or judging yourself. It's about getting more clarity in your life.

*Questions for women without children:*

← **My Diary!**

- Do you want to become mother?
- What do you hope for by being a mother?
- In which situations does this wish come up the strongest?

*Questions for mothers:*

- Recall the time before your pregnancy. What was it that really motivated you to become pregnant?
- Was it a conscious decision, or did it just happen?
- What did you hope for through your children?
- And how is it for you today to be a mother?

There are women who, out of a negative experience, absolutely do not want to have children. Such an attitude can also burden the uterus.

As I have mentioned already, to penetrate the uterus, to get in touch with its deeper layer, is a major exploration. To allow ourselves to open up and connect with old wounds requires a loving and protected environment—a tension-free zone. As soon as you feel threatened from the outside in any way, the fear of getting hurt will come up and this can prevent you from going deeper. Create a caring environment for yourself so you can develop a trusting love affair with your uterus, so it can open and reveal to you all its hidden treasures, needs, and troubles. If needed, lock the door and unplug the phone.

# Getting to Know the Uterus

## Getting to know your uterus

← **Try This!**

- Sit or lie down comfortably and close your eyes.

- Put your hand on the uterus and start breathing and smiling into it. With each outbreath, allow yourself to sink in a bit deeper.

- Bring your whole awareness into the uterus. With your inner eye, look into it; with your ears, listen to it; with your nose, smell it.

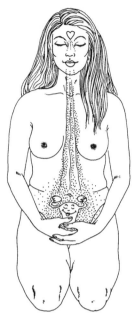

Getting to know the uterus.

- Take your time to get in touch with it, to get a feel for the uterus, to find out how she is doing and what she is carrying inside.

- Finish by filling the uterus with the fragrance of your heart, and then center yourself after that.

Don't worry if you do not have clear feelings straight away. There might be thoughts or pictures that don't mean anything to you. Or you might keep being distracted by other things. It is also very common that women get restless or are suddenly very tired and feel like sleeping. Try to stay awake and keep on breathing. If you fall asleep, it is relaxing and healthy, but the process of getting to know your uterus is about expanding your consciousness to dissolve old patterns, and while sleeping, this is not possible.

**My Diary!** ➜ **Dear Uterus**

A beautiful way to get in touch with your uterus is to write her a letter. Take beautiful stationery or your diary and start writing: "Dear Uterus," or however you wish to address her. You can also give your uterus a name that suits her, and then you can write and connect with her in a more personal way.

If it is easier for you, let the uterus write to you. Don't think much about it, just try it and see what happens. Perhaps she is very happy that you are listening to her. Or it can be that she is too frightened or timid, and she needs your support to be able to express herself. So take as much time as she needs, care for her, and whenever you remember, nurture her with all the love you have.

"Dear Uterus . . . "

The deeper you penetrate into the uterus, the less you will have words for what you are experiencing. Just let that be, then you will have entered the territory that goes beyond words. In this state, words can only dilute your contact with feeling, so stay with what you feel and deepen your loving connection with it.

# What Burdens the Uterus

## *Half-hearted sex*

Having sex in an absentminded way may negatively affect the uterus, because there is no energy or awareness there to care for and protect her. On top of that, sexuality intensifies everything. If you are absentminded, this pattern is enhanced. If a negative feeling arises, it will be stronger. Every sexual experience that is not enjoyed is stored in the body, and especially in the uterus.

## *Sexual abuse and violence*

Sexual violence, sex without care or love, as well as unresolved conflicts are poison to a weak uterus. From the depth of the uterus the whole organism, and even the environment around it, becomes filled with negative emotions. Violence is a shock to our system that gets deeply engraved in our cells, and influences the whole being. Deep distrust toward other people, and the terrible fear that the incident could be repeated, often accompany those women affected by violence for the rest of their lives. Often, abused women or children are confronted with violence again, and keep having terrible experiences until the deep wounds within them are healed, or until they fall apart com-

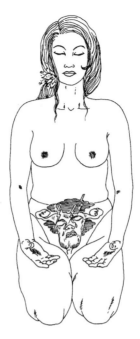

Burdened uterus.

pletely. Taking drugs or drinking is a very common way to try to get out of the vicious circle that being a victim of sexual abuse invites.

Even if it is impossible to forget an experience like this, I know many abused and beaten women who are nevertheless able to live a happy and relaxed life and are able to enjoy sex and their sensuality. Through my work with the Tao of self-healing, I have seen many abused women who have developed the inner strength to cut through their past experiences and enjoy a loving and healing sexuality.

*Contraception*    For the well-being of the uterus, it is important to use contraceptive methods that feel right for both body and mind, and that do not adversely affect the feminine nature. Your local women's health center can help you choose the best alternative. A properly fitted diaphragm is a good solution and also gives the uterus protection. The condom industry has made quite some progress and you can find condoms that are really nice and thin. Most pharmacies sell a wide variety of condoms—different materials, colors, and even flavors—or you can mail-order.

In the situation we live in today, where deadly diseases like AIDS and hepatitis are prevalent, it is a must to use a condom while making love, especially if your partner is ejaculating.

An unwanted pregnancy is always a disruption in a woman's life, no matter if she decides to have the baby or to get an abortion. I suppose we would all agree that an unwanted pregnancy should not occur in our modern world, and yet women are still confronted with it today, and it often happens in the most inappropriate situation possible. The relationship is falling apart, the living situation is unsuitable, the professional plans are not yet realized, the hope to travel the world remains unfulfilled—and on top of that, there is no money to afford a baby. An unwanted pregnancy always creates emotional turmoil.

*Unwanted pregnancy*

Insecure and overwhelmed by their emotions, many women, after struggling back and forth with the decision, choose to have the baby anyway, in spite of their personal situation. The negative thing about this is that the fears and emotions of the mother are transferred to the embryo from the very first moment of their lives. Therefore, one of the nicest gifts you can pass on to a new being is to welcome it and love it from the very beginning, from the moment of conception.

An abortion can be done with either a positive or a negative attitude. Mostly, an abortion is done out of a negative feeling, saying no to the baby, saying no to the situation, saying no to the partner, and so on. An abortion that results out of such circumstances will always be difficult to get over.

*Abortion*

In general, to say no means: "I do not want you, go away." On the other hand, to say yes means: "Yes I love you and I want you, you are mine." An abortion experience can be a chance to grow out of seeing your world in terms of black and white. If you have decided to have an abortion, try the following exercise. The exercise is about learning to love, and instead of holding and clinging to the beloved, to let it go, setting it free to find a better situation. To many women, including myself, it was a very helpful tool to open up a new perspective through this experience.

**Try This!** → **Before an abortion**

- Sit or lie down comfortably and put your hand on your womb and start to connect with the soul that has settled in your uterus. Do this until you feel true love and compassion for the little creature and you are able to accept your whole situation.

- Explain to the soul that you are loving it and that is the reason you are letting it go, so it can move and choose a better situation for its new journey on Earth. Do this until you are able to say goodbye to your new little friend with all your heart.

This process usually takes some time and can be painful. We are not used to letting go and giving freedom to the beloved. We link love with possession: "I love you and you are mine and shall never leave me." True love goes beyond that. This is a chance to outgrow that limitation, to move a bit closer to real love.

An abortion is a major intervention of the female organism. After an abortion, the body needs time to readjust. Give yourself lots of time to rest, eat well, and keep centering yourself. Acupuncture and Chinese herbs can support the healing process.

*Cold*  The uterus cannot handle cold that easily, like a cold bath after a sauna, swimming in cold water, or inadequate clothing in the winter. If you get too cold, always warm up and activate the uterus again. For this purpose you can use a hot water bottle, a hot bath, or massage your abdomen with a warming oil like rosemary or some home-brewed schnapps, such as Italian grappa.

**Uterus Removal!**  In the year 1822, the first uterus was removed. At that time, disorders of the womb were a big nuisance. Therefore, the first successful uterus removal was looked upon as a breakthrough for gynecology, and doctors were able to save many lives. But this form of surgical intervention was used not only to ease physical problems, but also to "cure" hysteria, melancholy, sloppiness, and manic states. The removal of the ovaries and uterus is actually female castration.

In Switzerland, a hysterectomy (uterus removal), including five days in the hospital, costs from about $1,800 up to $20,000 for private patients. I would say uterus removals are a very good business.

A friend of mine, a very intelligent warm-hearted professor was advised to have her uterus removed. After the operation her surgeon (male) brought her uterus into the room on a tray and said triumphantly to her: "Look Ms. Colleague, here I have done proper work." To add to this: my friend is not a professor of surgery, she is an ethnologist.

Years ago, when I lived in Ticino, the Italian part of Switzerland, my vagina was itching, not very badly, but it was itching, so I went to a gynecologist I did not know. After examining me, she came to the conclusion that in addition to the itchiness there was black shadow on my uterus, which she said was enlarged and in the wrong position. At the end of the consultation, she gave me three different types of antibiotics to take. And she gravely told me that I should come back to see her in a week, because the situation was very serious and it looked like I needed to have my uterus removed.

Here I was, standing in Lugano, with a bag full of medicine (and I hate medicine), totally confused and feeling fatally ill. I looked for a nice place near the lake to meditate over my situation. While sitting there centering myself, I realized that I did not feel ill at all. On the contrary, I felt very well, except that my vagina was itching. Still, I was a bit unsure. I traveled to find the doctor I knew to get another check up. The results of an ultrasound examination showed that there was no shadow on my uterus to be found, the uterus was neither sagging nor in an improper position. For the itching, she gave me an herbal suppository that gave me nearly instant relief.

*The medical trap*

In retrospect, I am grateful for that unpleasant experience. Along with all the other strange stories I keep hearing from women, it motivates me to continue deepening my perception and sensitivity to my body, so that I am able to trust and rely on my own feelings. But do not misunderstand me. I am not against an operation on the uterus. If the disease is severe enough, a hysterectomy can be the only solution left to keep a woman alive. There are many women calling me up as soon as they are diagnosed with cancer of the uterus, and out of panic they want to learn to heal themselves. In such a situation, the expectations surrounding the need to heal oneself can create even more stress, which can have just the opposite effect. The best time to learn the art of self-healing is when you are still healthy.

*Women with-out a uterus*

For women without a uterus, I would like to warmly recommend giving special care and attention to care of the uterus, even if it is physically no longer there. The energy patterns and emotions that caused the illness in the first place still remain, and need to be healed and cleared. Working with the energy egg can also be helpful, to prevent the sagging of other organs, which can happen more easily due to the empty space which the uterus has left behind.

# Healing Exercises for the Uterus

To do the following exercises successfully, you should be able to create a positive vibration within your body, for example with the help of the inner smile, or in any other way that helps you to get into a positive state of feeling. Do not use mental techniques or your imagination.

**Watch Out!** →

- During the exercises, if old memories or emotions overwhelm you and it becomes too much for you to handle, go back to your middle and center yourself until your breathing is deep and slow again. Connect with your heart and allow its fragrance to spread all over the body. In this way, old memories and emotions slowly fade away. Allow old negative pictures and feelings to come up only as long as you are able to encounter them with your heart. That's the way they can be healed.

- When you are suffering from a disease, well-chosen exercises can support you, but are no substitute for proper medical treatment from a qualified Chinese doctor.

## Entering the Palace

← **Try This!**

Remember your uterus as often as you can and incorporate it into your everyday life. In this way you will develop an awareness of your uterus.

## Cleansing the Palace

← **Try This!**

The energy egg, which you have already been introduced to, can be a wonderful help to unburden and cleanse your Palace. For many women, the uterus is in such a state of suffering and unhappiness, that this process can easily become overwhelming for them. Older women especially have to move very slowly and lovingly in liberating their uterus. The power of a mineral egg can be very supportive. We have been experimenting with different stones for the energy eggs for many years, such as: crystal quartz, milky quartz, smoky quartz, Chinese jade, milky jade, butter jade, obsidian, lapis, citrine, and others. Let the uterus choose the egg which suits you the best, rather than using a book about the healing power of stones to decide which one to choose.

Close your eyes, put one hand on your Palace and begin to connect. Look at the different stones and ask your uterus which stone could help to clear and cleanse her. Keep on breathing and feeling your Palace until you know which stone egg suits her. Remember to prepare the egg and insert the string, as you already have learned.

*How to choose the egg*

## The cleansing jewel

← **Go Deeper!**

- Sit comfortably and close your eyes, and hold your jewel (energy egg) in your hands placed on your womb area.

- Breathe and smile gently into your heart until it opens and starts to shine. Let the love and light from the heart flow down into your womb and into the jewel to charge them up with good vibrations.

- When you feel it is okay, lay the egg beside you and start massaging your breasts until they are overflowing with joy and energy. Let that feeling flow down into your Palace, and fill up your lips and pearls until they become alive and are pulsing. If you like, you can gently massage your clitoris and vagina to get ready to insert the egg. (You may have to move into a squatting position to do so.) Push the egg up with your finger as high as possible.

- When you have inserted the jewel, sit down again and close your eyes.

- Put one hand on your heart and the other on your Palace.

- Connect with a joyous feeling inside your heart, smile and breathe into it to activate it. You can also use the healing sound "haaaaaa."

- Once you feel connected with that healing love, breathe into the heart and while breathing out, let that loving feeling flow down like a shower to wash all the pain out of your Palace, and let all the burden from the uterus flow into the egg.

- As you sit there, remain connected with your heart and uterus, and allow the egg to pull everything out that makes the uterus unhappy and heavy. Hand it all over to the healing jewel.

- Do this as long as it feels right; do not push it. Stay with your feeling.

- Then take out the egg again and center yourself deeply.

*Purifying the egg*  Do not cleanse the egg with hot water right away; first rinse it with very cold water until all the energies are cleared again. It is not always possible to easily clear the egg of what it has absorbed. It often happens that an egg starts to look very dirty.

It can change colors, or may even crack when it has absorbed strong emotions and tensions. If it feels like it is difficult to clean the egg energetically, try putting the egg in the sunlight, or put it in the earth for a few weeks, or lay it in cold ashes—whatever feels like it works for you.

At the last Full Moon, we did our meditation around a little pond. Michelle, a young woman from Brazil who is very experimental and creative, put her eggs into the pond to charge them up and cleanse them before our meditation. Her eggs spent the whole Full Moon night in the pond, in the company of a family of gold fish. She said that she never felt her eggs so strong. Feel free to experiment, and whatever works for you, do it. Sometimes you may need to sacrifice an egg for the benefit of the uterus. You can bury it and give it back to the earth. After the egg is energetically pure again, you can simmer it on the stove again if needed.

## Liberating the Palace

← **Try This!**

This is another tool for cleansing the Palace.

- Take on the position of a horsewoman, close your eyes, and begin to enter your Palace until you feel in contact with it.

- Bring your hands over your head, palms facing the sky, and with the help of your breathing, charge your hands with healing cosmic light.

- Turn your hands down, facing the earth, and let the light energy from your hands flow through your body into your Palace.

- With your outbreath, let all the dark and heaviness flow from the Palace down to the ground.

- To finish, center yourself deeply.

## Activating the Palace

← **Go Deeper!**

After cleansing your Palace carefully, you can start activating it.

- Sit in upright position and open your heart.

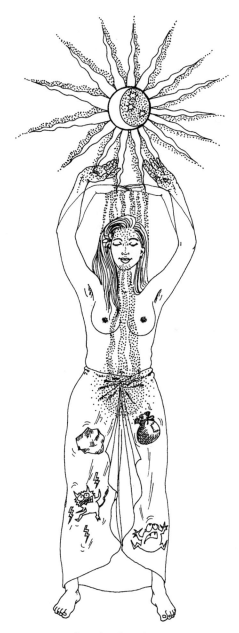

Liberating the Palace.

- As soon as you feel it getting warm and happy, let that feeling flow with your outbreath down to the Palace and fill it with that loving feeling.

- If the uterus is vibrating positively, start humming into it and just enjoy.

Activating the Palace.

This is a very beautiful meditation to do in a women's circle, but also good to do alone. In the end, take some time to cleanse and empty your Palace and then to center yourself.

← **Watch Out!**

If your Palace still feels burdened and wounded, it is better not to bring too much energy there. In this case you can do the humming into your center to strengthen it.

### The pulse of the Palace

← **Try This!**

This is a nice thing to do early in the morning before getting up.

- Lie in a supine position in bed, relaxed, and first open your heart. As soon as you feel its love, start filling your Palace with it.

- Keep breathing very quietly and enter your Palace deeper and deeper until you feel and hear your heartbeat pulsing there.

- As you lie there, feel your Palace pulsing, expanding, and becoming more alive with each breath and each pulse beat.

**Try This! →**    **Weighting the energy egg**

Prepare your energy egg with a little bag attached from the string and a lightweight object inside the bag—a stone, jewelry, or something else.

**Watch Out! →**

- This exercise is not for nervous women or those who have sleeping disorders.

- Only work with weight if you are able to center yourself and have mastered the microcosmic orbit

- Take the position of the horsewoman, both feet firm on the ground.

- Center yourself and open your heart.

- Put your hands on your breasts and let the loving feeling from the heart flow into your breasts.

- Massage your breasts rhythmically but slowly, until you feel connected with your genitals.

- With the outbreath, let the energy and heat from your breasts flow down and invite your vagina to open like a flower. If you like, you can gently massage your whole womb area, your lips and clitoris.

- When you feel ready, take your egg with the attached bag and insert it into your vagina and hold it firmly with your muscles.

- While breathing in, pull the egg up toward the uterus and with the outbreath, push it down again. Be aware not to make your back hollow and don't press your thighs together. The knees should be slightly bent.

- This exercise should not create heat inside you, just do it very softly and gently. Start with one minute and gradually increase the length of time and the amount of weight.

- To end the exercise, cleanse the uterus again, and let the microcosmic orbit circle to balance and spread any energies

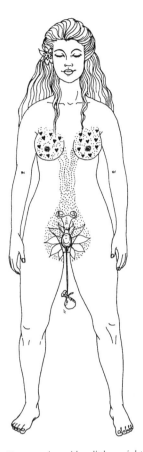

Egg exercise with a little weight.

that have been stirred up, and allow them to fall toward your center again.

For the protection of your Palace, be aware to keep its doors closed. The Taoists talk about two doors, the outer door refers to the vagina, and the inner door to the uterine orifice. At least one of them should always remain closed. The energy egg can be used for protection in difficult situations. Some women I know always use an egg while going shopping, while another one puts it in for journeys by plane. If you are leaving the egg in for a longer period, make sure you keep moving it once in a while so that no vacuum develops and the uterus is supplied with enough air.

*Protecting the Palace*

# Chapter 17

# HORMONES AND GLANDS

The word hormone comes originally from Greek, and it means to arouse or to move. Hormones are among the body's own chemical substances, and with the nervous system, they control the process of metabolism, and the development and reproduction of the body. The hormones influence the intensity of our love life and our emotional world. Our behavior, our perception, and our sexual characteristics depend strongly on the level of hormones in our bloodstream.

**The Love Hormones**

Many disorders of the female body and menstrual cycle are being treated today with artificial hormones, even though scientists cannot predict the long term consequences or negative side effects these treatments will have on a woman's body. The understanding that scientists have gathered up until now of the complex hormonal system and the way it interconnects with other body systems is still very limited and incomplete. Don't be surprised if some of your questions are left unanswered in this chapter. My major intention here is to give you a little taste of this very exciting and powerful topic and to awaken your interest so that you are more sensitive to issues surrounding hormones.

Most hormones are produced in the endocrine glands. The cerebrum has control over the whole system, followed by the diencephalon, where the hypothalamus is located. The pituitary gland coordinates all the endocrine glands and provides them with the signals they need to function properly. Among many others, surely the two most famous love hormones are estrogen and testosterone, the yin and yang of hormones.

**Estrogen: the yin of the hormones**

Estrogen is the queen of the female sex hormones and a reliable source of yin qualities. It is mainly produced in the ovaries; but the brain and the fatty cells are also able to produce and store estrogen.

*The effects of estrogen:*
- It promotes the monthly changes of the uterus, the female cycle.
- It gives women their round form, including the breasts and hips.
- It tones the skin and makes it smooth.
- It lubricates the vagina and strengthens the tissue and structure of the sexual organs.
- It develops the sense of smell.
- It enhances the cognitive abilities.
- It brightens up the mood.
- It prevents osteoporosis.
- It prevents and reduces stress.
- It sensitizes the sense of touch.
- It increases the action of oxytocin.
- It provides women with that certain something.

It is understood that these effects refer to the body's own natural estrogen. In taking artificial estrogen, there is always the danger of negative side effects. A higher risk of breast cancer is just one example.

*How estrogen affects sexuality:*
- Estrogen promotes the receptive libido behavior, the desire for penetration.

*What increases the estrogen level:*
- Building up yin

- Making love with penetration
- Oxytocin

*What lowers the estrogen level:*
- Removal of the ovaries
- Menopause
- Eating disorders
- Yang-oriented life style

Testosterone is responsible for male sexual characteristics. A woman's body also produces testosterone, but only about a tenth of the amount a male body produces. Women produce it in their ovaries and adrenal glands, and men in their adrenal glands and testicles. Studies have shown that career-oriented women (yang) have a higher testosterone level than other women.

*Testosterone: the yang of the hormones*

*How testosterone affects the female body:*
- Stimulates and activates the body
- Sensitizes the breasts and clitoris
- Makes women feel sensual and self-confident
- Awakens the desire to have sex, not for penetration, but for sexual fantasies, masturbation, and to have an orgasm
- Gives the motivation to find the right partner
- Makes women aggressive, irritable, and impatient
- Promotes women to define their boundaries
- Promotes the production of adrenaline, dopamine, and vasopressin

You will find more about the action of testosterone in the chapter on the male principle.

DHEA is the hormone found in the highest concentrations in both male and female. It is produced mainly in the adrenal glands, but small amounts are also produced in the brain, ovaries, and testicles. DHEA is the preliminary stage of most other sexual hormones and produces pheromones. It influences physical attraction.

*DHEA (Dehydro-epianrosteron)*

*The effects of DHEA:*
- Strengthens the immune system
- Acts as an antidepressant
- Reduces high concentrations of fat
- Breaks down cholesterol
- Promotes bone growth
- Supports women's libido

*How to raise DHEA production:*
- Meditation
- Physical exercise
- Reducing stress

*What reduces DHEA production?*
- Alcohol
- Chronic diseases
- Obesity
- Pregnancy
- Oral contraceptives

*Oxytocin*   Oxytocin is produced in the hypothalamus and is stored in the pituitary gland. It acts only in the presence of estrogen. Within an estrogen-rich female body, it can cause wonderful states—full of joyful feelings.

*The effects of oxytocin:*
- Awakens the desire of touch
- Diminishes mental abilities
- Makes skin sensitive to touch
- Causes contraction of the uterus in birth and orgasm
- Promotes caring and compassionate feelings
- Causes loving behavior
- Acts as a bonding agent in relationships
- Stimulates the production of milk
- Relaxes the body and causes a state of well-being
- Strengthens bonding between mother and child
- Raises the level of dopamine, estrogen, LH-RE,

prostaglandins, serotonin, testosterone, prolactin, and vasopressin

The release of oxytocin into the bloodstream is caused by having an orgasm and by touching. The American sexologist Theresa Crenshaw calls oxytocin "a super glue for relationships." The more couples touch each other or sleep in the same bed, the more they are activating oxytocin, regardless of whether they are loving each other or not. To maintain their level of oxytocin, women tend to become very affectionate, needy, and dependent.

*What raises the oxytocin level:*
- Stimulating the breasts by massage, breast-feeding, a tender touch or slight sucking
- A high level of estrogen
- The whole body being touched, like when sleeping close together
- A good whole body massage
- Massage or stimulation of the sexual organs
- Kissing and cuddling

*What reduces the level of oxytocin:*
- A low level of estrogen
- Alcohol and drugs
- A deficiency of being touched or having little sexual contact
- Dopamine

## Progesterone

Progesterone is a hormone that is very interesting and contradictory. Chemically produced, it is frequently used by pharmacology as a part of contraception and a method to treat sexual offenders. It lowers the testosterone and reduces active libido. In small doses, progesterone is slightly relaxing. It is successfully used to ease menstrual cramps, but at the same time, it prevents the reflex of an orgasm. A high level of progesterone can make women feel aggressive and irritable. It also is used to ease problems associated with menopause, and there are fewer side effects known than with the use of estrogen. There is currently a lot of research being done on this, especially in the United States. There are many products on the market that contain natural progesterone.

*Prolactin*   Pregnancy and breast-feeding raise the production of prolactin, which promotes milk production and is stimulated by estrogen. Prolactin reduces aggressive, yang-oriented sexual behavior. This is one of the reasons why many women do not feel like making love while pregnant or breastfeeding a child.

*Pheromones*   The one sexual fragrance that everyone naturally has is called a pheromone. It is not a hormone, but a chemical substance that can cause a certain reaction in someone else, via the sense of smell. It is incredible how such small molecules can control our behavior, without us being aware of it. The pheromones are spread via the skin, and they are found in higher concentration in the secretions of the body such as sweat, urine, menstrual blood, saliva, and sexual fluids. The way these sexual fragrances function is quite unique. Via the olfactory nerve, they directly stimulate the area of the brain that governs the basic instinctual drives, without passing through any other controlling and selection systems.

The effect of the pheromones can drive people into a very peculiar fondness. There is a new market flowering, originating in Japan, which sells used women's underwear. Believe it or not, you can order an unwashed lady's slip via catalog and pay lots of money for it.

The main question that arises for me in this context is what causes the sexual attraction between two people? Is it just the hormones, is it lust or love, or is it, after all, that your soul mate has entered your life? This mystery shall remain unsolved. I didn't include this section on hormones to confuse you, but to emphasize the immense power that they have to influence our lives. For those who want to know more about the love hormones and their action, I recommend Theresa Crenshaw's book, *The Alchemy of Love and Lust* (see Bibliography).

Instead of focusing on the health issues surrounding the glands, I would like to touch on the hidden powers they carry, offering their guidance on the spiritual path. Through connecting with the glands, it is possible to have profound and transforming experiences.

## The Secret Power of the Glands

Many of the old esoteric circles knew about the hidden power of the glands and have explored them in depth. The chakra system from India refers to the glands, and the Rosicrucians here in the West gathered great wisdom on the endocrine glands. The Chinese Taoists were also aware of the secret powers of the

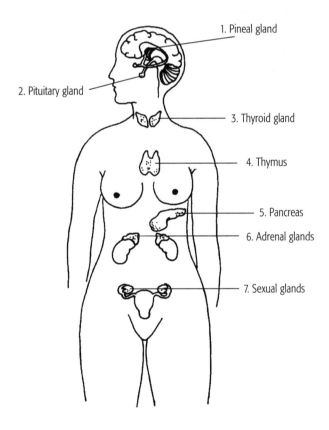

1. Pineal gland
2. Pituitary gland
3. Thyroid gland
4. Thymus
5. Pancreas
6. Adrenal glands
7. Sexual glands

The glands.

glands. Each of the glands is ascribed mystical or spiritual capabilities, independent of the production of the hormones. The glands can become an entrance to another reality.

### 1. Pineal gland: Mother of Spirituality
With the help of the pineal gland, spirituality can unfold. She teaches us to surrender our lives to the service of the divine consciousness. If we are in contact with her, she is like a compass and can guide us toward divine light.

### 2. Pituitary gland: Mother of Intelligence
The pituitary gland helps us develop intelligence and independence. She is the gateway to great wisdom and connects us with the powers of recollection. If we surrender to her, she will initiate us on the spiritual path and show us the way.

### 3. Thyroid: Mother of Growth
The thyroid helps us continue seeking, growing, and developing ourselves. She is the entrance to intellect and reason.

### 4. Thymus: Mother of the Heart
The thymus is also called the rejuvenator. Surrendering to the thymus will lead us to the highest form of human love. She helps us develop our artistic ability and is the entrance to beauty and harmony.

### 5. Pancreas: Mother of Transformation
The pancreas teaches us to digest and integrate food on all layers. If we surrender to her, she will guide us out of control and power, from ego to compassionate surrendering.

### 6. Adrenal glands: Mother of fire and water
The adrenals nourish the kidneys, the marrow, and the spine.

### 7. Sexual glands: Mother of the essence
They nourish the ovaries, uterus, vagina, and the breasts.

In the following exercise you will explore your endocrine glands and possibly connect with them. If you are not sure where the glands are located precisely, just relax and ask the gland to guide you. You just need to surrender to them—allow them to seduce you.

## Discovering the Secrets of the Glands

← **Watch Out!**

- A small quantity of a hormone can affect our well-being and behavior immensely. Therefore, our work with the glands needs to be approached with respect and care. Due to the complexity of the hormonal system, it is impossible to influence the production of only one particular hormone or one gland. You affect the whole hormonal system. Even if you are having problems with one particular gland, never work with one gland only. A gland can easily overreact when stimulated alone.

- Do not do the following exercise during pregnancy or while menstruating.

- Begin the exercises with the glands only when you are able to feel your inner organs, and are on good terms with them, and you have mastered centering.

### Getting to know your glands

← **Try This!**

- Sit in upright position, close your eyes, and open your heart.

- As soon as your heart has opened, put your hands on your ovaries, and let that loving feeling flow down to fill your ovaries until you feel them. Keep your awareness there and breathe softly but deeply until you begin to feel the quality of your ovaries.

- Then do the same with all the other glands. Take all the time you need to be able to feel each gland. Go to the adrenal glands, then to the pancreas, thymus, thyroid, pituitary, and then to the pineal gland.

- When you are done, lie down and center yourself deeply.

If you are able to feel your glands, go on to the next exercise.

**Go Deeper! →**   **Gland network**

- Sit on a chair in upright position, close your eyes, open your heart gently, and activate your breasts by massaging them.

- With your outbreath, let the loving energy and your complete awareness flow down into your ovaries.

- With your fingertips, massage the area of the ovaries softly until you feel them.

- Now bring your hands up and put them on your adrenals. While breathing in, draw the energy from the ovaries up to nourish your adrenals, and with your outbreath, fill the adrenals and let the energy spread within. As soon as you feel your adrenals clearly, bring that energy to the pancreas and do the same there. Then continue in the same way, drawing the energy up, gland by gland, to the thymus, thyroid, pituitary, and finally to the pineal gland.

- Do not put your hand directly on the crown point to connect with the pineal gland, but keep it an inch or two above the head, palm facing down, allowing your hand to circle slightly.

- It is very important after interconnecting all the glands to center your energy into an energy ball in your middle.

- When you are done, lie down for at least 15 minutes. This is the actual healing phase, so don't miss it, or you won't benefit much from this exercise.

**Sexual Glands as Key to More Life Force**

Within the ovaries, the sexual hormones support the egg cells to grow until they are mature enough to ovulate. According to the Taoists, the egg carries the precious essence of life within, and each egg that leaves the body without being fertilized is a waste of energy. Therefore, effective methods have been developed to maintain the sexual essence within to heal and strengthen the body. Ovarian breathing is one of them.

Ovarian breathing has the following effects:

1. It stimulates the production of sexual hormones.

2. It draws the energy and material essence from the egg.

*Ovarian breathing*

If you learn to draw sexual essence out of the egg cell, you can guide that energy into the microcosmic orbit and strengthen your whole body—your inner organs and the glands. This probably sounds a bit strange to you. I know that when I first heard about it, I thought it was pretty odd. To verify whether this dubious claim about drawing sexual energy from an egg cell was true or not, I participated in a fertility study. I was tested for two cycles, and every couple of days I had to go for blood tests to check the hormone levels, and have an ultrasound test that monitored the egg cells. To me it was very interesting to be able to visually watch the maturing process of my egg. A few days before ovulation, the egg and its protective cover were clearly visible. At that time, I didn't have a connection with my ovaries, but on this day that changed. After the examination, I began to practice intense ovarian breathing and kept doing it several times a day, up to the day my ovulation was supposed to happen. That day I had to go back to the clinic for another blood test and ultrasound. The doctor was very puzzled because the egg did not grow within these few days. In fact, it got smaller and there was no ovulation.

The next month I had to repeat the test, and this time I did not do any ovarian breathing, the egg was growing and ovulating as it was supposed to, and the doctor was happy. How I love experiments like this!

The energy from the ovaries is highly concentrated and has a very dense and sluggish consistency. It is absolutely necessary to refine ovarian power to your own energy level, which is finer. Use the microcosmic orbit for that. In addition to the nourish-

*Ovarian power*

ing effect the ovarian power has, it is also very yang, activating and warm, so it can cause heat within the body. Do not bring the ovarian energy directly into your organs, as this could overheat them and cause negative side effects, such as allergies or emotional imbalances.

**Watch Out! →**

Nervous or jumpy women should only do ovarian breathing if they are able to refine and integrate their energies by centering.

**Try This! →**  **Ovarian breathing**

- Sit on a chair in upright position, or take the standing position of a horsewoman.

- Close your eyes and open your heart.

- Fill your breasts with the fragrance of your heart and start massaging them until they feel full and firm.

- Let the energy and blood from your breasts and heart overflow down into your ovaries.

- Bring your hands down to cover the ovaries and keep breathing until you feel them clearly pulsing. If needed, massage the area slightly and keep smiling into them.

- Start to breathe slowly and deeply in through your vagina. This will create a slight suction in the uterus, which is drawing the energy out of the ovaries into the uterus. Continue breathing like this until you feel your uterus is filled.

- Do not leave the ovarian power in your Palace; let it flow and circulate into the microcosmic orbit until the energy has cooled down and is evenly spread.

- The microcosmic orbit is the way you transform and refine your sexual energy into life force, so don't leave it out.

- After that, lie down, center yourself, and remain centered for another 15 minutes. This is the actual healing and integration phase.

Here is one more exercise with hormones—one of my favorite ones.

## Hormonal shower

← **Go Deeper!**

- So that it is most effective, do the hormonal shower naked.

- Take the position of a horsewoman; close your eyes and open your heart.

- Massage your breasts in both directions, first firmly and then a bit softer.

- To activate the glands, massage gently around your nipples until the breasts are pulsing and overflowing out of joy and well-being.

- Let that energy flow down into your Palace and start with gentle ovarian breathing to charge your uterus. Keep smiling into the uterus to maintain a positive vibration.

Hormonal shower.

- Since you have already established contact with all the other glands, breathe in, and in one breath, draw the energy up from the uterus to all the other glands to the pineal.

- Breathe out through your crown, and push all the essence of your glands like a shower of healing fluid over your aura and your body. Enjoy this shower and absorb it into your pores.

- Then breathe that healing magic fluid again into your vagina and bring it into your uterus. If you want, you can repeat it.

- In the end, you need to lie down for at least 20 minutes to fall deeper into your center and integrate. Without the silent yin phase at the end, this exercise is just a shallow energy amusement and you won't gain any benefit from it.

*Ovarian breathing and menopause*

Ovarian breathing can be a very effective method to reactivate the decreasing estrogen production that accompanies menopause. If you tend to have hot flashes, just do it very slowly and gently, and make sure the heart keeps flowing into the ovaries.

*Pregnancy*

If you intend to get pregnant, gentle ovarian breathing can be used to strengthen the eggs to prepare for pregnancy. But stop as soon as you are pregnant.

# Chapter 18

# THE MAGIC OF
# THE SEXUAL VIBE

What is that certain something, enriching sexuality and keeping us under its spell? That irresistible magic seductively flirting with us, which keeps us hoping to come a step closer to the state of eternal bliss? What is it about sexuality that triggers such deep longing, the hunger for something greater, the wanting for something more? What is this potential, this tremendous possibility slumbering inside us? For millennia, we have searched to solve the mystery of sexuality. But neither scientists, nor philosophers, nor psychotherapists, nor sexologists have ever been able to reduce this phenomenon into a concept. Why? Simply because sexuality does not long to be analyzed or explained, but to be experienced.

**That Certain Something**

The recognition that sexuality and orgasmic experiences can be a door to higher states of consciousness has been fascinating people in the East and West down the ages. We have always had deep longings to develop methods to expand and capture those precious moments, and to liberate the potential held within them.

    The famous psychoanalyst and sexual researcher Wilhelm Reich has called that phenomenon the "orgasmic power" and has developed physical exercises to liberate the body from mus-

**Sexual Energy**

cular, energetic, and personal boundaries to set the orgasmic power free. According to him, only when someone has liberated his or her sexuality will he or she be able to live the potential of life. To ignore and repress sexual power reduces the level of life energy and its quality, and spoils the intelligence of a person.

*One energy— many faces*

There is only one life energy that presents itself in different colors, different lights. In our body, for example, depending on the energy center, emotion, or thought of the life energy flow, it manifests in different ways. If the life force flows within the sexual center, we call it sex, if the same energy is flowing through the heart center, we call it love. In most people the sexual centers are blocked, so the life force is stuck there. When this is the case, people are obsessed by sex. Sexual fantasies and dreams are their main interest and focus in life. Whatever they do, they are unconsciously pulled back toward sex. As long as the life energy remains blocked in the sexual centers, the potential of an individual cannot unfold. Female potential can only be set free out of the orgasmic state of fluid life energy.

*Women and sexual excitement*

Many women, because of their unhealed wounds and their negative experiences, are afraid of the intensity of sexual arousal. In my early days as a group leader, I worked mainly with mixed groups. Men were usually completely excited about working with strong energies, with intensity, sexual arousal, and ecstasy, but for women it easily became too much for them. Women frequently stepped out of the process by escaping into emotional reactions or negative thinking and projections.

To me, it is very important that women find access to their own sexual nature, so I started to emphasize that difference and focus on the patterns of female sexuality. This was entering new territory that my education and professional training did not prepare me for. Nobody I knew was focusing on the difference in the qualities of yin and yang in therapy.

In my work I am always supporting women to help them to heal themselves. Before women can start to work on their sexuality, they must build a physical and energetic foundation, so that the sexual intensity will be less threatening. And I see it happen again and again, that as soon as women are able to center themselves and connect with their depths and the silence within, it becomes very natural to let go and enjoy intense sexual ecstasy.

If a woman wants to develop her sexuality, she needs to be encouraged to have positive emotional and sexual experiences. The healing of female sexuality and its functions, like arousal, orgasm, and ecstasy, always arises out of lust, love, and sensuality, and never out of the repetition of painful, frustrating experiences of stress.

I am convinced more than ever that it is now impossible for a woman to develop her potential unless she has grown positive roots within. It is necessary to learn the art of self-healing if a woman wants to develop and explore her female ecstasy.

## Pelvis Roll

The pelvis roll can be done either in a standing position or lying down. I will describe the version in which you lie down to do it.

- Lie down on a padded surface that is neither too hard nor too soft.

- Pull your knees up, spread your legs slightly, and place your feet firmly on the ground.

- While breathing in, roll the pelvis up so that the back is slightly hollow.

- While breathing out, roll your pelvis down until the buttocks lift slightly.

- Continue to roll the pelvis back and forth in a relaxed and rhythmic way while breathing deeply through your open mouth.

- Let the movement become faster until the pelvis is moving on its own, without any effort or tension. Continue without stopping for another 15 minutes.

# Exercises to Strengthen Sexual Energy

← **Try This!**

- To end, lie quietly and fall into your center for another 10 minutes.

**Try This!** → **Compression of the lower abdomen**

- Take on the position of a horsewoman, close your eyes and center yourself, until the energy has condensed into an energy ball.

- As soon as you feel the energy ball clearly, let it roll down into your lower abdomen with the next outbreath. Push the solar plexus down to help.

- At the same time pull up your anus, vagina, and perineum slightly to create a feeling of pressure within.

- Keep that pressure for a while and then let go of the tension and relax your abdomen again.

Don't overdo this exercise. If too much heat is arising from it, balance out your energies with the microcosmic orbit. To end the exercise, center your energies in the middle again.

**Try This!** → **Vitalizing the lower abdomen**

- Take the position of the horsewoman and center yourself.

- Breathe strongly through your nose, and with your outbreath press and push the air and energy in and out of your lower abdomen, not more the 20 times in a row.

**Try This!** → **Dynamic meditation**

Dynamic meditation is not a part of the traditional Tao, but because it is such an effective method to liberate repressed energies and emotions, I want to introduce it to you. Do it first thing in the morning with closed eyes. It is best to wear a blindfold. The meditation has five different stages. There is a special CD available to use with the dynamic meditation (see author information, page 311).

*First Stage*

For the first 10 minutes, breathe deeply and chaotically through your nose, emphasizing the outbreath. Do this as intensely as possible and do not stop. Let your body be loose, and if it wants to move with the breathing, just let that happen.

*Second Stage*

The second phase is to express all your unexpressed feelings. Let it all come out, do not hold back and go totally into it. Use your voice at all times and let your body express whatever it wants: laughing, crying, moaning with pleasure, dancing, hitting, or yelling. Just be a witness and allow whatever comes.

*Third Stage*

The third stage is to activate your sexual center, and at the same time to watch your mind. Put both hands up above your head and start jumping up and down, as relaxed as possible. While landing on the soles of your feet, shout the mantra Hoo! Hoo! Hoo! (pronounced like "who," but stronger). Push the Hoo sound into your sexual center and your sacrum to liberate the trapped energy there. Women with back or knee problems should not jump in this phase, but rock their pelvis back and forth. Do the Hoo sound while the pelvis comes to the front.

*Fourth Stage*

The fourth phase is the yin phase. Stop all movement and remain standing, totally still. Breathe soft and deep. Do not move at all, do not cough or put your hair back, just freeze where you are and enjoy your yin qualities and center yourself internally, to strengthen your roots.

*Fifth Stage*

The last 15 minutes are to dance, to celebrate the beginning of a new day.

I would also recommend the Kundalini Meditation again, although it was introduced earlier (page 46). The shaking and dancing meditation is not only very effective, but also very popular among women.

## Sexual Response

Sexual response can be divided into three phases, which are all connected and flow into each other—the phase of lust, arousal, and orgasm.

### Lust

Sexual desire manifests as lust, libido, sex drive, or whatever we want to call it. For a yang-oriented woman, it can be the lust to be excited, or the desire to masturbate and have orgasms. For a yin-oriented woman, it can be the lust to receive, the lust to make love, to be penetrated. Several factors contribute to the flowering of the female lust:

- Personal attitude: whether or not a woman allows herself to feel sexual lust. This depends on her education, culture, and personal experiences.
- The ability to allow sensual feelings
- The physical and energetic condition of the body, the inner organs, glands and sexual centers
- The emotional state
- The personal circumstances of life
- Sexual relationships and partners

### Laughing

To maintain a sensual contact with yourself and with others, especially with your lovers, it is important that lust has a place in your life and is able to flower. Humor, laughing, and joyfulness are the best spices for a more lustful life. The laughing meditation is just for this purpose. Mostly people laugh only if they have a reason for it. The laughing meditation helps you to set your heart free by laughing without a reason for it. To be able to laugh is a must for women who want to liberate their sexuality. It is a very healing tool to keep the lust and laughter within, even if the situation inside or outside is getting heavy and painful.

**Try This! →**    **Laughing meditation**

- Do the laughing meditation first thing in the morning.

- Before even opening your eyes, start to stretch yourself and yawn like a cat to get yourself going.

• Start laughing loudly. The first few times this might be very strange to you and not funny at all. Anyway, don't worry, just pretend and laugh loudly: ha ha ha ha—until it happens by itself, naturally, out of your belly.

It is great fun to do the laughing meditation in a group of people or with your lover.

*Lack of sexual interest*

A boring everyday life, or a monotonous relationship maintained out of habit and duty are the most reliable killers of lust. When looking at a lack sexual interest, you need to distinguish between whether this is temporary, or if lust has never been felt in this relationship at all. In the second case, you need time and patience to overcome the problem. Sexual disinterest can develop, for example, out of feelings of disgust or aversion. If this is so for you, take it easy and slow. First start getting in touch with yourself, with your body, and with your organs and glands, until you are able to create a feeling of well-being within. The inner smile and laughter are the keys. The main causes of listlessness are:

• Being cut off from your body and emotions
• Unresolved emotions and traumas
• Negative sexual experiences
• Long-term draining relationships that are not going anywhere
• Unhealthy foods containing little energy
• Alcohol and drugs (also in the past)
• Emotions, stress, and lack of time
• Giving birth and breastfeeding
• Fear of getting pregnant

← **My Diary!**

Take enough time to investigate the main causes and sources for the lack of sexual interest or the frustration in your life. They may not be connected with sex.

*Sexual arousal!*

Sexual arousal is not just for pleasure and fun. It is needed to maintain a healthy body. In the state of sexual arousal, all your perceptions and feelings become more intense. It activates the glands and inner organs and promotes blood circulation, and the sexual organs are flooded with life force. The lips of the vulva swell, the vagina expands and becomes moist, and the breasts are firm and full. Sexual energy flows through the different sexual centers.

Being healthy and having a warm body with good blood circulation is supportive to sexual arousal. Each body reacts a bit differently and has its own needs and preferences. Find out what is exciting to you—what gets your sexual energy going.

Most of the time people are not connected with their sexual energy. They only feel it when it's stimulated by an outer impulse, another person, an image, a memory, a word—then they feel sexual as a physical reaction, but not as their state of being.

**My Diary! →** Think about the easiest way to get in contact with your sexual energy. Reflect on the following questions and write down what comes up.
- Which situations are helpful to you?
- What is sexually stimulating to you?
- Remember the situation in which you were the most sexually excited. Recall the moment and the feeling. What was it about that situation? Write down the whole event and how it evolved in detail.

*Erogenous zones*
There are areas of the body which feel particularly sensual and erotic, called erogenous zones. The clitoris, the G-spot, the breasts, mouth, and ears are known to be erogenous zones. But there are other areas of the body that can give you pleasure. You can explore your body alone or with a partner to find these highly sensitive areas. The erogenous zones of a woman are rarely limited to the above mentioned places.

There are women who dislike erotic and tender touch. Touch can be unpleasant or even painful for women with a yin deficiency, with emptiness of blood, a depleted substance, or an unbalanced liver. Or there are others who simply do not like to be touched.

## Sensual points

← **Try This!**

Go to the Appendix (page 295) for an overview of all the healing and sensual points in the book. It is very helpful to start exploring these if you have not done so already.

Find out how to please your senses. Be inventive. Use natural oils, fragrances, fabrics, clothes, sounds, foods, water, earth, your menstrual blood, saliva, whatever you wish. First explore your sensual responses on your own. Then, if you like, you can experiment with your lover.

*Sensual arousal*

Energy is the foundation of ecstasy. To surrender to the flow of sexual ecstasy means to give up control. Most of us never had the opportunity to expose our ecstatic animal that is hidden within us. On the contrary, we have been forced over decades to control our wild and instinctive behavior. After all, women should behave "properly." So do not be surprised if ecstasy and surrender are not possible for you spontaneously.

Dancing naked as wildly and freely as possible is a good remedy to practice letting go and ecstasy. Surrendering to your body, to your energy, and to music will affect your sexuality in a positive way.

*Ecstasy*

According to the Taoist view of life, to arouse the body is very vitalizing and healthy. A beneficial thing to do is to let the aroused energy flow through the microcosmic orbit and through your organs and glands. This strengthens your health and increases your sexual and sensual feelings.

*Sexual excitement and Tao*

Sexual arousal can grow out of a state of yin or yang. Arousal out of the yin state arises slowly and comes out of a peaceful state of being, out of depth and relaxation. It is long lasting and is enjoyed as nourishing and very healing. The sexual arousal from the yang state can be triggered instantly. It is short lived and creates heat and intensity. It is full of tension and excitement and is driven to reach the highest peak.

*Yin and yang of sexual arousal*

*Some causes of insufficient arousal are:*
- Low energy level, and not enough warmth in the body
- Yin deficiency; the physical foundation for sexual arousal is lacking
- Too much heat in the body; arousal can cause an unpleasant or nearly painful feeling
- Being nervous or jumpy, over-stimulation of the body (relaxation is needed)
- Mental blocks and limits
- Lack of experience
- Bad eating habits
- Coldness

*Self love*  Masturbation is a subject that is still a taboo for quite a number of people. Women who want to explore their sexuality miss a great deal if they leave masturbation unlived. Many sexual problems exist only because women have never explored the body and don't know what gives them pleasure.

In many big cities today you can find special sex shops that cater to women only. You can find some very nice things there that are especially made for women. Go uninhibitedly to look around and see what they have to offer, and let yourself be inspired. A vibrator or Chinese love balls might support you. The saleswomen are usually very helpful and understanding.

All the exercises you come across in this book will help you strengthen your energy, but only if you practice them. Many women have the idea that by reading a book, or even simpler, by just keeping it beside the bed, their lives will automatically be transformed. The yin energy within you can only be transformed by your own experience.

# Orgasmic Experiences

The orgasm can be the peak of sexual excitement, and for many people, it is the only time in life when they feel authentic and real. The intensity arises out of the union of opposites and the dissolving of all boundaries. While having an orgasm, we are touched by the breath of the divine, a state that triggers a desire within us to be able to catch that moment, to keep it forever. Many theories have been developed over the ages to explain the mystery of orgasm.

*Freud and company*

In the East and West, most of the hypotheses and models about orgasm originated out of male experience and a male orientation. For example, in the beginning of the 1900s, Freud made the claim that a clitoris-oriented sexuality is indicative of an immature woman; however, the vaginal orgasm is the expression of a mature and female woman. With this statement, Freud initiated a discussion that still occupies psychotherapists and sexologists, and orgasm theories continue to confuse many women today.

My intention here is not to tune into an endless discussion of orgasm. The orgasmic experience of a woman is so multifaceted and individual that it cannot be reduced to rigid theories. Such concepts only limit the unbounded states that female sexuality is able to experience.

*How important is an orgasm?*

Many women live life without ever having an orgasm and don't feel that they miss it. Other women suffer because they are not able to experience orgasm. Some women need it daily, and others—like the American ex-prostitute Anne Sprinkle—talk about mega-orgasms, which last about 15 minutes. She claims she needs to have one every couple of months to maintain her well-being. There are a number of women who are able to have an orgasm while masturbating or being caressed by a partner, but not while having intercourse. Other women have spiritual experiences while having sex. As you can see, the female orgasm is very individually experienced and valued. Obviously for men, orgasm usually is more important than for women, and they generally invest much more in having a great orgasm than women do. To reach that longed for climax, men seem to know no limits or taboos.

*Clitoral, vaginal, or overall*

A very common question for modern Western women is whether an orgasm is clitoral, vaginal, or overall. Because of endless publications and claims, women are becoming insecure

225

about themselves and their sexuality. To that confusion I could add the statement: "Women, forget about clitoral or vaginal. The real female orgasm is *uterine*." But how could such an assertion or hypothesis help a woman in any way get to know her own orgasm? The best is to forget about all you have ever heard and read about orgasms.

### Better, higher, and horny as hell

The achievement-oriented orgasm I am claiming here has grown out of male rubbish and has nothing whatsoever to do with the quality of a female orgasm and the art of loving. To me, achievement-oriented sex seems to be more of a symptom that a person is not really connected with his or her feelings or with the divine. In this limited state, there is no access to the healing and nourishing power of love, the main ingredient that invites sexuality to open to a state of bliss and joy. And as long as that magic door remains closed, the emotionally and spiritually poor long for the orgasm to be bigger, better, and ever-more-lusty!

### Perfect orgasm for a woman

The Eastern arts of love have become very trendy lately. Several books I have come across on Taoist sex contain the nine steps for the perfect female orgasm, and guidelines for men to satisfy a woman.

To me, these kinds of guidelines are a nice gesture in that they try to please women. There are not many cultures in the world truly concerned about the sexual well-being of women. But the motives of such Taoist lovers are not really coming from a space of love and compassion for women, but from gaining some personal benefit out of it.

The theory of nine steps to the perfect female orgasm does not correspond with the understanding and experience I have. The fact that I have been asked about it again and again suggests that it has become an issue for many people, so I feel obligated to mention it.

226

## "The Nine Steps of a Female Orgasm"

*1. Level of the lungs:*
The woman sighs, breathes heavily, and salivates.

*2. Level of the heart:*
The woman, while kissing the man, extends her tongue out to him. (According to old Taoist scriptures the tongue corresponds with the heart.)

*3. Level of the spleen, pancreas and stomach:*
As her muscles become activated, the woman grasps and holds the man tightly.

*4. Level of the kidney:*
The woman experiences a series of vaginal spasms. At this time, the secretion begins to flow.

*5. Level of the bones:*
The woman's joints loosen and she begins to bite the man.

*6. Level of the liver and nerves:*
The woman undulates and gyrates like a snake, trying to wrap her arms and legs around the man.

*7. Level of the blood:*
The woman's blood is boiling, and she is frantically trying to touch the man everywhere.

*8. Level of the muscles:*
Her muscles totally relax. She bites even more and grabs the man's nipples.

*9. The entire body is energized:*
She collapses into a "little death." She completely surrenders to the man and is completely opened up.[1]

---

[1] Stephan Chang, *The Tao of Sexuality* (San Francisco: Tao Publishing, 1986), p. 97.

I find it very interesting that men are always questioning me about the levels of a female orgasm. They want to do it right, but they have become insecure because the partner did not show the physical signs mentioned in the book. Their most common question is, "How do I get my lover to the next level?" Maybe you are a bit confused by this discussion now, or you are smiling. In my women's seminars, this issue often brings a lot of laughter. However, I am also aware that many women are confused because of such theories and books. Maybe their partners have books and videos on this and they want or expect them to be like that.

Don't bother about any of this. Don't let anyone dictate what you are supposed to feel. Female orgasm loves freedom and has a will of its own. To put it into a pigeonhole destroys all its beauty and aliveness.

## Implosion and explosion

Of course, there is no way to avoid mentioning the yin and yang aspects of orgasm. I am sure that you are becoming more and more sensitive to this polarity and could write your own chapter on this.

Normally, sexual tension climaxes into an explosion followed by a feeling of relief and relaxation. The main intention of the Taoist and also Tantric art of love is to let the energy of orgasm flow inside. The female Tao teaches us that the implosion within can only happen in a state of total surrender and letting go. The yin orgasm is also called the valley orgasm.

A yang orgasm is short, intense, and ends with an explosive climax. A yin orgasm carries into a profound feeling, a state of bliss, with a long-lasting and nourishing impact. A yin orgasm does not necessarily arise out of stimulating the body. The source of female sexuality is to be sought in a totally different place.

## Orgasmic ability of a woman

Worldwide, there is still quite a small percentage of women who experience orgasm. How do we understand this? It cannot be that so many women are sexually disturbed or uptight. I am sure that having an orgasm is simply not as important for women as it is for men. If having an orgasm were so important, women would invest much more energy into attaining the ability, but many women are not interested in pursuing this in their lives.

Women rooted in their yin essence have access to an abundance of experiences within them. They are able to be in a state of bliss and joy at all times, even without having sex. Sensuality is a natural state, independent of having sex or being sexually stimulated. That is why women are seldom as possessed or driven by sexuality as men are. Fulfillment does not depend on having an explosive climax.

In case you are one of the women who have never experienced an orgasm, don't worry. Relax. If it is important enough for you, you will eventually have one. But don't hurry; take your time to slowly learn to enjoy your body and connect with it. In this book, you have all the tools and information you need. Many women before you have succeeded on this journey. In order to explore your own potential for orgasm, it's a good idea to first learn about your physical response on your own. And as long as you don't get too pressured, exploring it with your lover is also fine, too.

*Training for orgasm*

Another common question women have is whether or not they lose energy when having an orgasm. This depends very much on their emotional state: they could lose or gain energy while making love. Of course, men lose more energy than women do because ejaculation diminishes their physical substance.

The following techniques spread the feeling of arousal and excitement within the body. You can combine these exercises with the energy egg exercises.

*Expanding sexual arousal and orgasm*

**← Watch Out!**

Only do these exercises as long as they do not create stress or tension within you, and you are able to enjoy experimenting with them.

The "Big Draw" is a method I learned from Mantak Chia. At first, this technique caused a bit of confusion, at least in me. The main goal of this exercise is to draw the energy of the

*The Big Draw*

orgasm up and allow it to spread within the body. When I first learned it, I had been meditating for many years and my higher energy centers were activated and quite open, which helped my energy to flow upward. So as soon as my sexual energy was aroused, it flowed upward on its own, and this was happening so naturally that I was not even aware of it. So when I tried to pull the orgasmic energy up, I was trying to manipulate my energy to do something that was already spontaneously happening. Of course, these intense experiments threw me completely out of my center. My heart was overheating and becoming very restless, my emotions became intense and overwhelming, and my sexual energy evaporated and disappeared in the middle of it all.

So it is important to remember from the very beginning that a woman's sexual energy can be very sensitive and you can easily overreact while applying techniques, and very often they are not needed anyway. If you regularly practice the microcosmic orbit and your energy flows freely and naturally within your body, and your awareness is moving more and more inward, sexual energy is transformed in a very natural way. Nevertheless, here are some exercises to explore your sexual energy.

**Try This!** →   **Orgasmic flow through the microcosmic orbit**
Experience has shown that it is more natural for women to allow their orgasmic energy to flow upward through the front channel, rather than it flowing up the back channel. For women with an open heart, it often happens that all the sexual energy flowing into the heart causes a major love attack and feeling of joy. But what can happen in this case is that at the same time, the sexual energy disappears. While circling the energy within the microcosmic orbit, you can bring some energy back to the sexual center, especially when this happens while making love, just to keep the energy flowing. Don't forget to put your tongue touching the palate to close the orbit so the energy is able to flow fluidly.

## Let the orgasm energy flash your organs

← **Try This!**

This is one of the most stimulating health exercises and it is best to do first thing in the morning. The exercise is most effective in the horsewoman position.

- Close your eyes and open your heart.

- Start massaging your breasts until your whole body feels alive.

- With your outbreath, let the energy that has gathered within your breasts flow down into your pelvis.

- Massage your lower abdomen to energize it.

- Lovingly massage your rose until it opens up.

- Stimulate your sexual energy in its preferred way. You can also use a vibrator if you like—whatever works best for you.

- Continue to arouse your sexual energy and then stop before the urge to have an orgasm comes up, and then draw the aroused energy up with the help of your inbreath and your awareness, and let it flow through your organs.

- Come back to your rosebud and play with your pearls to raise the arousal level more and more, and while having an orgasm, draw the energy up and let it fill your whole body. The perineum plays an important role in this. It usually takes a while until you are able to have an orgasm and at the same time close and pull up the perineum. Keep trying and it will happen.

- Before going to work, remember to center yourself properly, otherwise it might be difficult to function efficiently.

## Orgasmic flow within the glands

← **Go Deeper!**

You can also do this exercise with the glands. It is a wonderful exercise, but only do it when you have enough time to rest for at least an hour afterward. And remember that only practice makes perfect.

*Chapter 19*

# THE RED DRAGON

The red dragon is the name that the Taoists have given to the monthly bleeding of a woman. You are already familiar with the language of the dragon for the different qualities and quantities of bleeding and the symptoms of menstrual problems. In this chapter, we look into the healing and magical power of menstrual blood, which is not only a part of the Taoist system, but of many other cultures as well. I will also comment on traditional Taoist techniques that are recommended by many Taoist masters to slay the dragon.

## The Magic and Healing Power of Menstrual Blood

Since primeval times menstrual blood was used as an effective magic potion. The high content of pheromones and hormones gives the blood "magical" powers that can seduce a man and drive him crazy with passion. In the past, when a woman wanted to draw a man's attention and love, she would conceal a small blood-soaked rag within his pillow. To trigger a man's passion, drops of blood would be secretly mixed into his food. But female blood was not only used with positive intentions. Menstrual blood has also been used by practitioners of black magic to place evil spells on their enemies.

*Healing power of urine and blood*

In 1979, during my second trip to India, I was continuously suffering from intestinal problems caused by amoebas. I was strictly against using any type of prescription drugs at that time in my life, so I decided to go for a fasting cure in a Gandhi ashram located in a small village in central India. The natural medicine doctors there touched me very much. They all looked a little like Gandhi himself, and were very concerned about my health. In their broken English, they tried to convince me to drink my juice of life. It took me quite a while to realize that they were talking about drinking my own urine!

At that time, being only 22, I thought this was very weird and funny. And only many years later, after many attempts, was I able to drink it. Now I am convinced about all the benefits a urine treatment can have, but frankly it is not a healing method that suits me. But don't let my opinion prevent you from making your own experiences. You can only really know if it suits you by trying it. (There are several books on this subject available from health food stores.)

Now urine therapy has become very popular here in the West as well. And many urine drinkers are sharing their experiences openly. Mantak Chia is convinced that when a menstruating woman drinks her morning urine, it is very beneficial to her health, especially if she has hormonal imbalances or is suffering from menopause problems. He also recommends this for women who want to tame their dragon. It can be very healing and soothing to put a few drops of morning urine into your eyes with an eyedropper, and while menstruating, the effect is even stronger. You can also try taking a few drops in your nose.

Both menstrual blood and urine have a very nourishing and healing impact on your skin. Women suffering from skin problems can treat their skin every morning with the first urination in the morning, with or without blood. I am always surprised how many cases this helps. Another nice thing to do is to put blood on your energy points to strengthen them while menstruating. You can collect the blood by inserting a small natural sponge in your vagina.

Blood is also very good for plants. A friend of mine works in an intensive care unit where they bring patients after surgery. Just recently, she told me that since she has come to my seminars, she has become more conscious about the power of blood and is not able to throw out all the gallons of blood that is drained and collected as waste after surgery. There is a garden right next to the ward she works in, and for the last few years, she has emptied the collected blood into the garden. She told me that all the plants and flowers have become much more radiant and healthy.

To continue, I would like to introduce some methods to use the power of blood within the body.

### Filling the sea of blood                    ← Try This!

- Sit upright in a comfortable position and close your eyes.

- Massage your breasts until the blood has gathered there and they become strong and firm. Charge the blood with the feeling of love from your heart, until the breasts are filled and the blood begins to overflow.

The sea of blood.

- With the outbreath, guide the enriched, healing blood down to fill your Palace.

- Contract your Palace very softly and gently until the uterus opens up.

- While sitting silent and relaxed, continue to breathe and feel how the sea of blood is slowly becoming full.

- Sit for at least another 20 minutes, and in a deep state of silence, let the sea of blood heal your Palace.

- When it is possible for you to really feel this, you can go on to the next step.

**Go Deeper!** → **Brewing your blood pill**

- Pour your heart energy into the sea of blood.

- Start circling your energy, awareness, and feeling (just like you would stir a saucepan) in your sea of blood.

- Continue until the blood condenses into a blood pill.

Brewing the blood pill.

- You can bring the blood pill to any place in the body that needs healing and support.

- To finish, let the pill circle into the microcosmic orbit, and don't forget to center yourself as deeply as possible when you are done.

In the traditional Tao, there are methods to slay the dragon, which means there are methods you can use to stop the monthly bleeding. People keep asking me about these methods, so let's look at this issue.

**Taming the dragon**

There are books on the market, all from male writers, where they give women instructions for how to stop their menstruation to rejuvenate and heal their bodies. According to my experience, women should be careful about applying these techniques, as they can be quite harmful.

Originally, a recommendation to stop menstruating was given by the master to a woman disciple on the spiritual path. The techniques to tame the dragon were part and parcel of a whole spiritual concept. In this case, to be able to stop bleeding was part of the physical training on a particular spiritual path. I would question any other motives to tame the dragon, like the wish to look younger or wanting to stop the period because of the pain, or as a natural contraceptive. Before a woman starts to slay her dragon, it is important to clarify her real motives.

*Keeping the blood*

There is another point to be considered here. In the last fifteen or twenty years, many recommendations and teachings from the wise old masters have been translated from ancient scriptures by a very different kind of people. The translators of these texts are usually male. This makes me wonder if the techniques they write about are just their mental concepts, or a clever idea to make money, or even misunderstandings of the original material. Or have these techniques been thoroughly tested and proved valid? We need to ask critical questions: How healing are these techniques? And how meaningful is it to stop menstruation with forceful techniques utilizing the will?

Many of these techniques are extremely yang-oriented and violent to the feminine essence, such as the Deer Exercise—and can precipitate physical disharmonies and female problems. A deer has never been known as being particularly feminine. In the context of this book, it does not make sense to present these exercises to you, because they can cause more harm than good, especially if you learn them from a book.

I have observed that it is easier for a yang-oriented woman to influence and manipulate her menstrual cycle. In the body of a woman addicted to drugs, or a woman with eating disorders, such as bulimia or anorexia, or in anemic women or sports-women, it often happens that menstruation stops because the body cannot afford the extra energy needed to maintain the menstrual cycle. When the female parts of the body are depleted over a long period of time, the monthly bleeding dries up. Menstruation also stops naturally during pregnancy and when a woman is breastfeeding.

According to my experience, forceful manipulations by yang-oriented methods have nothing to do with the female way. So I am recommending that women focus on the essentials—to learn to open up to receive the divine, to initiate a spiritual pregnancy, consciously and lovingly.

# Chapter 20

# ENTERING THE HEAVENLY PALACE

The uterus is the gate to the Heavenly Palace, giving a woman security and warmth. But it can also be the entrance to hell, a source of infinite sorrow and pain. So take care of your uterus. Do the exercises to strengthen and empty it carefully until it has found its natural state of sensuality, and you are able to perceive and enjoy your Heavenly Palace. Every uterus is a vivid and sensual organ. How much time a woman needs to access that inner quality varies, and this process requires a certain determination. For a woman to liberate her uterus, she must swim against the stream of the collective. But only those who swim against the stream can reach the source. It requires energy, inner strength, and resolution.

**The Gate to Heaven or Hell**

Women have not received much support on this path as of yet. An awakened, alive uterus has a strong magnetism that can help other uteruses become alive, but only if a woman is ready for it. If she insists on remaining stuck in a superficial and mind-oriented life, she will only become enmeshed in struggling against her own inner hell trapped inside of her, and continue to irresponsibly project her negativity on to other people.

A uterus does not liberate itself spontaneously or intuitively by pure chance. Women who want to experience the uterus as a door to a new dimension have to deliberately decide on the way of freedom and self-liberation. In most contexts, I do not like to use the words "have to," but in order to liberate female sexuality, such a commitment is absolutely needed.

The future lies in our hands. But many women meekly allow their life to be guided by the will of the masses, as if they were dangling behind an "out of order" sign. They define themselves only through being a mother and relating to others, guaranteeing their financial and emotional dependency at the same time. Mothers who want to maintain financial independence deal with a great deal of pressure and strain. They often have neither time nor energy left to be able to free themselves from the vicious circle of survival in order to develop genuine individuality.

That does not mean that mothers cannot shake off their chains. Even though in some respects it is more difficult for them, mothers have had the experience of pregnancy. They have gone beyond the romantic dream of having a husband and a baby, and are already standing on the solid ground of reality, handling a real child and the responsibilities and challenges that arise from that. And this in fact is a very good situation for beginning the journey.

*Female potential*

The time has come for women to detach their sexual potential of openness, receptivity, pregnancy, and giving birth from the biological reproductive cycle, so they can also realize these capacities in another dimension. The female principle guides us to find deep fulfillment within ourselves, to be able to give birth to our spiritual self instead of investing and diluting most of our inner strengths into the outer world of relationships, families, and an entertaining social life. Openness, receptivity, pregnancy, and giving birth—the female qualities—all originate in the uterus. The uterus is a very sturdy receptacle embedded in a protected place. It is our own choice how we use it. Either it can become a dumping ground for negative energy or we can entrust it with more creative and innovative responsibilities.

In the beginning of this book I introduced the three energy centers or Tan T'ien. You have gradually learned to activate, charge, and be centered in—in many different ways—the lower Tan T'ien over the course of working with this book. Maybe by now you are able to feel your inner field of medicine. Even though I am convinced that the lower Tan T'ien of a woman is located in the uterus itself, up until now we have been doing all the centering exercises in the area above the uterus. And I can only recommend that you go on doing so. You will notice yourself that it has a totally different quality. Centering yourself and strengthening the middle always refers to the area above the uterus. If the uterus is not entirely healed, it can affect you very negatively to gather energy there.

# The Uterus: The Female Tan T'ien

The female Tan T'ien.

The following exercises I recommend only to women who have set their sexuality free and who are able to enjoy the deep silence within. They have the potential to magnify undigested emotional and sexual problems, especially if you are not really energetically involved in the exercises, but only doing them in your imagination.

← **Watch Out!**

241

*Spiritual embryo*

Developing a spiritual embryo, also called a Body of Light or the Golden Elixir, is a major focus of the Taoist path. Male Taoists have evolved techniques that aim to get them pregnant in a spiritual sense, by trying to turn their yang nature into yin in the hope to achieve immortality. To achieve such an exceptional goal requires incredible strength, which they mobilize by hard physical discipline and untiring training of their metal powers. The interesting thing is that in most schools where they focus on these practices, women are not allowed, even today.

The female body is naturally intended to become pregnant. Within the uterus, we have a beautiful space where something new can emerge; a woman's body is especially designed for it. It is part of a woman's nature to develop spirituality. The male Tao is goal-oriented, striving for immortality. On the other hand, the female Tao reveals its natural loving and healing powers in the here and now.

The spiritual embryo.

I have met many women practicing the Tao according to male instructions and principles. But honestly, the result has not convinced me that these techniques are appropriate for women at all. (And that is one of the major reasons I started to develop the female Tao.) These women have strongly developed their yang aspect, and this only serves to weaken and overpower their yin nature, and prevents women from surrendering to the deep silence within, where yin has its roots.

*The female Tao*

Many women I have spoken to have had experiences similar to mine with traditional Taoist exercises. It feels as if we have already integrated that aspect. And the more we keep manipulating our energy and body, the more our precious yin essence is destroyed. That is why many women avoid getting deeply involved with traditional Tao. They instinctually feel that the male approach does not bring them back home. So for a woman on the path, there is nothing left to do but to relax, to be able to consciously enjoy female energy so the natural potential of spirituality can unfold.

The treasures of the female Tao support women to empty and heal the uterus, to create the space needed to initiate a spiritual pregnancy. In the protected depth of a woman's womb, the female power of healing love can mature until it is ready to overflow and manifest itself. The following exercises are only for pleasure-loving meditators who are able to enjoy both the silence within and healing laughter.

## Spiritual Pregnancy

← **Watch Out!**

Energies can enhance your basic state of feeling. If you start to fill your uterus with energy, this can bring up repressed energies or diseases. Only do the following exercises when you feel your uterus is light and free and you are able to connect with your natural state of sensuality. As a preparation to initiate a spiritual pregnancy, you need to be in a total yin state, utterly passive and silent, to be open and empty, ready to receive.

**Go Deeper!** → **The Golden Elixir: preparation for spiritual pregnancy**

The following exercise deepens the process of filling the sea of blood that you already know.

- Sit in upright but comfortable position, close your eyes, and breathe slowly and deeply until you are connected and rooted within.

- Open the third eye with the help of your middle finger. Hold your finger there until the third eye is pulsing and opening.

- Via the third eye, start to connect with the divine light and while breathing in, draw it into your heart.

- With your outbreath and the healing heart sound "Haaaa," let the divine light flow deeply into your heart and into your breasts, until they become light, vibrant, and joyous.

The Golden Elixir.

- Massage your breasts until the blood has gathered there and they become full and firm. Keep smiling into your breasts until the blood is fully charged with loving and divine energy, until the blood and energy overflows.

- Let that stream of healing energy flood down into your Palace.

- Contract your inner door slightly (the uterine orifice) to connect and open your Palace.

- Just sit and relax and enjoy the slow filling of the sea of blood.

- Then put your awareness to the crown until it begins to pulse and open up.

- Very gently contract your uterus and receive the divine light in your Palace.

- Sit and watch how your blood absorbs the divine healing light and gets transformed into a golden magical elixir.

- Sit utterly silent, open, and receptive, and enjoy the state of inner fullness.

*Getting pregnant*

It takes time to properly prepare and initiate spiritual pregnancy. It is important to remember that the female grows slowly, but steadily. Female essence is only destroyed by forcing it, by being impatient or in a hurry to achieve something. The Full Moon is a good time to initiate spiritual pregnancy. Decide which qualities you want to absorb to fertilize your female essence; the healing light, the fragrance of the heart, the silence, the Moon—choose the quality and truly connect with it.

Receive it in your Palace to initiate the pregnancy. But the initiation is just the beginning. After that, you will need to capture and nurture the precious seed within day by day. It is your responsibility to provide an ideal environment, a joyous state of yin for it to grow. Feed it with your love and the silent state of meditation so it can grow inside of you. Take time every day to support and nourish your inner process so that something new and wonderful can mature inside you until it is strong enough to overflow and blossom. In this phase of pregnancy, it is essential to surrender your life to silence, to meditate, and to stay in loving touch with your environment.

*Full Moon meditation* The Full Moon night is the night for women, because the healing yin powers are very powerful at that time. I would like to invite you to join the next Full Moon Meditation. It does not matter where you are. Keep the night free for this meditation, either alone or with other women. If you are getting together with others, make sure you don't talk. A good way to tune in and begin is to let the Palaces dance freely. At 10 P.M., if the weather allows, go outside together to sit in a circle in the moonlight. Otherwise sit next to a window.

**Watch Out! →**

For women who have not liberated their Palace yet, it is best to do the Full Moon Meditation above the uterus, in your center.

**Try This! →** **Full Moon meditation**

- Sit in an upright but comfortable position. Close your eyes and open your heart with the help of the healing heart sound.

- Let the fragrance of your heart flow down into your Palace.

- For the next 15 minutes, fill your Palace with your heart energy, and at the same time hum gently into it.

- Be as open and receptive as possible and breathe slowly and deeply to receive the elixir of the Moon.

- Enjoy the silver fluid of the Moon entering your body and allow it to flood and heal each cell of your body and your Palace.

Full Moon meditation.

- To mix the essence of the Moon with your own energy, chant the mantra "Om" directly into your Palace, tenderly and softly.

- Continue as long as you feel like it.

- Remain sitting in the moonlight for the whole night, if you wish.

The number of women meditating with the Full Moon is constantly increasing, and this is wonderful. In this way, female healing power is strengthened and spreads more and more all over the planet!

**247**

*Part Five*

# RELATING
# WITH
# THE YANG

# Chapter 21

# YANG, THE MALE PRINCIPLE

As long as we are involved in sexuality, we are in a world of polarity, full of opposites and contradictions. As long as these two opposites are not integrated within our being, we swing back and forth between the two extremes and this will always create tension within and without.

**Yang is Different**

So far we have only focused on the female principle—yin—the mother of everything that exists, which gives birth to yang. The Taoist cosmology teaching says: "When the yin has reached its deepest depths, it will turn into yang." We have already taken a detailed look at the dualistic principle of yin and yang. At this point, I would like to add some aspects that can be fundamental to understanding sexual relating.

*Birth of yang*

Chinese letter
for yang.

- When yin strives for unity, yang aims for separation.

- When yin longs for community, yang moves into hierarchy.

- When yin surrenders, yang controls.

- When yin has reached its naturalness, yang develops technique and science.

- Out of relaxation arises excitement and tension.

251

- Feelings are the roots of the mind.

- While yin withdraws into the deepest point, yang shines at the peak.

- Yin's nature is to be, yang's is to do.

- Yin is creating peace and yang is stirring things up.

Women react very differently to yang energy. While many have left yin and learned to move with and adjust to yang, for others, yang is a threat, one that they try to avoid. To find our lost unity, it is important to be able to understand and integrate yang as well as yin.

*Yang essence*  Women who are rooted in their yin qualities can afford to be open, soft, and sensitive. Then, the yang seed within them gives them inner strength and self-confidence. The yang principle, which rules the male body and the male sexuality, functions just the other way around. The soft and sensitive yin seed within a man, full of feelings, needs to be protected by outer strength. Yang takes on this function of protection.

*Fire*  In Taoist symbology, the yang element is characterized by fire and the yin element by water. Fire generates energy and radiates warmth; it expands and strives to reach the peak. Fire is intense and alive; it is the expression of vitality, strength, and passion.

Water is needed to regulate fire. If fire gets out of control, it can become very destructive. On the other hand, fire can warm the water and bring it to a boiling point, but too much fire evaporates water, just as too much water can drown the fire.

*Yang as protection*  Yang-oriented behavior is a survival strategy for both men and women who are not connected with their internal strength. There are as many women who are afraid to live and show their strength and power as there are men who are frightened to get in touch with their inner weakness and show their true feelings. The female hides her strength and the male hides his weakness.

To develop female sexuality, one cannot avoid surrendering to the depths of yin. On the other hand, to develop male sexuality, one needs to learn how to generate yang energy.

## Cultivating Yang Qualities

Contrary to yin energies, which accumulate slowly and steadily, yang energies can be generated quickly. Yin's home is in the state of being, silence, and surrender, whereas yang is in its element in activity, movement, and controlling energy.

There are different methods to generate yang energy. Unconsciously, a man is always looking for new possibilities to get in touch with his yang forces, with his outer strength. For us women, it is often quite baffling how much time, energy and discipline men invest in yang activities, to be good at something, or to prove their value to themselves and others. Yin needs to feel good to be able to be good. Many women get stuck by not feeling really good and consequently their activity remains average. Yang feels well when it is doing good. Yin does well when it is feeling good.

*Physical activity*

It makes a big difference whether a man is consciously building up his yang or whether he is driven to do it unconsciously. The way that a man activates his yang will depend on the element he uses to generate that quality. The professional field will also influence which method a man uses to get in touch with his yang. The most direct ways to generate yang are physical activity, exercises, and martial arts.

*Intelligence*

Mental activity can also generate a yang state, a feeling of strength. Logic, being critical, collecting information and knowledge, having an overview, a good orientation, or a strong opinion can serve the same purpose as physical exercise.

*Status*

To be honored or respected is another way to build up a yang shield, but this apparent security only exists in the mind as fantasy. A yang quality that is built on acknowledgement and confirmation from the outside is weak and dependent. One doesn't get in touch with one's internal power in this way, it is only borrowed. The choice of a status symbol depends on each person's social environment; houses, cars, women, being a part of something, or assuming responsibility are among the more common ones. In spiritual or religious communities, the status symbols are a bit more distorted or even perverted. They can manifest as being the most humble or loving, for instance, or can take many other forms. Just look around life and you will notice this phenomenon yourself.

*Power*  Ego and power trips are part of exercising power. To prove one's power, making somebody feel small to be able to feel great, always indicates inner weakness and insecurity. Power games can be very tricky. Many therapists, group leaders, and so-called gurus use this method to try to feel strong within themselves.

*Stress*  Emotions, tension, and stress can create heat within the body, which from an energetic point of view can have a vitalizing yang effect.

*Personal freedom*  The feeling of being independent and free can generate yang energies.

*Secrets*  If no method is effective enough to stimulate the power of yang to protect the inner self, there is always the escape into the secret world. A typical female ritual is to initiate each other into hidden secrets, to feel close to each other, to dissolve all boundaries. A man, on the other hand, needs his secrets to protect the innermost self, a world that needs to be respected by women.

# Chapter 22

# YANG-ORIENTED SEX

**W**hen sexuality is ruled by the yang principle, we talk about yang-oriented sex. Yang sex strives to be more exciting and intense, strives to create more lust and horniness, strives to play in and with the fire. Yang reveals its potential by being on top, it blossoms at the peak of climax, and so it is always driven to achieve these heights again.

**To Play With Fire**

Another main characteristic of yang is in its outward orientation—it is extroverted. Because of this, it reacts to and depends on outer images, pictures, confirmation, structures of power and achievement.

An increasing number of women are living a yang-oriented sexuality, even though their potential is rooted in yin, in the qualities of water. Yang-oriented sex arises out of an overflow of energy and fire. To fulfill its biological function, the male sex depends on having power and energy. Having sex with a woman requires lots of courage. For a man, it means that every time he makes love, it is a journey back to his origin, an attempt to return to his source. The required tension can only be built up out of an extreme yang state. Just as there are many women who are not connected with their yin roots and yin qualities, there are also men who have no access to their yang sources; they are unable to kindle and light their own fire.

*Male virility*

The fastest and easiest way for a man to connect with his yang energy is via sexual arousal. Sexuality is for many men the only possibility to perceive and define themselves, and so sex becomes very important to them. Sexual excitement gives men vitality, power, and self-confidence. The size and hardness of a penis turns nearly every man into a hero, at least for a few moments. That state of strength, that tiny little moment of being on top of the world, awakens the hunger for more. Only a few men have the strength and sensitivity to keep their fire under control so they are able to stay on top of the world.

## Yang Patterns

*Strong yang*

Men with strong yang energy and corresponding yang behavior are usually sexually aroused quite easily. Without any effort, they are able to dominate their surrounding,s by energy, radiation, mood, and personality. In the presence of a man with strong yang energy, a sensitive yin woman may have difficulty being able to perceive her own tender inner voice. On the other hand, it is difficult or nearly impossible for a strong yang man to understand the yin nature.

So, we women should not be so naive as to expect the impossible. It is a waste of time to expect that such a man should be able to recognize the needs and feelings of a woman. A woman with such a partner needs to take her own free space to feel herself and not lose her personal perspective, so she can clearly articulate her own needs, feelings, and limits.

Strong yang types have difficulty getting in touch with their inner yin qualities; therefore they tend to depend on being close to or sexually in touch with a woman.

*Weak yang*

Getting sexually involved with men with a weaker yang can be more complicated. It seems to be an energetic law that we always feel attracted to what we lack inside ourselves, to have a chance to integrate the weak or missing piece. If a man has no access to his own source of yang to become sexually aroused, he will try to distill it from the tension and energy without. This can be through fantasy, something forbidden or perverted, conflicts or stress, or simply through basic hunting and conquering instincts. In long term relationships, or in being too intimate with a particular woman, it can be very difficult for him to have an erection because the needed tension is missing.

A lack of yang is a major reason that male sexuality is increasingly getting out of control. In search of that last peak of natural tension, some men go on triggering their sexual force any way they can, in order to have some sexual sensation. While striving for some physical reaction, they are not in the most sensitive state about themselves and are easily disconnected from their feelings. In moments like this, they don't realize that the fire is burning until they are suddenly overwhelmed by it and completely lose control over their sexual actions. They may not even know what is happening to them. Unconsciously, they surrender to their unconscious emotions and sexual fantasies. Rape, perversion, and child abuse are the sad but logical consequences of this energy gone awry.

    The majority of men can only learn to regain control over their fire with the help of a woman, but if a woman is not present and rooted in her femininity, and takes on the yang aspect instead, the fire will get even more difficult to control.

*Controlling and surrendering*

It is interesting that the male hormone testosterone can change into the female hormone estrogen. This indicates that the laws of yin and yang also rule the hormonal system.

*Testosterone —the male hormone*

*General action:*
- Vitalizes and activates the body
- Causes aggression and promotes defining one's space or territory
- Enhances self-confidence and assertion
- Strengthens the cognitive abilities
- Increases the mass of muscles in relation to body fat
- Causes masculine sexual characteristics
- Promotes the production of adrenaline and dopamine

**257**

*Its influence on male sexuality:*
- Activates the sexual drive in men and women
- Enhances the hunting instinct, the drive for adventure and affairs
- Induces sexual images and fantasies
- Awakens a desire to masturbate
- Regulates production of sperm

*What increases the testosterone production:*
- Sexual excitement
- Sexual fantasies
- Competition and sport
- Confrontation and tensions
- Winning, controlling, and being in power
- Eating meat
- Alcohol (except beer)

Testosterone is mainly produced in the testicles, but it has no direct influence in causing an erection.

*Testicles*  The testicles are the biggest yin reservoir of a man. After ejaculation, testosterone promotes the growth of hundreds of thousands of sperm. The yang force changes into yin: the male testosterone stimulates the production of sperm, which is the yin component in the male body. Likewise, the ovary power is the yang force in the female body.

A burning fire requires fuel. Male sexuality must have a good physical foundation to keep the fire burning. This does not necessarily mean that the stronger the fire, the more lustful the climax. It depends very much on the roots, for the deeper the roots, the higher a tree can grow. The stronger the yin roots, the more yang can blossom.

Unfortunately, a yang-oriented sexuality happens mostly at the cost of precious yin power, the physical substance. The burning of yin substances creates energy and causes an intense feeling of aliveness and lust for a few moments, and ejaculation is one form of it. To derive a few moments of pleasure and satisfaction, the precious yin essence is sprayed out of the body.

We have already looked at how strongly we are trapped in collective patterns in connection to female sexuality. Male sexuality is just as manipulated by the collective. A man's orgasmic potential is prevented by unconscious destructive sexual behavior patterns. If a man is ready to break out of these deeply manifested patterns, he needs to learn the art of keeping the semen in the body. By appreciating the yin qualities (semen), and integrating them within the body, it is possible for a man to establish a solid foundation that will allow him to experience an unlimited sexuality.

Most men think that sexual satisfaction means to climax into ejaculation. In fact, ejaculation brings an abrupt end to sexual activity. Because of the physical exhaustion and relaxation, the emptiness and depth that follows is bearable for a while. But in the long run, he does not feel at ease in this empty yin space, so he strives again to be on top, and the game starts all over again.

Young men usually have a surplus of yang energy and life force, which they release by ejaculating. But the more a man ejaculates, the weaker his yin substance becomes, which is the solid foundation for an exciting sex life. An important issue for men in the Tao of sexuality is to learn to separate orgasm from ejaculation. But this is only possible if a man is rooted in his yin qualities. The inner roots make it possible to let the orgasmic energy flow inward to fill the emptiness. As long as a man lives his sexuality by emptying it out, it will not be possible to experience inner ecstasy and sexual power as a permanent reality.

The Tao teaches us to strengthen our inner organs, our glands, and our sexual force. The healing potion for that is found in the semen. The first step for a man who wants to maintain his sexual power is to learn how to connect with his semen power and to guide that nourishing essence from the testicles via the microcosmic orbit into organs and glands, to strengthen the yin parts of his body. Later on, the same can be done in a state of sexual arousal.

*Orgasm and ejaculation*

*Power of the organs*

**259**

## Male Sexuality and the Five Elements

Each organ has an influence on the physical, energetic, and mental planes. Their functions are very complex, so I will only go into a few functions that help us to expand our understanding of male sexuality.

### Wood

The liver, which is assigned to the wood element, plays a central role within male sexuality.

#### The liver

- Regulates physical tension. It gives stimulus to the penis for erection.

- Plays an important role in dealing with stress and processing impressions.

- Vitalizes, energizes and generates yang energy.

- Reacts strongly to visual stimulation, because the eyes are the opening to the liver. Through visual stimulation the male penis can grow and be ready for action within seconds.

- Thanks to the liver, men have a pleasant method to reduce stress—through sex.

### The lustful valve

Only a few men have natural access to their feelings, and are able to move comfortably on the emotional plane. Most men have learned to cut off from feelings and successfully repress them from the reach of conscious perception. Often they only notice feelings when they reach a point where they are involved with inner tension, stress, sex, or being hurt.

The liver reacts a bit indifferently to the energetic impulses it receives. Whether the impulse is one of joy and an overflow of energy, or an impulse arising out of stress and unprocessed impressions, the liver passes the impulse unfiltered on to the penis. There might be a visual stimulus and the male organ takes on its erect posture. Only a few men are able to feel the difference between real lust and a stress symptom. The only thing that counts is the state of tension within the liver, the signal that initiates erection.

For a man, sexuality that climaxes into ejaculation is a very pleasant way of stress management. In this way, emotions leave the body unprocessed. For women who are not connected with their uterus, sexual contacts of this kind can be very burdening. Negative emotions, stress, and tension are absorbed by the uterus and stored there. From that center, negativity will spread all over her being. Because of this, a woman can develop an aversion toward sex, or it can be that she becomes negative and pessimistic, constantly frustrated, nagging the husband and children.

The solution is not that women withdraw from men or put their effort into changing them, but that they develop and strengthen an independent power of love that transforms the negative. If a woman has sex absent-mindedly, or cuts off from her feelings, especially if they are not good, or escapes into a fantasy, it can be very harmful to her. Her inner presence and power are missing, which can only invite negativity to enter and spread all over her body.

The liver fire stimulates sexual tension, and can be triggered not only by activity and stress, but also through warming and heating foods and beverages. A partner with strong liver fire can be very strenuous to be with, because he tends to be horny, moody, or irritable quite often. The liver fire reacts to restrictions and rejections by being edgy and aggressive, which again stimulates the liver, especially in the summer. For a woman who finds herself being around such a "liverish" person, it is important that she not absorb such a vibration. She should take her own space to strengthen the cooling and healing water qualities within, and be especially loving with herself, while remaining centered. She can protect herself and her own liver with the power of her heart.

If you are able to influence your partner's eating habits, do as follows:

**Hints for Healing!**
←

*Avoid:*
- All chemical supplements in foods and beverages
- Hot, spicy, and fried foods
- Alcohol (except bitter beer)

*Recommended:*

- Natural foods, raw foods, and lots of vegetables. Yang types often do not like this because of the opinion, "a real man needs meat."
- Little meat—best is beef
- Fish, but avoid other seafood
- Bitter taste

**Healing Points!**

→

- Press Liver 2 and Liver 3 to draw the heat down.

*Fire*  In yang-oriented sexuality, little importance is given to the heart and its needs. The two important energy centers—sex and heart—are not interconnected. The heart is not being supplied with enough energy and becomes weak.

When the heart is dried up, you will find an unpleasant coldness and lack of feeling that manifests in arrogance, cruelty, or hatred. In mixed seminars, this is a point that has always been very difficult. How can we bring men in contact with the quality of a loving heart? All the tools that help women, like the opening of the heart, the gland exercises, and so forth, seem often to be boring for men.

On the other hand, I keep observing that a man's heart begins to awaken when he starts meditating and working on his sexuality, and when he uses his semen power to fill the inner self and to nourish the heart. Women who have opened their heart could help men with this task. The easiest way is to silently let the elixir of your heart flow into his, until it has the strength to become alive and liberate itself. And a man with an open heart is more fun to be around.

*Earth*  The earth element, which manifests through the spleen and pancreas, can become an important guide in becoming more responsible about sexuality. The message of the Tao is to live sex consciously, out of the middle, so that it becomes healing and not hurting for everyone concerned. For this a man needs a strong center. Otherwise he will be manipulated by the unconscious and destructive compulsions of our collective conditioning. Centering exercises and natural foods are very supportive to strengthen the earth element.

The yin water element strongly influences male sexuality as well. *Water*
The kidneys, which manifest water qualities, are responsible for the lower gates and for ejaculation. Premature ejaculation can be a sign of a weak water element. Wet dreams can be another indication of a weak water element. A strong water element is needed to root the yang power within.

One of the main functions of the metal element is being *Metal*
responsible for vitality or chi. If a person has a low chi level, sexuality will be, of course, naturally weakened. The lung is part of the metal element, therefore good and deep breathing, and getting enough fresh air, is a must for men who want to improve their sexuality.

# Chapter 23

# DEALING WITH MALE SEX

Men are not always the way we would like them to be. When they have sexual desires and preferences that do not correspond with our own wishes, our capacity to love and understand is strained and tends to diminish rapidly. The "yang flash," the state a man gets in when his fire energy is stimulated and he is sexually aroused, is a very popular way for men to get in contact with their power and to move from the plastic world of the mind into experiencing life directly.

But for a woman this is different. Making love is an opening and an absorbing of something different from herself. So making love does not necessarily put her in contact with her strength.

Whenever I ask women and men to recall their most cherished sexual experience, I usually get very gender specific answers. In general a woman remembers a wonderful moment full of depth and intimacy, and men remember the most exciting and fortuitous chance encounter. No wonder it is the highest art of love to unite these two extremes.

Women's search for identity and liberation has not passed without leaving its footprints on men. In the last number of years, we have witnessed a tremendous nagging criticism of male qualities and male behavior. Women have put a great deal of effort

**In Search of Male Identity**

in convincing their partners to participate in couple therapy or in a self-exploration group to develop their feminine sides—wanting them to become softer and full of feelings. Super-machos were transformed into nice understanding super-softies. But the experience has shown that the endless counseling sessions that discuss and analyze our relationships have not brought the opposite sexes any closer, at least not sexually. Too often, male power has just fallen by the wayside.

Realistically, women cannot be serious about wanting men to act and feel like women. It is better for a woman to develop the female qualities she is missing inside herself, to be able to influence her love life according to her desires. That gives her the freedom to accept men the way they are, instead of wasting her energy trying to change them.

When it comes down to having sex with a woman, men have become confused and insecure. Out of the fear of rejection or condemnation from their wives or lovers, they do not communicate their true desires and preferences. Let's be honest, there are some terribly uptight and prudish women who have banned male sexuality out of their lives and relationships.

## Men and feelings

Feeling corresponds to the female principle and the mind to the male principle. This does not mean that men are not able to have true and profound feelings, rather the contrary is true. But because yin is located deeply within yang, the emotional plane is hidden in the depths of the male unconscious. For those men who continue to live a yang-oriented sexuality and lifestyle, this area remains untouched and unexplored. The male mind functions like a bodyguard, protecting that vulnerable and tender state within, and often does not let anyone or anything near enough to touch it.

But there is a deep longing inside of us for aliveness that is only possible through feeling, which keeps pulling men down in the unknown mysterious depths of yin. Sex has the ability to bring those foggy states of feeling back to life. When it comes to sex, men often tend to lose their connection to reality, because they never learned to move in the world of feelings in an easy and natural way. From quite a young age, boys are trained to behave properly and become "real men." If daddy is not able to fulfill mother's ideals, at least the son has to be pressed into the ideal image of a man for her.

*Men's fear*

The fear of losing control and falling into the abyss of yin is the major motive for anti-woman patriarchal societies. Here men are fighting the female within, which has been transferred to the outer physical woman. This inner fear makes it impossible to treat women with true love and respect. In many areas of life, this fact is hidden. But, when it comes down to sex, the fear and heat men have toward women becomes visible in one way or another. This inner conflict prevents men from living in a relaxed way on a higher energy level, and leads them toward destructiveness instead.

*Fantasy and reality*

Feeling can make us confront our reality. But many men try to avoid feeling by escaping into the world of fantasy. They may use sexual fantasies to build a dream world that is detached from reality. Repressed unconscious longings nourish those dreams. In sexual relationships, fantasies cause lots of confusion and misunderstandings. A fantasy will never become real and imagination can never replace a real feeling.

## Sexual Fantasies

Of course, women also have sexual fantasies, but they arise out of the male principle. Sexual fantasies create feelings that are not present in reality. People are always real, and therefore no one ever corresponds exactly with someone else's dream. To meet, feel, and love someone is only possible in reality.

From my experience as a sexologist, I am quite sure that most men stimulate their sexual energy mentally. To build up the required tension to be able to make love with their long-standing wife, they stimulate themselves with sexual fantasies. Of course there are also exceptions to this.

*Pornographic material*

Sex films are watched predominantly by men. That's why they play to a male audience. Within the last twenty years, especially in Europe and Asia, the sex trade has moved out from the edge of society and established its place as a part of our everyday life. Sex films on TV are raising the ratings, sex shops are located in the most exquisite shopping areas, phone numbers for anonymous sex fill the daily newspapers, and in general, a business dealing in sex has become socially acceptable. Worldwide this tendency is increasing rapidly. Via the internet, pornographic material is spreading uncensored all over the planet, available to children as well as adults.

We should not underestimate the effect that all this has on our sexual behavior. Young children who orient and inform themselves about life with sexually explicit videos absorb a very unrealistic image of sex. Since videos of this kind are often used as a masturbation aid, the images get mixed up with a person's life energy and take their place in the deep layers of the unconscious.

Very few people seem to be fully aware that these videos are always unreal and that what they watch are paid actors and actresses posing fabricated sexual encounters. Female sexuality is mostly presented in a way that does not correspond with the real desire of the majority of women. These videos are especially deceptive to women, who often get the impression that all other women except them like hard sex, and they begin to feel insecure about their own sexuality. When they don't feel turned on by the posed sexual practices they see, they start to feel that they have a problem with sex themselves.

*Perverted sex*

Sexual practices that arise out of anything other than a natural aliveness are perverted. People with perverted sexual behavior and those who are into violent sex are never willing to change their sexual behavior or preferences of their own will, and this is a very difficult issue for a sexual therapist to deal with. About 90 percent of the sexual delinquents undergoing treatment have a relapse, even after many years of intense therapy. In my work I keep observing that victims are much more motivated to begin therapy than the culprits. As long as the violators' sexual preferences continue to give them pleasure, no matter what they are, there seems to be no real motivation to change. Why renounce a few intense, gratifying moments? These people are only persuaded to participate in therapy under legal or family pressure, but intrinsically they remain unconvinced of any need to change their habits.

Sexual practices that involve sadomasochism, rape, child abuse, or any sexual contact that is ruled by a lack of respect or an uncaring attitude are destructive. And according to me, these destructive patterns need to be dissolved. Women need to begin to charge the global sexual vibration with positive yin qualities. Time will not allow us to ignore the sexual reality and current developments any longer, just because we don't want to be confronted by them.

*Destructive sex*

*There are different patterns with which women react to violence and cruelty. They are:*
- Powerlessness, helplessness, paralyzing fear
- The "ostrich policy" of not looking, or going unconscious when it gets uncomfortable
- Cutting off from feelings

- How do you react to destructive sex and violence?

  **← My Diary!**

  If you have experienced sexual violence yourself, this question might feel very unpleasant to you, and bring you directly in contact with the pattern you are using to try to deal with it.

- How do you react to sexual violence in newspaper reports, or on TV, or while watching a video?

- The next time you are reading or hearing about such news, be aware of your reaction. Is your breathing changing? If yes, how? Are you absorbing the negative vibration of it?

## Is It Possible to Change a Man?

That men should change is a very common request among women. And men would also like women to be different. Wanting to have an educational influence on a grown-up man is a thankless task, especially if a woman wants to influence her beloved's sexual behavior for the "better." Male-hood does not want to be questioned. If a woman cannot resist doing this, don't be surprised if you trigger the opposite. Most likely when you criticize or question your partner's sexual behavior, he will withdraw and put his sexual focus where he will receive confirmation. Most men get an allergic reaction to a woman wanting them to change. This aversion is usually deeply rooted in early infancy and connected with the behavior of a mother who was continuously trying to change the little boy, "Do this, don't do that."

## Sons and mothers

Women have special relationships with their sons. The mothers who have not healed their own sexuality often wind up abusing their sons out of the unmet unconscious sensual desires and needs of a mother. For many women, the son is the only male being that they allow to be close and the only one they allow to be affectionate with them. Women tend to spoil their sons much more than their daughters.

Especially for a single mother, or a woman who feels neglected by her husband, the son becomes a much too important figure in her life, and she might try to place him in a role that is unnatural. If a man does not give a woman what she thinks she needs, at least she has the power to shape her son according to her needs. This can cause severe sexual and emotional problems later on in a man's life.

In Zürich, walking down the Bahnhofstrasse, I am always astonished to see how perfectly these cultivated gentleman are dressed, in their gray suits, matching tie, shirt, and socks, clean and tidy. It is nearly unbelievable to me when I think that years back, they were a hoard of little yang monsters, dirty, noisy, and completely wild. Their mothers have created a miracle, that those very lively rascals are walking around today, gray on gray with the perfect crease, without a grumble. At least from the outside it appears that they are living an orderly, regular life.

The mother is usually the first female being a boy experiences. The way she deals with the boy's early infant sexuality marks and manifests the man's sexual behavior later on in life. Whether a woman confronts a child's body and sexual organs with natural joy and acceptance, or if she ignores or abuses them; it is out of these basic experiences that a child constructs his life and relationships. A child is in a very open and receptive state, in a deep unknown. It absorbs and takes on all the unconscious feelings and unspoken words as well—all the double signals and emotional confusion presented by the mother.

Switzerland is one of the strongholds for "hobbies of pleasure," sexual perversions, and this not by coincidence. The people here are living such an orderly, diligent, conscientious, and reliable life. These are obviously all the qualities women want, and that's why they continue to insist on training their sons in this way. Later on in life, the repressed and accumulated hatred toward the first woman in their life, the mother, is triggered by sex. Then these men pay lots of money to prostitutes to beat them up or put them in diapers or stimulate them with violence. There are many different manifestations of misguided sexuality.

The yang from his nature needs freedom and adventure, and is attracted to wild animal-like intensity. If a boy from his early childhood on is restricted and controlled too much, and has no space of his own, this can have disastrous consequences for his sexuality later in life. In a similar way for the older man, imprisonment is the best nourishing ground for sexual perversion and violence to flower.

*Early infant sexuality*

271

# Chapter 24

# SEXUAL RELATIONSHIPS

In this chapter we will look into our sexual relationships. Even if we are dealing with the togetherness of the sexes, we won't deviate from the essential focus of this book, the liberation of female sexuality. There are far too many women who make their sexuality and personal development dependent on their partners.

**Togetherness**

Although there are many beautiful partner exercises, I will only introduce you to one. My effort is to support women to get in touch with their own power to liberate their sexuality, whether their partner is into this or not. While many therapists and teachers say that fulfilled sexuality depends on a great sexual relationship, I say that for women this is not the case. At any rate, I would like to inspire women to develop a new perspective toward sexual relating.

One of the highest arts in a woman's life is to remain focused on her inner liberation while having a love or a sexual affair. To deepen a sexual relationship to the point where the healing quality of love develops can be quite demanding and is only something for mature lovers. Only people who can assume complete responsibility for their lives with all its consequences are ready

*For mature lovers only*

for this. While sharing sexual energy with someone else, a woman is always confronted with unconscious patterns that need clearing and healing. With awareness, mutual respect, and love, she can dissolve them. Without continuous alertness and the intention to do so, sexuality reinforces neuroses and generates more and more conflicts.

*From monolog to dialog*

Sexual relating becomes complicated and unsatisfactory if it arises out of an inner deficiency or dependency. It makes a huge difference if two people are sharing their love and freedom, or if they cling to each other out of fear and neediness. Either their sexuality remains a monolog or it develops into a true sharing and a dialog.

A true love affair, a dialog and exchange between two beings, can only result out of freedom and abundance. It is entirely your responsibility which qualities you bring to your relationships.

*The development of inner freedom*

Inner freedom does not develop from one day to another, after a weekend workshop on personal enlightenment, or reading a book on meditation. The liberation of the female is very subtle and gradual, like the lasting nature of water, always flowing, leaving its trace in even the hardest stone. Life is definitely on our side, always creating a new challenge and chance for us to grow.

At first sight, this appears to us a bit differently. Mostly, we are attracted exactly to the person who will confront us with our old patterns, which we were hoping we had left behind. Or we are trapped in a relationship that is difficult to bear; enduring jealousy, struggles over possessiveness and self-doubt. And an endless discussion of the relationship with your partner and all your girlfriends robs you of your last spark of energy. Suddenly, all the profound experiences and insights you had in meditation are fading away and the next lover's quarrel is pre-programmed.

In a sexual relationship, women often lose track of their inner power, freedom, and higher perspective. We keep intending not to repeat our unconscious negative experiences before getting involved with another partner, but there is no shortcut. Unconscious patterns will continue to draw our attention as long as they have not become conscious and completely dissolved. And it is guaranteed that you will find a partner who will initiate the next step necessary for you to grow.

To choose the way of self-liberation does not necessarily mean: "Dear Bill, I have had it. You are too egotistical and insensitive. I need my space now to set myself free. See you later." Liberation does not mean to walk out of a difficult situation, but to learn how to solve or heal it. Once you have learned what you needed to learn, you can still decide to say goodbye nicely.

Many people base their relationships on a decision to stick together so that one does not feel lost and lonely in this cruel world. The partner should give us security and warmth, and should love us unconditionally no matter how we are or how we look, and this should remain so exclusively and forever. All I can say is, good luck! According to my vision of life, the main purpose of relationships is to help and support each other to grow.

- Begin to investigate the expectations you have about your love affairs.

- What do you expect from your partner?

- Take enough time to explore this touchy issue and to write about it as honestly as possible.

Let's look at the different forms of relating a bit more closely. Sexual relationships are always a continuous back-and-forth between tension and relaxation, the world of dreams and reality, between imprisonment and freedom, conscious and unconscious actions.

# Women in Relationships

*The meaning of relationship*

**← My Diary!**

**275**

*Being in love*    The way a relationship starts is of great significance. Most start off with being in love, triggered by a mood or by the love hormones. Being in love can cause a magical euphoric state, which is there day and night. Being in love is a wonderful experience. Enjoy these wonderful intense feelings, then they are all yours.

Make sure that the best feelings you have do not all flow outside of you toward the other person. In the end, there will be nothing left for you or in you. Sooner or later this will make you unhappy, because you will begin to depend on the other person transferring his good feelings to you in return. And if that person is not doing it in the same way as you are doing it with him, inevitably you feel disappointed. You give all, your best, and do not get anything back.

It is enough that someone is inspiring you to connect with your own feeling of love and aliveness. If a love affair happens in this way, it will happen very naturally. If there is something else for you to learn out of the situation, then it will be more difficult. Just trust in life. What has to come, comes naturally, and what does not have to come does not come. Trust is the best preparation to stay open for the right thing to happen. It would be a pity if you repress your most beautiful feelings just because the other person is not ready to love or willing to share his love with you.

Next time you are in love, take time for yourself from the very beginning. The following exercise will help you internalize your feelings of love, so you will stay connected with them whether the other person is returning your feelings or not.

**Try This! →**    **Internalizing being in love**

- Close your eyes, and allow the feeling of love without getting sentimental or thinking about it, and breathe deeply.

- Allow the feeling to expand so that the wave of love spreads all over your body, until all your inner organs and glands start to dance and sing.

- To end the exercise, let all that good vibration flow into your middle, and condense and store it there so you will have access to it whenever you want.

- Being in love is always a state of opening and overflow. Your center easily dissolves in that state of euphoria. Therefore, it is necessary to center yourself even more than usual.

- Make sure that your feelings move deeper and don't get stuck in the head, but strengthen your heart. Love is the best food for the heart.

- Make sure that while falling in love, you are being in love, not falling out of yourself. Fall deeper into your center.

- Being in love means being alive, and if you spread that magical potion within your body it can be very healing.

**Hints for Healing!**
←

*The first time*

Each sexual relationship starts with the first time, which is usually a stressful situation. It is a whole new territory and we do not know what is going to happen. What if I do not like it? Or, Is it going to be too much for me? Can I still say no? But I am sure you know all this.

Here is a little consolation for inexperienced women. Only a very few women experience the first time making love as extraordinary. For most others, at least for nearly all the women I know, after the first time they were wondering, "Was that all?" How satisfying the first intercourse winds up to be also depends on the partner and his experience and abilities in dealing with women.

*One night stands*

Even though holiday affairs and "one night stands" can be physically very straining, they can also have a healing effect on women. Many women are blocked sexually because of an idea that they should only make love to a man who is seriously interested in having a long-lasting relationship. To break away from this pattern is a very important experience in woman's life. But this expression of liberation should only take place **while using a condom.**

Frequently changing sexual partners can have a very negative effect on women, especially if it stretches over a long period of time. Sex happens not only physically, but it is also, whether we are aware of it or not, a sharing of energy in other dimensions. Especially for a sensitive woman, melding her energy field with many other energy fields can be a major irritation and may disturb her being very deeply.

After every sexual adventure, take enough time to rebalance your body and energy field. Center yourself, clean and refine your whole system, and meditate a lot, until you are deeply connected with yourself again. Making love is similar to taking in food. It takes time to digest food, and it takes even more time to process the foods so they are transformed into blood and nutrients. When you make love to a person, you take something new into your system. And a female being needs time to absorb and process this. Making love with a condom is a big help, so the body does not have to absorb all the energy and information carried within the sperm.

*Being a lover*  Easy, frequent sexual contact with one person will create a sexual relationship with that person. Many women find themselves in the role of lover. Sexually, this can be very exciting and arousing, especially if you are a secret lover. It is also significant if the woman having a love affair has a steady partner or not. If both lovers are in a similar situation, it is balanced.

For a single woman, the situation is quite different if her lover is married or has a steady girlfriend. Such a situation is a great gift to help us discover the deep patterns in our personality. If he gets up after making love to you and takes a shower to go back home to his woman, that is a very precious moment for you. If you can remain alert and center yourself, keep your positive vibration within, and not fall into painful old clichés, these moments can reveal hidden treasures within you. Being a secret lover gives you the opportunity to encounter your fears, your dependencies, and your dreams. It is an ideal situation in which to see and dissolve them, to become free of them. You have enough time for inner exploration without being disturbed by anyone—it is a very precious gift. Enjoy this state as long as you can, for sometimes circumstances can change with lightning speed.

If I write about a partner and not a female partner, this is not because I mean to discriminate against sexual relationships between women. I myself do not relate sexually with women, so I can only refer to the experiences I have as a sexologist and a group leader. And I keep learning from my lesbian girlfriends. If a woman has decided to develop her sexuality, it does not matter if she is a lesbian, a heterosexual, or single. I have observed that many lesbian women are often hurt women. Having a loving relationship with another woman can be a chance to heal old wounds together in a protected space.

*Loving a woman*

Just as in a heterosexual relationship, the foundation and motivation of a relationship between women needs to be right. If you have a girlfriend, tune into whether the relationship arises out of a positive feeling for a woman, or out of a negative feeling or hostility or fear of men. You should also be aware that the over-emphasis of yin in a lesbian relationship can create an overload of emotion (water) between you. The fire of passion is easily drowned in the swamp of emotion.

# Chapter 25

# EVERYDAY LIFE

After my boyfriend and I decided to split up after being together for ten years, I started a new phase of my life with a trip to Thailand. I needed time and distance to digest the end of that relationship. I was very moved by the separation with him. It cast a shadow over all the other things happening in the world. Full of stirred up emotions, I found myself stranded in a little mountain village, where I stayed for some time. There were no sanitary facilities and I will never forget how terribly cold I was at night. But the mountain tribal people I lived with impressed me very much, especially how they managed their relationships.

A Lahu woman is married about four to five times in her life, and the marriage is executed by following a ritual. If a man and a woman like each other, they begin to flirt, and finally they ask the most important man of the village to marry them. Whenever the man has the time to do it, the couple will bring the best tea leaves they can find and a little money, and he performs the marriage tea ceremony with them. Once they have drunk the tea, they are officially a married couple.

After some time or maybe years later, if they do not like each other anymore, they begin to fight very loudly, and the whole village can hear it, until it is decided that they can divorce.

**Forms of Liberty**

Again, the couple looks for the best tea leaves, and this time they have to pay a little more money, and when the most important man of the village can find time, he will again do a tea ceremony with the couple. But this time, they do not drink the tea, but spill it together and then they are divorced. I was very touched when I learned how easily these people found each other and split up again. But unfortunately, as deeply rooted in our culture as we are, it is impossible for us to take on such simple customs as those of the tribal people in Thailand.

*Using our liberty*
At least in developed countries, we women are finally in a situation where we can decide for ourselves how and with whom we want to live our life. We could live in freedom—but only a few women choose to do so. Most women are not aware of the possibilities they actually have and remain living in traditional patterns. We still find too many women completely stuck in senseless, destructive relationships.

This section about sexual relations in marriage I would have liked to skip, because it is one of the most unrewarding and difficult issues to solve. A lot of psychiatrists, psychotherapists, sexologists, and many others are earning a fortune from it. Not to waste our time together, I want to keep this short. I just want to point out the sore areas of sex and marriage. The alliance of marriage is a contract between two people and the government, and sometimes God is pulled in as a witness. The marriage is actually the setting up of a little company: the family. That company's function is to bring children into this world, and once that has happened, sexuality has fulfilled its main purpose between husband and wife.

Children always affect the love life of a couple. Parents sacrifice a significant portion of their life energy and a part of their sexuality for them. Children are both a challenge and a big responsibility. They need a mother around the clock, and less won't do. They need to be loved and nourished, and the fact that they need attention all the time restricts the flow of sexuality between their parents drastically. It requires a lot of understanding, love, and maturity to be able to develop sexuality together under such circumstances. The treasures of female sexuality support women to transform their purpose-oriented partnership with a man into a union of true love.

*Healing love*

To develop healing and meditative qualities in a relationship, energy and awareness are needed, as well as spending lots of time together. Because many couples are caught up in emotional entanglements, they arrange their lives together because of their children, or out of convenience or comfort. They do not have a loving sex life, and slowly they lose their aliveness and ability to love in the bargain.

Quite a number of men in their late 40s have come to me for counseling recently because they have sexual problems. The situation was similar for all of them. They were successful businessmen, married for about twenty years, and for several years their wives did not want to make love anymore. Consequently, they felt insecure and harbored negative feeling toward the women. Most of the couples did not share a creative activity or a hobby together. What he likes to do she doesn't like to do, and vice versa. After they sketched their situation and complained about the wife, I usually asked them the question, "What do love about your wife?" Most of them, after thinking it over, said that they love the way she takes care of the house, her cooking, or how big a help she is in their business. Do I need to say more?

Sexuality in our everyday life is very demanding. If this area is to remain full of love and light, it requires time and willingness from both partners.

## Hints for Healing Relationships

*Time:*

Love affairs need time and space to grow. Create love niches together to relax, meditate, and enjoy.

*Place:*

Make yourself a sensual love nest. For couples living together, it is best to have separate bedrooms. Especially for women, it is important to have the space to withdraw to find themselves again. Be creative in finding nice places to be together. Being out in nature, especially during the Full Moon, can be very special.

### Rhythm:

Everyone has his or her own rhythm. If one adjusts too much to the rhythm of another, there is a possibility of losing touch with one's own nature. It's good just to be aware of this. The more you adjust to your partner's rhythm, the more difficult and unsatisfying a mutual sexuality can become.

### Communication:

Words are also needed. Learn to speak and share with your partner about your sexuality. But only talk about what you are experiencing. Try to be aware of your intentions and the undertone in your voice. Either you can communicate something to become more clear and conscious or you can use words to try to educate or accuse him. How you go about communicating will affect your beloved and your relationship with him in very different ways.

### Tuning in:

Many sexual problems and disharmonies accumulate because the partners do not take the time to tune in with each other. To tune in before making love is as important as it is to tune in before making music. In an orchestra, before they begin to play, the musicians take the time to tune their instruments, so the symphony will be harmonious. In love it is the same: two people always need time first to attune with each other, or there can easily arise a note of discord or misunderstanding between them.

### Meditation:

The healing potion for lovers is a daily meditation together, to meet in empty silence, without any other intention. Reserve at least 20 minutes for this every day, in the morning or in the evening. Let the following exercise inspire you.

## Tuning in meditation

← **Try This!**

- Sit opposite each other in an upright and comfortable way. If you want you can touch each other.

- Close your eyes and start breathing slowly and deeply. Bring your awareness inside yourself, until you are centered and relaxed.

- When you are ready, you can start humming together for 10 to 20 minutes. If you like, you can use meditation music and incense.

- After the humming, remain sitting silently for another 5 to 10 minutes.

# Sexual Techniques

How important are sexual techniques to ensure that women have a happy love affair? There are masses of literature about sexual techniques from both East and West. Many of these techniques have neither been questioned nor verified. Often they are wrapped in great theories and ideas, which when lived in reality, are not necessarily healing to our sexuality, even if many of these techniques come from ancient Eastern scriptures. Also, it can be a little presumptuous to trust a translator or author of such a book. We cannot really ascertain his true intention in writing about sex, and on top of that, it is unlikely that methods that worked for Eastern people thousands of years ago (as these authors claim), have the same effect on us today. We not only have a personality structure very different from the Eastern people who lived thousands of years ago, but we also have a completely different lifestyle and culture. Most people become interested in cultivating their sexual energy only when something in their sex life goes wrong. However, if you only have a few sexual problems, they can be solved by a simple technique.

*Taoist loveplay*

Taoist tradition knows countless numbers of positions for making love which are meant to have a healing effect. Different positions activate different reflexology zones in the sexual organs.

The various positions have some very witty names. For example: "The Screaming Monkey Clinging to the Tree," or "The Donkey in the First, Second or Third Month of Spring," or "The Horse is Kicking."

If the recommended positions are to have the desired healing effect, the man has to use special thrusting techniques, and it should be done several times a day over the course of a specified number of days. Shallow and deep thrusts are to be done in certain rhythms, like one deep nine shallow and this in cycles from three to eight times in a row. Every Taoist master will have his own recommendations about what position, how often, and how long, etc.

*Concrete example*
I would like to point out one of the shadow sides of the so-called healing love techniques. A few years ago, a 30-year-old man from Santo Domingo attended one of my seminars on the Tao of sexuality with his Swiss wife. In his home country, the man learned a special sexual technique from a voodoo woman, which helped him solve a chronic problem with constipation. If he practiced it daily with his wife, he was fine, but if he missed a day, he became constipated again and didn't like that.

Since he couldn't convince his wife to do this exercise every day (actually she refused), he dragged her to the seminar. It came out during the workshop that he wanted me to convince his wife to do this healing love act with him, so he could have his natural bowel movement every day. Unfortunately, he didn't know me well enough when he signed up for the course. During the seminar, I did my best to make Mr. Macho understand that no woman likes to be used as a laxative. In the end, he was very angry with me, but at least his wife felt a bit relieved.

## Developing Sexuality

To develop feminine potential is a long, holistic, and in the beginning not always an easy process. Be patient with yourself and your environment. A lasting transformation rarely happens from one day to another. Each woman has her own pace. Especially for older women, it is important to be gentle with yourself and not expect too much from yourself too fast. Each phase of our life has a different rhythm. A young and healthy woman has the capacity to learn and move faster than an older woman does. There is no hurry; just do the best you can. And remember that each of our cells stores information. It takes at least seven years for the body to renew all the cells, so it takes time to change our inner chemistry and the vibration of the body.

It is also good to get support from the outside. In bigger cities, there are more and more women's groups dealing with female sexuality in which participants have the possibility to learn more about themselves in a protected space. The best is to find a group that emphasizes depth and silence, where women do not talk much, but enjoy a mutual deep yin silence. This is an incomparably nourishing space for healing, one that I would not want to miss in my life.

## Sexual Therapy

There arise moments in a woman's life where conflicts and problems overwhelm us and blur our vision. It can be helpful to find a neutral person to support you in finding creative and healing solutions. If you are having a sexual conflict, it is not so easy to find the right person to contact. They should be well-qualified and also have the ability to deal with sexuality in a natural and conscious way that is sympathetic to the female. Unfortunately, especially among therapists, there are many yang-oriented women who may not be able to provide the needed female support in your situation.

### Where do I get help?

Finding professional help to work on sexual problems is a delicate matter. No doubt psychotherapy and analysis are interesting and a way to explore new facets of one's personality. But sexuality, and especially female sexuality, does not change by talking about it. The healing quality that sex needs in order to change and blossom doesn't arise out of an intellectual atmosphere.

As a woman, I would recommend going to another woman to talk about sexual problems. Even though there are many male professionals working in the field of sexuality who are especially

287

interested in helping women, I am convinced that male therapists or doctors are not appropriate in the field of women's sexuality. Especially in the case of insecure or hurt women, and which woman does not belong to this category? I often hear about abuse and encroachment in therapy situations. So be aware of that, especially when you feel needy and helpless. Several studies have proved that abuse and encroachment among women and children happen mostly in a nice, understanding environment by people they really trust. The female way is all about trusting yourself. Don't lose your focus on that, especially when you feel you need somebody. Pay attention to that little voice inside you when it does not feel good about something. Respect your strange feelings and allow yourself to stop the situation, or to speak up about it. People who abuse or take advantage of others are often very calculating and plan their encroachment very carefully, step by step. It usually begins with a very subtle, tiny detail, a very small crossing of boundaries, too small to even mention. And usually, if you do gather all your courage and speak up, it is not welcomed and appreciated. You might even be punished or humiliated for doing so. Be aware that if you do speak up, the reactions you get from abusive people can be very tricky. Their goal is to make you feel insecure, to convince you that your perception and your intuition is wrong. But nevertheless, do it anyway. Women are very sensitive; we are able to recognize all these little, subtle, power games, so we can step out and avoid getting trapped.

I am strongly convinced that male therapists are not the right people to help a woman heal her sexual wounds in a way that really suits and strengthens her femininity. The male nature certainly has many great abilities and skills, there is no doubt about that. But let's be real—dealing with their own sexuality, or with the sexuality of a woman in a healing way, has never been an art men have made headlines with. With all our respect and love toward men, let's not be naïve and hand over our sexual responsibility.

**Sexual abuse**  For the past few years, sexual abuse has become very trendy. You do not know how many phone calls I get from women who would like to work on their suspected sexual abuse, an experience of which they have no real memory. Many of them were pushed by their therapists—both male and female—into assuming they had an abuse problem. I am aware that there are many children who are sexually abused, and many suffer from this abuse, but many have learned to deal with it in a creative way. And there are also many sensitive women who have not really been abused. I do not know why therapists and doctors are so eagerly focused on trying to provoke a possible abuse memory in clients, but for some reason, this has also happened to some people.

It is really easy to get a woman to suspect she has been sexually abused. On the inner journey, most women encounter the abuse issue, but not necessarily because they have been affected personally by it, but because they have entered deeper layers of the subconscious, where collective experiences are stored. It will never be possible for a single woman to process all this information. Once you have tapped in to that channel of global misery, it is very difficult to heal the suffering of the whole world. The deeper you go into that channel, the more you are sucked into the swamp. But the therapists who are not familiar with the depths of this inner world don't understand this phenomenon. So just be more responsible and alert!

Therapy is always an unreal and superficial situation. It can give support, which can be helpful at times, but therapy can never really help a woman connect with her inner strength. Sexual abuse will remain an issue in a woman's life as long as she cannot access her own female power, and old wounds are not completely healed. The path of self-healing is especially suitable for abused women. They can begin to learn to trust themselves, instead of submitting to or holding on to somebody or something outside. In this way, they can learn to decide what's good for them and to say no whenever it is needed. Only by developing individuality and consciousness are we able to connect with our positive forces, so we are no longer affected and controlled by the dark destructive forces within and without.

# CONCLUDING REMARKS

I consider it every woman's responsibility to develop the healing qualities of female sexuality and to get in touch with its hidden power. If we want to create new values in our society, the female potential needs to be revealed and used consciously. Being rooted in our yin nature, we are able to move freely and more effectively in yang fields of society and can accomplish our life's calling more deliberately.

**Out of a Female Perspective**

A yang performance tends to involve quantity at the expense of quality. Yang wants to be stronger, more important, and more powerful even than nature, which is exploited, manipulated, and destroyed to fulfill personal desires. Yang wants to collect and hoard material goods, and to do so, other humans are unscrupulously exploited and used. For a little change and entertainment, one can go to the next street corner and purchase a few minutes of lust and love. Yang expansion has stretched beyond the boundaries of the healthy expression because the yin has become too weak to root the yang; the yang forces have gotten out of control.

Men—and also women who are dominated by the male principle—often cannot handle the yang position of power and responsibility, or even the expression of their sexuality. Power

*Abuse of power*

291

builds up yang energy. Through uncentered power, insecure and immature people quickly disconnect from the yin qualities of compassion, surrender, or even being realistic. Once people are blinded by power, they lose their original focus and goal.

Many people in a position of power are corrupted by it, forgetting the purpose of their job. Blinded by their status, they start to focus on personal benefit and enrichment, instead of accomplishing their originally assigned task.

To be able to assume responsibility and consequently live and realize it implies that, if the situation requires, we need to be strong inside and truthful enough to be able to lose face. This requires solid yin roots, to be woman enough to swim against the yang tide and maintain our integrity, even when people misunderstand us, or reject or fight us and our intentions. Empty and insecure people who are depending on approval in a position of power are not able to do this, for they are equating being in power and being popular with survival.

*Less is more*  Women still don't understand (or have forgotten) what it means to live and act according to the yin principle. It does not involve passive submission to life out of fear or dependency; it involves a conscious decision to live the female way, the way of Mother Nature, which includes the conscious development of inner qualities. Surrendering to yin allows women to open for both old and new ways of living, which they are able to encounter with open eyes and an open spirit, without fear and negativity. Thanks to their inner roots, women can surrender to the open emptiness of the Tao and allow themselves to be touched by life and surrender to the natural flow and that incredible gift of being alive.

To live out of yin means to have an inner fullness, and not to depend on material substitutes for satisfaction. If women place their awareness increasingly into focusing on the development of inner qualities and riches, there is no need to define ourselves as a mother, lover, or wife. You have the right to be that natural and beautiful woman that you are. Just give yourself the permission and space to be yourself. As long as a woman's worth is tied to whether she is having children or not, women continue to establish a sense of self-worth by having children, and their energy is absorbed by that responsibility. The times require that we invest all our female strength in the liberation of the uterus, and use our female potential to give birth to the healing qualities.

Togetherness, compassion, and surrender arise out of the female principle, not fighting and egoistic power games. But why is it that women are still exchanging envy and cruelty and fighting each other? It is a sad fact that I see quite often through my work. There are always women, mostly yang-oriented women, trying to block and destroy my work out of an unnecessarily destructive rivalry. Women can only react in this manner when they are not rooted deeply in their yin and they live their life at the extroverted and superficial level.

*Together*

In the professional world, and in politics, the women who have dedicated their life to yang qualities are the ones who succeed. Unfortunately, in the development of these yang qualities—developing a sharp, calculating mind, ambition, promoting oneself in a man's world—women always pay for it with their female essence. Yang-oriented women who do not nourish the female qualities within, will eventually disconnect from their true nature and roots. Sooner or later this creates a deep vacuum, which they try to compensate with approval or attention from the outside world. Without that, they feel insecure, frustrated, and empty, which goes toward promoting yang-oriented behavior.

Female potential will never develop out of male qualities, and as long we fight the male-predominant world with yang methods, we limit our effectiveness. Female power doesn't manifest by fighting, but by its soft, loving, and enduring nature. Feminine potential unfolds in the healing of female essence. The more we are connected to our female essence, the stronger the intimate ties between us. The best way to heal this lost trusting union among women is to sit together in deep silence and depth, to strengthen and support each other to heal our world and ourselves. The female contribution to a more peaceful and natural society can happen every moment anew by making the first step toward the reconciliation of yin and yang.

**An old Taoist saying recommends:**

*Do, without doing*
*Do without being busy*
*Taste the tasteless*
*Recognize the big in the small*
*And the many ways in one*

*Repay enmity with kindness*
*Plan the severe as long as it is still light*
*Do the big, as long as it is small*
*Start the difficult thing in life always lightly*
*The big things in life start when they are small*

*Therefore the wise woman*
*Is never doing the big things*
*Therefore she can complete her greatness*
*The one who easily promises, seldom keeps one's word*
*The one who takes many things lightly, will experience difficulty*

*Therefore the wise woman*
*Because she is not taking it lightly*
*Will find nothing hard.*[1]

With these words from Lao Tzu, I would like to close and say goodbye to you. Having reached the end of the book, on one hand I feel that so much has not been said, and on the other hand, each word is one word too much. Female sexuality is such a complex and varied issue, it will never be possible to consider all the aspects at once, especially using words.

---

[1] This is my own translation of Chapter 63 from the *Tao Te Ching* and I have adjusted it so that it speaks to women.

# HEALING POINTS

The healing points you came across in the book can be activated and nourished in many different ways: by pressing, massaging, or working with healing oils. You can put hand-picked herbs on them or strengthen them with your menstrual blood. It is important that you get to know the individual qualities of each point by connecting with it and feeling it. Let the points take you on an exploration. But do not over-stimulate a single point.

B—Bladder Meridian

LI—Large Intestine Meridian

GB—Gallbladder Meridian

H—Heart Meridian

Liv—Liver Meridian

L—Lung Meridian

St—Stomach Meridian

Sp—Spleen Meridian

K—Kidney Meridian

Ren Mai—Directing Vessel

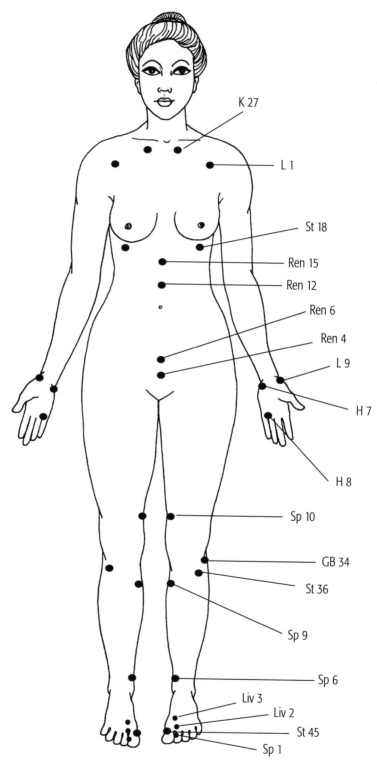

The human body, front view.

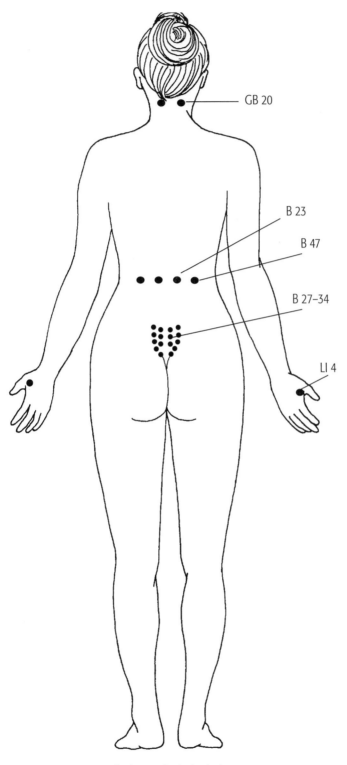

GB 20

B 23

B 47

B 27–34

LI 4

The human body, back view.

### B 23—*Ravine of the Kidneys*

*Location:* These points are located between the second and the third lumbar vertebrae, two finger-widths next to the spinal column.

*Action:* One of the most important points for strengthening and nourishing the kidneys.

### B 27—B 34

*Location:* Sacrum

*Action:* Vitalizes female sexual organs

### B 47—*Door of the Wandering Soul*

*Location:* Between the second and the third lumbar vertebrae, four finger-widths next to the spinal column.

*Action:* Can help people get the feel of sense orientation in life, has a positive influence by diffusing fear and emotional states.

### LI—*Connection to the Valley*

*Location:* On the back of the hand on the muscle which comes out when thumb and index finger are pressed together.

*Action:* Promotes digestion, good for detoxification; helps relieve constipation.

### GB 34 *Yang Well at the Hill*

*Location:* In a depression on the front edge of the head of the fibula.

*Action:* Harmonizes and releases stagnation in the liver; eases cramps.

### GB—*Wind Pond*

*Location:* Below the base of the scalp, depending on the size of the head, 3 to 4 inches apart, between both big muscles of the neck.

*Action:* Clears and nourishes the brain, removes or reduces liver yang.

### H 7—*Door of the Spirit*

*Location:* Within the fold of the wrist in the extension line of the pinkie finger.

*Action:* Nourishes the heart blood, liberates the opening of the heart, reduces stress and jumpiness.

### H 8—*Palace of the Little Yin*

*Location:* In the depression on the back of the hand, about two finger-widths below the fingers between ring and pinkie finger.

*Action:* Reduces fullness of the heart and calms the spirit, when feeling restless, having strong dreams, or problems sleeping.

### Ren 4—*Door of the Original Well*

*Location:* Three finger-widths below the belly button on the front midline.

*Action:* Tones kidney yin and yang; regulates uterus and menstruation; nourishes the blood.

### Ren 6—*Sea of Chi*

*Location:* Two finger-widths below the navel.

*Action:* Eases exhaustion, strengthens spleen; helps dissolve vaginal discharge and mucous deposits in the lower abdomen.

### Ren 12—*Middle of the Stomach*

*Location:* Four finger-widths above navel.

*Action:* Strengthens stomach yin; drains dampness.

### Ren 15—*Tail of Lovey Dovey*

*Location:* On the middle front line, seven finger-widths above navel

*Action:* Powerful point to calm the spirit caused by yin deficiency; strengthens the heart blood.

### Liv 2—*Travel Between*

*Location:* On the top of the foot between the first and second toe, close to the margin of the web.

*Action:* Relieves liver fire, symptoms of heat; cools the blood.

### Liv 3—*Great Surge (Wave)*

*Location:* On the top of the foot in the depression of the big and second toe, about a finger-width above Liv 2.

*Action:* Harmonizes liver and blood flow; calms the spirit.

### L 1—*The Main Palace*

*Location:* Outer chest area, three finger-widths below collarbone.

*Action:* Helps exhaustion, stagnation, and tension in the chest; eases coughs.

*L 9—Deep Abyss*
*Location:* In the depression of the wrist fold underneath the base of the thumb.
*Action:* Tones lung chi and yin.

*St 18—Root of the Breasts*
*Location:* Vertically below the nipple in the fifth intercostal space, four finger-widths lateral to the Ren Mai.
*Action:* Regulates functions of the breasts; dissolves stagnation.

*St 36—Three-mile Point*
*Location:* Four finger-widths below the kneecap, lateral to the anterior crest of the tibia.
*Action:* Exceptional point to strengthen chi and blood, especially for physically and psychically weak people.

*St 45—Evil's Dissipation*
*Location:* one finger-width from the lateral corner of the second toenail.
*Action:* Clears stomach heat; has a sedative effect.

*Sp 1—Hidden Clarity*
*Location:* Approximately one finger-width from the medial corner of the first toenail.
*Action:* Regulates the blood; promotes a stagnant blood stream and stagnant uterus, used for diminishing bleeding.

*Sp 6—Meeting of the Three Yin*
*Location:* Four finger units above the inner ankle on the posterior border of the tibia.
*Action:* Promotes building blood; drains retained water; regulates menstruation and uterus; relieves pain in lower abdomen; cools and moves the blood (do not stimulate during pregnancy).

*Sp 9—Yin Well on the Hill*
*Location:* On the inside of the leg, below the outward bulge of the inside of the knee, below the head of the tibia.
*Action:* Drains dampness out of the lower part of the body, from the legs and the meridians.

*Sp 10—Sea of Blood*
*Location:* With the knee flexed, located four finger-widths above the upper edge of the kneecap on the head of the thigh muscle.
*Action:* Regulates menstruation; supplies uterus with blood, and nourishes blood.

*K 1—Bubbling Spring*
*Location:* On the sole of the foot between the balls of the foot.
*Action:* Nourishes yin, roots the spirit, promotes harmony between heart and kidneys.

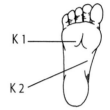

K1–The Bubbling Spring.
K 2–The Burning Valley.

*K 2—Burning valley*
*Location:* In the middle of the vault of the foot, halfway between the outer ball of the big toe and the back side of the heel.
*Action:* Clears heat and cools the blood.

*K 27—Conveying Palace*
*Location:* Directly in the depression of the outstanding bones of the collarbone.
*Action:* Spreads and transmits yang energies, stimulates kidneys, receives and holds chi.

# BIBLIOGRAPHY

Achterberg, Jeanne. *Woman as Healer.* Boston: Shambhala, 1991.

Anand, Margo. *The Art of Sexual Ecstasy.* Los Angeles: J. P. Tarcher, 1989.

Chang, Jolan. *The Tao of Love and Sex.* New York: Viking, 1993.

Chang, Po-Tuan. *The Inner Teachings of Taoism,* Thomas Cleary, trans. Boston: Shambhala, 1986.

Chang, Stephen T. *The Complete System of Self-Healing.* San Francisco: Tao Publishing, 1986.

———. *The Tao of Sexuality.* San Francisco: Tao Publishing, 1986.

Chia, Mantak. *Awaken Healing Energy through the Tao.* Huntington, NY: Healing Tao Books, 1986.

———. *Awaken Healing Light of the Tao.* Huntington, NY: Healing Tao Books, 1993.

———. *Healing Love through the Tao.* Huntington, NY: Healing Tao Books, 1986.

———. *Taoist Secrets of Love.* Santa Fe: Aurora Press, 1984.

Cleary, Thomas. *The Essential Tao.* San Francisco: HarperSanFrancisco, 1992.

———. *The Immortal Sisters.* Boston: Shambhala, 1989.

———. *Sex, Health and Long Life.* Boston: Shambhala, 1994.

———. *The Spirit of the Tao.* Boston: Shambhala, 1993.

———. *Vitality, Energy, Spirit.* Boston: Shambhala, 1991.

Connelly, Dianne M. *Traditional Acupunture: The Law of the Five Elements*. Columbia, MD: Traditional Acupuncture Institute, 1994.

Crenshaw, Theresa L. *The Alchemy of Love and Lust*. New York: G. P. Putnam's Sons, 1996.

Douglas, Nik, and Penny Slinger. *Sexual Secrets*. Rochester, VT: Destiny Books. 1979.

*Essentials of Chinese Acupuncture*. Beijing: Foreign Language Press, 1980.

Flaws, Bob. *Fire in the Valley*. Boulder, CO: Blue Poppy Press, 1991.

———. *Sister Moon*. Boulder, CO: Blue Poppy Press, 1992.

———. *Prince Wen Hui's Cook*. Brookline, MA: Paradigm Publications, 1983.

Giovanni, Maciocia. *The Foundation of Oriental Healing*. New York: Churchill Livingstone, 1989.

———. *The Practice of Chinese Medicine*. New York: Churchill Livingstone, 1994.

Gray, Miranda. *Red Moon: Understanding and Using the Gift of the Menstrual Cycle*. Boston: Element, 1994.

Hammer, Leon. *Dragon Rises, Red Bird Flies*. Barrytown, NY: Station Hill Press, 1990.

Kaplan, H. S. *The New Sex Therapy*. New York: Brunner/Mazel, 1974.

Kaptchuk, Ted J. *The Web that Has No Weaver*. New York: Congdon & Weed, 1983.

Kushi, Michio. *The Gentle Art of Making Love*. New York: Avery, 1990. This title is currently out of print.

Lowen, Alexander. *Love and Orgasm: A Revolutionary Guide to Sexual Fulfillment*. New York: Macmillan, 1965. This title is currently out of print.

Nitsche, Gunter. *Silent Orgasm*. Koln: Taschen Verlag, 1995.

Osho. *Das Buch der Frauen*. Munich: Heyne Verlag, 1997.

———. *Meditation: The Art and Ecstasy*. Rebel House, 1992.

———. *Tantric Experience*. Boston: Element, 1994.

Pross, Roswitha. *Eros-Rose-Eros-Rosenbuch*. Freiburg, Germany: Eulen Verlag, 1998.

————. *Frauenkorper neu Gesehen—Ein Illustriertes Handbuch.* Berlin: Orlanda Frauenverlag, 1987.

Reed, Michael. *Acupressure for Lovers.* New York: Bantam, 1997.

Reid, Daniel. *The Complete Book of Chinese Health and Healing.* Boston: Shambhala, 1994.

Ross, Ashoka. *The Wonderful Little Sex Book.* Berkeley: Conari Press, 1987.

Tannen, Deborah. *That's Not What I Meant!* New York: Morrow, 1986.

Voss, Jutta. *Das Schwarzmond-Tabu.* Zürich: Kreuz Verlag, 1988.

Weed, Susun S. *Breast Cancer, Breast Health: The Wise Woman Way.* Woodstock, NY: Ash Tree, 1995.

Wile, Douglas. *Art of the Bedchamber.* Albany, NY: State University of New York Press, 1992.

Wong, Eva. *The Teachings of the Tao.* Boston: Shambhala, 1997.

Worwood, Valerie Ann. *Aromatics.* London: Pan, 1987.

Wühr, Erich. *Gesund Durch Chinesische Heilkunst.* Munich: Graefe & Unzer, 1997.

# INDEX

**306**

**M**aitreyi D. Piontek is a nurse, author, and sexologist. She studied meditation in India, and she has lived in Asia, where she studied various Eastern healing methods. Her training as a therapist and her twenty-five years of practical experience combine to make her uniquely equipped to help others in her workshops and lectures. She travels all over the world to initiate other women into her work and trains therapists to integrate the female principle into their work. She lives in Switzerland and can be contacted through Weiser Books or at her website: www.tao-of-sexuality.com.

**Seminars and Lectures**

For information about seminars and lectures please contact Maitreyi Piontek at the following fax and e-mail addresses. If you want information about the meditation CDs (if you can't get them in your local bookstore) or if you want details about ordering eggs for your own use, you may want to subscribe to the newsletter at:

www.tao-of-sexuality.com

or contact Maitreyi Piontek at her Woodstock address.

*To contact Maitreyi in America:*
Maitreyi Piontek
P.O. Box 460
Woodstock, NY 12498
E-mail: MaitreyiPiontek@cs.com
Fax: 1-866-572-6888

*In Europe:*
Maitreyi Piontek
Postfach 255
8024 Zurich, Switzerland
E-mail: MaitreyiPiontek@cs.com
Fax: 41-1-262-2280